About the Author

Anne-Marie worked for many years as a production manager for BBC Television at international sporting events. With deteriorating eyesight due to a genetic disorder, Stargardt disease, she chose to leave in 1999. After the birth of her son in 2001, and his subsequent interest in dance, she became associated with Hasland Dance Studios in Kent and is now a partner. From writing broadcast facility and dance school show information documents, she finally found the time during lockdown to write the book she has been planning for more than twenty years.

Winter of Sumatra

Anne-Marie Maple

Winter of Sumatra

Olympia Publishers
London

www.olympiapublishers.com
OLYMPIA PAPERBACK EDITION

A CIP catalogue record for this title is
available from the British Library.

ISBN: 978-1-80439-063-4

This is a work of fiction.
All the characters originate from the writer's imagination. Any
resemblance to actual persons, living or dead, is purely coincidental.

First Published in 2023

Olympia Publishers
Tallis House
2 Tallis Street
London
EC4Y 0AB

Printed in Great Britain

Dedication

For Michael

Acknowledgements

Thank you to Shelagh and Len for their input and encouragement.

Prologue

Sounds penetrate as he wakes. Birdsong, buzzing insects, strumming crickets. His heart beats in time to the lazy double pulse of a jungle morning.

Everything is pain. Eyes closed, he stretches fingers, toes; rolls wrists, ankles. Head movement is excruciating so he stills, willing the agony to subside. With careful fingers, he probes his stomach, chest, collar bones, neck. He allows one eyelid to open, revealing an iridescent blue dragonfly hovering just above. He blows. It vanishes. Now both eyes are open. Cautiously, he turns his head. Pain stabs. Overwhelming exhaustion. He loses consciousness.

Coming to, he rolls to one side to throw up. Wiping his mouth, he catches sight of giant ants marching over buttressed tree roots, a relentless moving shadow, stripping all in its path. A deep breath and agonised exhalation as he pushes up to hands and knees, the earth damp but solid beneath trembling hands. Enduring waves of dizziness and nausea, the pounding inside his head, he sits down to confront the endless evergreen.

Now, he stares at the broken aircraft tail, caught in thick foliage – gun turret open, but intact.

"Tail-end Charlie," he whispers. As rear gunner, he has survived. The rest of his crew is not so lucky. Intense humidity has doused the flames but the twin engines and wings are shattered. Debris is everywhere. The fire from exploded fuel tanks has left a grey mangled mess, barely recognisable. He continues to stare, mind numb, in shock, unable to process.

Time passes. Thirst demands attention. He stands, legs wobbling like those of a newborn foal, he holds on to a branch until the worst of the nauseating dizziness passes. He can hobble slowly, stiffly and painfully. Dreamlike, he shuffles between vine-encrusted trunks that soar away into the canopy. As little light penetrates the broad-leaved monstrous trees, he stumbles, clutching at their encircling offspring of spindly saplings. He has no sense of direction, mindful only of his thirst and his pain.

It is dusk. He is walking, aware of biting insects. The air is oppressive, so humid, still hot. He hears thunder rumbling, crackling. Ahead, lightning forks flash white between giant silhouetted trees. He welcomes the rain, sucking wet leaves as they brush his face. Tearing thunder cracks like rifle fire. He stops, turns, listens. Again, the crack, but this time bullets rip into the bark above his head and he is off, running, staggering, falling, crawling and running, running. Adrenaline surges. Rain pours. Assaulted by panic, he is prey, running for his life. He must keep running and running until his legs give way. Collapsed, he lies on his back, mouth open, choking as he battles for air and water. As the rain intensifies, he crawls into thicker vegetation. The flight hormone streams away with the water, down through soaked clothing, draining every sensation, until there is only oblivion.

The storm has passed. He lies and listens. Daylight has gone. Cicadas replace the drumbeat of the rain, calming, cathartic. He is aware of small nocturnal animals out foraging. He hears owls, nightjars, frogs or maybe toads? He is not sure.

Now, he senses alarm. Increased scurrying, flapping wings, sharp calls. Eyes closed, he listens and there, there it is. Unhurried, the stealthy pad, pad, pad, of a larger animal, a hunter. The predator is close. He can hear its breathing. A heavy coughing breath and now, the unmistakable deep grating growl of a tiger. So close, but he does not try to move. Too tired. So much pain. He is resigned, barely making the effort to hope, to hope this will end quickly.

PART ONE

Chapter 1

July 1941

Sitting at his desk, John Crawford seems to derive no benefit from the recently-installed ceiling fan rhythmically rotating above his head. With a hundred per cent humidity, and the temperature well over ninety, beads of perspiration trickle down his forehead, the salt stinging his eyes, making them water. Wiping his face on the sleeve of his open-necked shirt, he frowns at the long memorandum received from London. Since the Nazi occupation of the Netherlands the previous May, the Dutch government has relocated its headquarters to London, apparently closing its eyes to the Japanese threat in the East Indies. With great deliberation, he drops the document into his filing tray and stands up, stretching long arms above his head, rolling the tension out of his shoulders. Collecting his jacket from the back of the chair, checking the rolled-up tie is still in his trouser pocket, John leaves his office, stopping only to switch off the ineffectual fan.

"Good afternoon, Mr Crawford. Leaving us so soon?" His secretary, Anna, smiles knowingly, raising an eyebrow.

"I've had enough for today," he replies. "A shower, a stroll to the club and a stiff drink is what I need to start the weekend." He winks at her before pushing open the outer office door and heading to his car. Anna chuckles to herself, watching her boss make his getaway before the shift ends and he is bombarded with complaints about increased security measures. London may decree he is over-reacting, but Anna knows John Crawford is convinced the Japanese threat is all too real.

Out in the sun, the battered Austin is a furnace, so he rolls down the windows, hoping to let any slight breeze stir the hot moist air. As the engine sputters into life, he turns out of the car park, driving home along newly surfaced roads, reclaimed from the peat swamps by ever-optimistic Dutch engineers – leaving behind the huge oil storage tanks that dominate the skyline.

John's bungalow, one of an identical line of eight, is set back from the road. As with all the Dutch-built houses around the Pladjoe refinery, the lawns are perfectly manicured with exotic flower beds neatly bordering each property. It is not the residents, all employees of Royal Dutch Shell, who are responsible for the regimented aesthetics, but an army of considerably less well-housed Malay locals, who keep the jungle at bay and the houses immaculate.

John's maid sits on the veranda, folding laundry.

"I get drink for you, Mr John?"

"No thanks, Lai. I'll have a quick shower, then head down to the club. If you haven't started on dinner yet, Emily and I can eat there?"

"No started, Mr John. You home early! Okay, I go home after you go to club?"

"Of course, Lai. We can manage. You get off and we'll see you in the morning."

Lai watches Mr John go inside. The smile remains on her deeply lined face. She has grown fond of the Crawfords over the past two years. She feels needed, appreciated, not taken for granted. Not all her friends are so fortunate, resenting their pale European employers who openly flaunt their wealth, their entitlement. On leaving the bungalow, Lai will walk home along

18

the rough dirt tracks that cross the swamp, down to the Musi river, to the shack on stilts she shares with her extended family. With so many mouths to feed, she is relieved to have this job and a considerate employer, one who even remembers to pay her regularly.

Plumbing in the bungalow is basic, but the water pressure is just sufficient to remove the dust and sweat of the day, so John feels refreshed as he emerges from the bathroom, towelling himself dry. He dresses in pressed lightweight trousers and a short-sleeved shirt – not forgetting the tie and jacket he will need for the dining room. He chooses a cotton print dress and a pair of sandals from Emily's wardrobe, being fairly sure she will not be suitably attired for dinner. Club rules are strict and he is not in the mood for an argument about the dress code.

Entering the bar, John orders a large gin and tonic with ice and lemon, starts a tab and books a table for two. Few members are about at this early hour, so it is cooler in the bar where he finds a table and selects a ten-day-old British newspaper. It is all war, of course. The 'Battle for Britain' being fought in the skies over southern England and the Channel. His frustration with the Dutch lessens as he reads of the situation in Europe being 'on a knife-edge'. Refolding and returning the paper to the 'English' pile, he collects his drink and wanders out to the pool area.

At this time on a Friday, the pool becomes the domain of the members' children. As school is over for the summer, he finds a pack of feral creatures, romping, screeching, splashing as if half are actively drowning, and all thoroughly enjoying their longed-for freedom.

An ear-splitting squeal assaults his ears as a small form erupts from the water, hurling itself at him.

"Daddy!" He lifts his glass to safety as the eel wraps itself around him. "Hello, Daddy," cries his ten-year-old daughter, Emily.

"Hello, you," he beams, bending down to kiss the girl's wet head.

The two are seated at a formally laid dining table. Emily chatters away in her usual manner, a stream of consciousness, impossible to follow. Her father listens, somewhat inattentively, but practised at nodding and gesturing in almost all the right places. Other members begin to drift in from the bar. All notice the pair, some more than a little envious of their relaxed intimacy. John Crawford, at thirty-eight, is still an attractive man. A little over six feet with dark unruly hair and vivid blue eyes. A widower, he is seen as a potential husband for one of their single friends. John Crawford, however, enjoys the company of his daughter, his only child. John Crawford has absolutely no interest in the matchmaking efforts of his friends' wives.

"I have to go out tomorrow, darling. Would you like to come along? Work won't take long and we can go *wild* in the jungle if you like."

"Yes, please!" Emily nods enthusiastically. "Where are we going?"

"A couple of hours inland. We can take the ferry and drive most of the way, then we walk. There's some land I need to take a look at, but it shouldn't take long."

"Just us, Daddy?"

"Yes. Just the two of us. I'll ask Lai to pack a picnic and we can make a day of it." Emily wriggles on her chair in excitement. A whole day with Daddy on a jungle adventure. She wonders how she will possibly sleep tonight.

"Can we play survivors in the jungle? Can we pick figs?

What birds will we see? Can you show me how to…" a cascade of questions flows across the starched white tablecloth as he drinks in her words, delighting in the enthusiasm and intelligence of his beautiful daughter.

Back home, John settles Emily down to read in bed, then sits at his desk, looking out through the living room window. His attention is caught and held by a breath-taking sunset. A deep orange glow, bleeding into a purple sky with grey wisps of cloud foretelling overnight rain. He reaches to pour a measure of brandy from the crystal decanter, set on a silver tray, beside a pair of bulbous brandy glasses. Swirling the golden liquid, inhaling its deep tones, he sips, enjoying the rich flavour, the colour in harmony with the amber sky.

From a locked drawer, John removes the packet delivered by hand to his office earlier in the week. The large manilla envelope is sealed, with his name and the words 'Top Secret' scrawled across the thick paper. Eager, he slits the envelope open with a paper knife and removes the contents. He carefully spreads out a map, tracing his finger across the page, to a large open area, marked with the number '2'.

Although British, John Crawford, a land surveyor, is employed by the Royal Dutch Shell oil company, based at its largest refinery, Pladjoe, on the banks of the Musi river at Palembang in South Sumatra. As such, British Intelligence sees him as just the right sort of chap for a secret land reconnaissance mission. Contact is made from Singapore, and the RAF delivers the documents to him via Pangkalan Brandan, the Palembang aerodrome.

In the accompanying notes, John discovers that the RAF will requisition the civilian aerodrome at the end of the year, to station allied squadrons as part of the defence force for Singapore, Borneo, Sumatra and Java. Pangkalan Brandan will be codenamed P1. In the event of an attack on Palembang, its two oil refineries being considered a priority target for the Japanese Pacific Fleet, P1 could be exposed, so a secret second airfield, P2, would be required as an allied base. According to RAF flight reconnaissance, an area just over forty miles west of Palembang could be suitable. He studies the coordinates to plan his route for the morning.

Before turning in, John checks on his daughter. Emily is already fast asleep, fingers curled on the pillow beside her head. He continually worries whether he should have uprooted her from all she knew in England. Laura's death had shattered their lives. His decision to move to Sumatra intended to give them both a chance to recover, to make a new start.

John and his wife had been so excited to find another baby on the way, but complications had arisen and both Laura and their son had died during the birth. He had been completely devastated. Only the responsibility of caring for his young daughter in her distress had kept him going. The offer from Royal Dutch Shell had come out of the blue – a heaven-sent opportunity to escape their grief. Despite Britain's policy of appeasement towards Hitler, war had loomed on the horizon. As the Nazis expanded their territory into the Rhineland, so John and Emily's retreat to the Far East seemed the right thing to do.

He remembers the dreadful rows. Emily's maternal grandparents insisting she remain with them because that is what Laura would have wanted. How they had lost their only daughter and now he was selfishly taking their granddaughter to the other side of the world. It was Emily herself who had settled the issue. She had absolutely refused to be parted from her daddy, so he had stopped feeling guilty and booked their passage. How relieved he had been – he could never have left without her, even though he desperately needed to get away. John would never forget his beautiful wife, Laura, and the wonderful years they had shared. He had worked so hard to put his memories away, locked deep in his heart, from where they would be retrieved, when time and distance made the loss more bearable.

More and more, he sees Laura in Emily. She has her mother's straight dark brown hair, the olive skin of her Spanish ancestry and large brown eyes with thick long lashes. For now, she is all legs and arms, fawn-like as she gambols along at his side when they are out walking together. Never still, skipping and jumping on to every wall or rock and chattering, always chattering like a little monkey, full of ideas and observations. Emily adores their 'jungle adventures' as she calls them. For him, these so-called adventures are a way to spend precious time with his daughter, to teach her about the indigenous plants and animals. More importantly, he must teach her how to protect herself, how to survive in a world he had once thought so secure. He cannot lose her. After Laura and their son, he cannot lose Emily.

Chapter 2

John watches the sun rise while he drinks coffee on the veranda. The air is warm and damp from the overnight rain. Lai is in the kitchen giving Emily breakfast and putting together a picnic of sandwiches and cake, purchased from the club, with two large corked bottles of water. Lai would like to have added fruit, but Emily assures her they will pick figs in the jungle.

"We'll bring some back for you too, Lai." The girl has not stopped talking of what she will do on her adventure. Lai nods and smiles, running an affectionate hand through Emily's sleek brown hair. Inwardly, she cannot help picturing her own grandchildren, the same age as Emily, already at work at the Europeans' club – cutting grass, raking leaves from the pool, preparing vegetables and washing dishes in the stifling kitchen. For them, there will never be picnics or jungle adventures, just the daily drudgery, necessary for survival.

The early morning breeze on the river brings relief from the constant humidity. Local workers pull the old wooden ferry, hand over hand, expertly guiding the rudimentary craft to the little jetty. A ramp is folded down for John to drive off and the car bumps down to a dirt road which runs parallel to the Palembang railway for about thirty miles, heading inland. Emily waves at a passing train, at the few passengers she can see in the windows of its painted wooden carriages. As the road continues west, she watches the train turn south, down towards the small port of Oosthaven, from where most passengers will travel by ship to

Java, across the Sundra Strait.

"It's Shanks' pony from here, Emily." Her father hefts a large backpack onto his shoulders and they set off across grassland. Both wear thick cotton trousers tucked into leather boots, white shirts with rolled-up sleeves and broad-brimmed hats. Emily carries her own small backpack containing her water, sketchbook and pencils.

"Company, halt!" John commands in his best regimental voice, which makes her giggle. They stop for him to consult the map. "Right. You stay here with our stuff and I'll take a little look around. Okay? See if you can do a sketch for me. That'd be really useful." He removes a small rug from his pack and Emily settles down to draw.

They are in a vast area of grassland. Except for the dirt road, which passes within a few hundred yards of where Emily sits, they are surrounded by jungle and swamp. John scratches his chin where the weekend stubble itches. Drainage will be necessary to remove any standing water from the lower ground, but it will be simple enough to measure the elevation with poles and line and take it from there. The area is certainly long enough for a runway, but it can't be surfaced, as tarmac would make it visible from the air. Fortunately, the central area appears to be on higher ground, sloping down gently on either side, so it will drain naturally, making it easier to pack down. Bumpy landings no doubt, but manageable. He will need hard standing to prevent stationary aircraft from sinking into the boggy ground, but if he clears foliage around the perimeter, right back to the largest trees, the jungle canopy should provide adequate cover. He can camouflage accommodation blocks and aircraft hangers, so the location is definitely promising. He decides to come back with some trusted men to carry out a full survey, reporting back to

Singapore with his proposals by the end of the week.

"These are called epiphytes," he explains to Emily, pointing to the colourful orchids. "It means a plant that takes its moisture and food from the air, not from the host plant it lives on."

"Otherwise, it would be a parasite!"

"Good girl. You've got it."

"What's this one again?"

"A saprophyte. Look. Do you see? That one is wrapped around a dead branch and that's the difference. It's a fern of some sort. I can't give you its exact name. I'm only an amateur."

They wander companionably through thick foliage, perspiring in the heat and humidity.

"Here's a parasite, Em. Can you remember its name?" He points to an enormous flower, with five dark orange and white petals. Each petal is the size of a large dinner plate.

"Raff something. Hang on, it's on the tip of my tongue," she makes fists, screwing her eyes up in concentration. "Raffesia!"

"Almost. You forgot the 'le'. It's rafflesia."

"It stinks, Daddy!" She holds her nose dramatically and moves away. "It's like rotten meat left in the sun. Yuck!"

"Careful!" he reaches for her arm as she trips on a large root.

"Why are the roots above the ground?"

"This is a freshwater swamp forest," he explains. "During the rainy season, the winter if you like, this low ground is often flooded and the roots are submerged, sometimes for months. Now, in July, it's much drier and the loose soil erodes away, leaving the roots exposed above the ground. They're called 'buttressed'. Understand?" She nods. He crouches, crumbling soil through his fingers. "It's not as dark as the earth down by the river at home. That's a peat swamp. When it floods there, the water is more brackish, not so clear as it is here. That's why most wild animals prefer it here. Some fish, too, prefer the clearer, fresher water."

"I've seen the Musi flood, Daddy. It's a good thing Lai's house is on stilts. I wouldn't want her to float away."

He grins. "Absolutely not! We couldn't manage without her. Speaking of Lai, how about that picnic. Are you hungry?"

"Ravishing!"

He laughs. "Or even ravenous?"

"Stop laughing at me!" she pouts, punching him playfully.

"I give in! I surrender!" He feigns being winded.

They follow the sounds of flowing water and find an outcrop of rock overhanging a natural pool, fed by a stream snaking down through the forest. John lays out the rug and unpacks the sandwiches. They sit contentedly, munching the food and swilling water from their bottles. As the day reaches its hottest hour, all around is peaceful. Only the insects remain industrious. Sitting by the water, the air feels a little cooler. They relax, listening to the odd twitter and call, but mostly, they hear only insects and running water, endless, hypnotic.

"I wish Mummy was here with us. She'd love it. I really miss her, Daddy."

"Me too, Em. Me too." He strokes her hair and she turns towards him. The wistful smile is so like her mother's. His heart contracts and he cannot speak. Moved by the glistening tears in his eyes, she shuffles closer, slipping a small slender hand into his – offering comfort, her infinite love.

"Shall I throw you in?" Emily squeals, jumping to her feet. "Yes, you definitely need to go in," he reaches out as if to grab her. Giggling, she scurries away, dropping down from the rock to the water's edge.

"Oh look!" she calls up. "Look! I've found a cave!" John climbs down to join her, to view the great discovery. Where flood water has eroded the rock over thousands of years, it has created a natural hollow, deep and high enough for a man to stand or lie down. It is dry and has recently been occupied – the musty animal odour is strong.

"Come away, Emily," he takes hold of her firmly and moves back.

"Why?"

"It's an animal's home. We shouldn't disturb it."

"But I want to look inside."

"No," he says more forcefully. "Animals are wild. They detest humans, the smell of humans. Let's leave well alone. Come on." Disappointed, she clambers back onto the rock to help pack away the remains of their lunch.

"Did we scare it away when we came here?"

"Perhaps." He is thoughtful. "There have been other people here though."

"How do you know?"

"Are you sure you want me to tell you?"

"I'm sure!"

"Well, back there," he points to a spot a little way off, "I could smell a human had been to the lavatory."

"Daddy! That's disgusting!"

"You wanted to know," he grins ruefully. "No other animal has that smell and the footprints confirm it. It must've been earlier today though. We had rain last night so any older prints would've been washed away."

"Other adventurers like us?"

"I doubt it. Not out here. Poachers, maybe." He stops to listen, hearing a faint cry. "Stand still, Emily. Be quiet a moment." They listen. She shuffles her feet impatiently. "Ssh!" He puts his finger to his lips.

The sound comes again. A short, almost duck-like call. No, not a duck, more like a kitten. He hasn't heard a cat mew since

28

leaving England and it sounds completely out of place in this setting. He moves cautiously in the direction of the noise, Emily on his heels, her finger still pressed to her lips. Now, she hears it too and they exchange a disconcerted look. Both silently wait until it comes again – locating the sound, she points to the buttressed roots of a huge tree.

"Under there," she whispers. John crouches, trying to see into the dark recess between the twisted roots. There is movement, and a little black-tipped nose with white whiskers protrudes, sniffing the air. Emily gasps as she glimpses orange fur with tiny black-striped markings, realising it is a very young tiger cub.

"What have we here?" John inches forward, speaking quietly, crooning. "Come on, little one. Out you come. You can't hide in there all day."

"Where's its mummy?" Emily looks around fearfully, imagining an enormous angry tiger ready to pounce on her.

"She can't be close," John replies. "She would've come to its calls if she could."

"Daddy! Look!" He rises and walks over to where Emily crouches. The earth is churned and damp, with a dark sinister stain. Touching the tips of his fingers to the ground, John lifts them to his nose.

"Blood!" He casts around, finding more streaks, as if something bleeding has been dragged across the soil. Understanding, he glowers, becoming enraged. "Bloody poachers." Emily does not reprimand him. He looks so angry. She turns back to the cub finding bright black-rimmed eyes watching her from the safety of its hiding place.

She plucks long grass to tempt the cub, wiggling the stalks around in front of the tree. A paw, larger than she expected, with sharp black claws, pats at the air, not quite able to reach the grass. She edges back, continuing to wiggle the stalks, tempting the cub. Cautiously, it emerges, dusty and frightened. Before her father can stop her, Emily has scooped the cub into her arms and is cuddling it.

"It has more stripes than I thought," she says, so casually that John just stares, scratching the back of his neck, completely amazed by her confidence.

"Erm, that's because it's Sumatran. They do have more stripes. It's not a pet, Emily." His tone entreats her to be careful, wishing those claws were a little further from his daughter's face.

"Well, it can't stay here on its own, Daddy. We'll have to take it home." He shrugs, shaking his head in exasperation. Emily is right. What else can they do? They can't abandon the poor creature. It will certainly die if left alone out here.

All the way home in the car, Emily cuddles the cub close to her, burying her face in the soft baby fur. It is restless, opening its mouth wide, giving short sharp cries.

"Poor mite must be hungry," guesses John. "We'll have to stop at the Charitas hospital. There's no vet I know of here, but Peter may agree to take a look, and the nuns might be able to rustle up a feeding bottle and some goat's milk if we're lucky."

The ferrymen keep their distance, dark eyes riveted on the girl with her cub. Mortally afraid of tigers, they believe the only safe tiger is a dead one.

Chapter 3

Doctor Peter Janssen removes his white coat, slips a cotton apron over his head and washes his hands thoroughly.

John had first met the doctor a few months after Peter arrived in Sumatra, when a weeping Lai had brought in one of her grandsons. A nasty burn on the boy's forearm, from the oven in the club's kitchen, had been ignored all day by the chef and other kitchen staff. The boy had tried to be brave but his arm was a livid red and likely to become infected. Seeing the pain in the tear-filled eyes of the under-nourished child, John had driven him to the Charitas hospital, a Catholic mission established by Dutch nuns, where locals could receive free medical treatment.

The tall imposing Dr Janssen had been surprisingly gentle, and the boy had emerged from the treatment room beaming, his arm freshly bound, sucking on a boiled sweet. Each man had sensed the compassion in the other, an understanding of the need to care for the local people. These workers formed the foundation of the colony, and, as with all foundations, they had become the dirt beneath the careless boots of the European immigrants.

Rapport had developed into a friendship, and the two men socialised together on the rare occasions they were both free. John learnt that Peter had also come to the East Indies to escape personal tragedy. While Peter had been visiting a hospital in Switzerland, his wife, a nurse at the Amsterdam hospital where they both worked, had been shot during the German invasion of the Netherlands. The couple had no children, so Peter fled the chaos of Europe for the relative sanctuary of the Charitas hospital at Palembang.

"Well, this is a first for me!" Peter remarks in his deep guttural accent. "I will examine your little friend, Emily," he smiles genially, "if you promise it won't *bite*!" He emphasises the word and mimics taking a huge bite, causing Emily to step back in alarm. She is a little intimidated by this large man with close-cropped fair hair and booming voice, even if he is her Daddy's friend.

"I can't thank you enough, Peter. I didn't know where else to go." John shrugs, raising his palms. "We couldn't just leave it out there. It can't be more than a few weeks old."

"Well, I can tell you that 'it' is a 'she', weighing in at just under ten pounds, but not much else. I am not used to so much, er, so much…" he casts around for the right word.

"Fur?" supplies Emily. He flashes her a wide grin.

"Quite right, young lady. Definitely more fur here than on my usual patients." His laughter comes easily and Emily decides she likes him after all. The noise brings a knock at the door of his examination room. It opens, revealing a nun, pristine in long white robes, who bustles in. Immediately, she backs out again, her eyes widening in horror, one hand rising to cover her gaping mouth, the other clutching the rosary hanging at her waist. She is utterly speechless. The prolonged silence amuses the doctor greatly, as it is most unusual.

"Ah, Sister Catherina! Come in! Come in and meet my friends, John and Emily Crawford and – do you have a name for her, Emily?" The child shakes her head. "Then it must be your job to think up a good name." He gives a single nod to confirm this decision and another wide smile – which Emily returns, nodding her agreement.

32

Sister Catherina cautiously re-enters, recovering from her initial shock. She is young, pretty, diminutive. Emily thinks she looks like an angel, although angels should be smiling and peaceful – whereas this angel looks completely terrified.

"It's a *tiger!*"

"Ten out of ten for observation, Sister." Peter's shoulders shake with suppressed laughter.

"*She* is only a baby, Sister." Emily is indignant. What a fuss about a little cub. "And she's very hungry. Please could you give her some milk?"

Sister Catherina regains some colour, although she still clutches the wooden rosary beads as if they provide divine protection.

"Please, Sister," intervenes John. "We wondered if you had a baby's bottle and teat we might borrow? And maybe some goat's milk if you have any?"

The cub, now cradled in the child's arms, suckles greedily from the bottle. Emily smiles up at the two men, delighted with her maternal role. Sister Catherina, having provided the warmed milk in a bottle, finds she is needed elsewhere. The doctor has enlarged the hole in the teat to increase the flow. It is all guesswork, but it seems to be doing the trick.

"So, what next?" asks Peter. "What will you do with her now?"

John runs a hand through his hair and sighs deeply. He looks at his friend, his eyebrows raised in indecision.

"I can just imagine," Peter's eyes twinkle mischievously. He puts on a high-pitched voice, "Why, Mr Crawford! What a large kitty you have in your garden!"

They all laugh.

"Seriously, John," he adds, "You need to think about this."

Emily's eyes focus appealingly on her father, but she says nothing.

"Dusit Zoo opened in Bangkok a couple of years ago." John scratches his chin where the weekend growth is itching again. "I don't think there's anywhere else in this part of the world."

"No, Daddy! Please not a zoo! She'd hate being shut in a cage," wails Emily. "Can't she stay with us until she's grown up and can go home to the jungle?"

"Without her mother, she can't learn how to hunt and won't survive." John tries to reason with his distressed daughter.

"Then *we'll* teach her! Won't we, Daddy?"

Peter feels desperately sorry for the little girl. She has so much to learn about life's cruelties, and no mother to provide guidance. He does not envy John's overwhelming responsibility in raising his daughter single-handed.

"I wouldn't know where to start, darling," entreats John. "Tigers hunt deer, wild pigs and such. How on earth could we teach her how to hunt and kill what she needs to survive? We don't have the skills. Humans make so much noise, tramping through the forest, any prey is long gone before we can even see it, let alone catch anything."

"We *have* to try, Daddy!" Tears run down Emily's flushed cheeks and into the cub's fur. Sated, the cub has fallen asleep in the girl's arms, blissfully unaware of its uncertain future.

"Let me find a crate for her, just for tonight," suggests Peter. "We're all tired. I'll come over in the morning as it's Sunday and we can talk about it then. Do we have a deal?"

Lai looks on in dismay as John places a large crate, containing a sleeping tiger cub, on the kitchen floor. Returning to the car, he fetches a sleepy Emily and sits the fractious child at the table to eat.

So, not the promised figs. Instead, a dangerous wild animal. Lai places a bowl of fragrant rice with a mild fish curry and bean sprouts before Emily, encouraging her to eat. She serves Mr John before retreating to the relative safety of the living room, pretending to tidy, although nothing is out of place.

After Lai has gone home and Emily is in bed – the crate, at his insistence, still in the kitchen rather than her bedroom – John pours himself a large brandy, flopping down in his armchair. Spying Emily's *Jungle Book* on another chair he picks it up, turning the well-thumbed pages until he finds an illustration of Kipling's tiger, Shere Khan. Thankfully, the cub is female, unlikely to be saddled with such a ferocious name.

Wearily, John pulls himself out of the chair, taking his empty glass through to the kitchen. Rescuing the feeding bottle and milk from the crate, he prepares for the cub to wake and the long night of feeding ahead.

Chapter 4

"That should do it!" Peter hammers the final nail into the wooden roof of the small enclosure he and John have built with wood and wire, begged and stolen from the hospital, oil refinery and neighbours.

Emily sits on a rug, in the shade nearby – a recently-fed cub sleeping peacefully in the crate beside her.

"How about 'Tiggy' after Mrs Tiggy-Winkle? Or 'Mopp' after Miss Moppett? No, I don't like either of those." She is searching for a suitable name from the eponymous heroines of Beatrix Potter's books surrounding her. "I like Jemima, as in Puddle-Duck. Not Flopsy, that sounds silly. Maybe Ginger? It's the right colour after all."

The men smile, admiring their handiwork and the girl's endless capacity for chatter.

"Beer?" offers John.

"I'm a Dutchman! I was weaned on beer! Thanks. So, this little one has a home for a few more weeks, but it's only delaying things, John."

"I know, but it'll have to do for now. I've so much else on at the moment." He has to organise the land survey for the intelligence services as well as manage new tank installations and security complaints.

"Not Mrs Tittlemouse. That won't work. Gosh, there are too many boys' names here – Johnny, Jeremy, Benjamin, Peter…"

"Hey! Nothing wrong with Peter! I'll set Mr McGregor on

you!" She giggles as Peter stands, hands on hips, pretending to be the angry farmer who chases Peter Rabbit around his garden.

"Jemima! I want to call her Jemima. What do you think?"

"She's not a duck," they say in unison.

"Why don't you ask Lai?" suggests her father. "She may have some good, more local names. Jemima is a bit... *English*?"

Emily disappears indoors in search of Lai while the two men move the crate, with its sleeping occupant, into the cub's new lodgings.

"In your professional, medical opinion," John smiles. "When do we start introducing meat?"

"Absolutely no bloody idea!" Peter raises his beer bottle to John in salute.

Emily bursts through the door leading out of the kitchen. "Indah!" she yells. "Indah. Lai says it means beautiful and she is, isn't she, Daddy?"

Word spreads quickly. A steady stream of children come to the door, asking if they can see the tiger.

"Her name is Indah, with an 'h' at the end," Emily announces importantly, as yet more enraptured children gather around the little enclosure. They stand in silent awe as Emily lifts the cub from the crate, bringing her out for them to stroke.

"She's in her element," John turns to Peter, who is smiling benevolently; enjoying the sight of the children, for once forgetting the differences in colour and class in their eagerness to touch the cub.

"I think the war may come here." John's face suddenly becomes sombre, shaking Peter from his reverie.

"What's brought that on?" replies his friend, frowning in concern. "I understood peace negotiations between Japan and

China were going ahead?"

"The Japs have made some kind of deal with the Vichy French in Indochina which has upset the Chinese. The Americans have already embargoed scrap metal and closed the Panama Canal to Japanese shipping. I heard they've now frozen Japanese assets, so if sanctions continue and the US cuts off their oil supply, where do you think the Japs will turn for their oil?"

"Pladjoe refinery?"

"Got it in one!"

"But that would bring the US in, surely? As well as Pladjoe, there is the smaller Sungei refinery which the Americans own."

"Sadly not. The Americans have said they're not getting involved in the fighting. Not in Europe, nor here. It leaves us incredibly vulnerable."

The pleasant mood of the afternoon slips away as the two men continue to watch the children gathered around Indah: a new generation, living under the shadow of war, facing an uncertain future.

PART TWO

Chapter 5

January 1942

Pulling up at the Palembang aerodrome, now the 225 Squadron HQ, John dashes through the pouring rain, concerned he will be late for the briefing.

Following the bombing of the American Naval Fleet at Pearl Harbour in December, there is a great deal of speculation among the staff at Pladjoe – the international oil embargo on Japan has made the refinery a valuable prize – and some of John's colleagues are sending their families down to the relative safety of Java. As the Japanese air force now occupies most of the airfields on the Malay peninsula, allied Blenheim and Hudson bomber squadrons arrive daily at Palembang, together with Hurricane and Buffalo fighters – all in preparation for the defence of Singapore and Sumatra. With the Americans finally entering the fray, even a few B17 flying fortresses have come through to refuel on their way to Java.

"Attention everyone! I want to introduce John Crawford. John works for the Dutch at Pladjoe refinery but is also helping us. He is responsible for setting up P2 – the secret airfield I mentioned at our last briefing – so he has our thanks." RAF Squadron Leader David Fawcett faces a group of British and Australian air force personnel, seated in rows. He leads the men in muted applause, gesturing for John to take a seat, before turning to point to a large map of southern Sumatra, hung on the wall behind him. "We are *here*, the civilian airfield, now called P1, north of the town, which is *here*." He jabs a finger at Palembang. "To the south, on the other side of the Musi river, *here*, are the two refineries – Pladjoe is the much larger Royal Dutch Shell installation to the west and *here* is Sungei, which belongs to the Americans." He turns back to the men, and seeing they are attentive, he continues. "Now, *here* is P2, forty or so miles to the west. Approximate flying time is thirty minutes from P1, so about an hour from the coast and the Bangka Straits, *here*." He now points to the east, past the town, to where the river forms a delta that flows out to the sea, to a narrow channel between Sumatra and Bangka Island. "*This* is where the Japanese Southern Expeditionary Fleet will enter the Musi, sailing upriver to Palembang to attack the refineries." He looks around to see that the men have understood. "Okay, you know which base you've been allocated, so let's get the bombers over to P2, pronto. Remember, it's an unsurfaced runway, so hard to spot from the air. You have the coordinates, but radio in if you need assistance. Any questions?"

John sips the strong black tea as he sits with Fawcett in a cupboard loosely termed the office at HQ. The squadron leader looks exhausted. Black circles bulge under his pale green eyes, and although his hair is mostly light brown, grey streaks at his temples emphasise his pallor.

"I've been speaking with the Dutch troop commander in the town. A Colonel Vogel," Fawcett tells John. "He has about two thousand infantry and a thousand Dutch Home Guard. We have forty Blenheims and thirty-five Hudsons, including two Australian squadrons. It's not much of a defence force, I'm afraid, so we're recommending all civilians leave for Java immediately, from where they'll be evacuated to India. I really think it's time for the staff to go, John. I appreciate you've essential workers at the refinery, but the rest should get out while they can. The colonel said he'd provide lorries, and there's also the train, to get everyone down to Oosthaven."

"I've closed up my house already," explains John, "and moved my daughter out to P2."

"Ah yes, the little girl with the tiger. I know all about *her*. A feisty little thing."

"Are you referring to my daughter or the tiger?"

"Your daughter, actually." Fawcett smiles and the lines around his tired eyes crinkle with humour. "She tells me she's training the tiger so it can go back to the jungle."

"Has she been bothering you too? I'm so sorry. It's an impossible situation. I've tried to reason with her. At least out by the airfield, Indah, that's the tiger's name, has more room."

"Indah with an 'h' at the end?" Now Fawcett's face breaks into a broad grin, as John puts his head in his hands; totally embarrassed.

"I've told Emily, that's my daughter's name, though I'm guessing you already know that too?" He pauses, and the squadron leader nods, still amused by John's evident discomfort. "I've told her, she's not to let Indah go near the airbase. Please understand, when we found the cub back in July, not far from P2, we had no choice but to take it home. Poachers had shot and taken the mother. We built an enclosure in our garden. It was okay for a few weeks, but the bloody thing quadrupled its size in a month and we were getting complaints. In the end, I moved them both out to P2 as I've been working there most of the time. The spot where we found the cub is about a mile from the airbase and I'm far happier Emily is out there, with Indah, rather in the town or at Pladjoe, with all the air raids. I couldn't persuade our maid to go with us as she has a large family right on the river. I'm so worried about them, but what can I do? The Dutch aren't going to evacuate the locals. I just hope they'll be okay."

Fawcett steeples his fingers under his chin, pale eyes assessing.

"Where at P2 have you put them?"

"I had our engineers build us a basic cabin, a little further out, past the other barracks. Indah is secure in a wire enclosure, so she can't wander into the base. Emily takes her back to where we found her and has set up a little camp – but I insist they're back at the cabin well before nightfall – there may still be poachers about, even though the flood levels are quite high at this time of year."

"Well, the child will have to go if we withdraw to Java. No tigers permitted, I'm afraid."

"Of course!" John looks alarmed. "Emily's my priority, above anything else. One of my engineers who is permanently stationed at P2, Mike Harman, is keeping a close eye on her when I'm over here. His family left when the Americans joined the war. If the squadrons withdraw to Java, he'll make sure Emily goes with him and I'll join them there."

"Good. As long as we've got that straight." Fawcett looks relieved, pleased to have his concerns about the girl resolved. "Now, I need to talk to you about the refinery. We're planning to locate six anti-aircraft guns at Pladjoe, but if the Japs get through, can we neutralise the refinery? The entire installation must be destroyed rather than fall into enemy hands."

"We're considering flooding the river with oil from the tanks and setting fire to it as the Japs come up the Musi. We'd have to get the locals to safety first, though."

"Mm. It's a possibility. In the meantime, I've discussed plans with the Dutch colonel – we'd like your men to help set charges to blow up the installation, including the storage tanks, if it becomes necessary."

"God almighty! Will it really come to that?" John whispers, pinching the bridge of his nose with his thumb and forefinger, spreading them across his closed eyelids and slowly down his face, in a gesture of exhaustion mingled with despondency.

Chapter 6

February 1942

Anna bursts into John's office, startling him with her cries. "Mr Crawford! Mr Crawford! Singapore is being invaded!" As white as a sheet, the secretary is visibly trembling. "The Japanese have landed in the north and are advancing on the city! The Australian troops are taking terrible losses."

He guides her to a chair and fetches a glass of water.

"Let's try to keep calm, Anna. We knew this was coming. Is there any word from Squadron Leader Fawcett? Has he taken losses?"

She shakes her head. In her thirties, Anna Weiss is an attractive woman, tall and athletic. She wears a navy sleeveless dress and her thick blond hair in a long rope-like plait, most unlike the linen suits and perfect chignon – her usual office attire.

"Listen to me, Anna." He leans down and takes her gently by the shoulders. "You and Thomas must go now." Anna's husband, Thomas, is an engineer with Royal Dutch Shell. "Get yourselves on to one of the lorries going down to Oosthaven and over to Java. There are Dutch troop ships to take you to safety."

"What about you?" In her distress, Anna allows tears to run freely down her cheeks. "What about Emily? Should she come with us?" Unnerved by the complete change in his secretary, usually so calm and confident, John realises she has been under the illusion, so common within the Dutch community, that the war is a European affair. Despite all his warnings and the air raids, she has never believed herself to be in any real danger, safely tucked away in the Far East.

"We'll be fine. We'll join you in Java in a few days. Emily is with Mike Harman. You take Thomas with you, Anna. All married men leave with their wives. Tell him from me, that's an order! I don't want any heroics. Okay?"

He watches Anna through the window as she rushes to find her husband. He hopes Thomas will agree to go. John has insisted only single men, who have volunteered, will stay to put their plan into action. As for Emily, if he is unable to get to P2 in time, the ever-reliable Mike will get her to safety.

It had been a difficult conversation with his stubborn daughter. Eventually, he had persuaded her that, thanks to her training – of which he actually knew very little – Indah would be able to survive on her own. He had no idea if his words held any truth, but there was simply no alternative.

Emily had finally agreed to stay near the base and, if John is away when the order came to evacuate, to release Indah before departing with Mike. He hopes he has not been unfairly stern, but he had needed to stress the importance of staying close to Mike, without bringing Indah onto the base. Everyone at P2 took their meals in the mess, so Mike should have no difficulty keeping an eye on her.

"Squadron Leader?" John makes the call on the field telephone rigged up to P1, to facilitate communication between the refinery and HQ.

"Ah, John. I imagine you've heard the news from Singapore?"

"Yes. I'm ordering the rest of my staff to get out – just the volunteers remaining now."

"Good. The air raids have cost us dearly. Our remaining fighter squadrons are trying to provide air cover for evacuees sailing from Singapore. They're heading for Java but under enemy fire. Fortunately, our bombers are safely hidden at P2, ready to hit the Japanese fleet entering the Bangka Straits."

"When do we expect the Japs to land at Palembang?

"A couple of days, so we'll keep in touch. Are you and Colonel Vogel all set?"

"We'll be ready." John finishes the call, fear rising through his body, inching towards his brain, where it could paralyse his mind so completely he would be unable to act. He forces the panic down, leaving it to swirl uncomfortably in his stomach, gritting his teeth in grim determination to get the job done.

Fawcett stares at the map, furrowed lines of worry etched deep into his forehead. The evacuees fleeing Singapore – in a strung-out flotilla, made up from military and civilian vessels of varying sizes – are sailing south, hugging the east coast of Sumatra, passing through the Bangka Straits, hoping to reach Java. At the same time, the Japanese fleet, with its aircraft and troop carriers, destroyers and other support ships, will reach the Bangka Straits within the next two days. Banging his fist down hard on the table in frustration, he knows there is nothing he can do to prevent the evacuees encountering the fleet but provide limited air cover and pray for a miracle.

John shakes hands with Colonel Vogel, commander of the Dutch garrison, who is coordinating the ground defence of Palembang and the refineries. They have met socially on previous occasions as the colonel is a friend of the Charitas doctor, Peter Janssen. Unlike the ebullient Peter, John finds Vogel very cold and formal, in fact he has never really taken to the colonel.

"Good afternoon, Crawford," barks out Vogel. His grip is self-assured, but his eyes do not meet John's, wandering restlessly, mistrustful.

"Good afternoon, Colonel. Thank you for coming out to Pladjoe. As you requested, I have twenty or so volunteers assembled to help set the charges around the storage tanks and pump room."

"My men will handle the explosives, Crawford. Your men must oversee the positioning and provide assistance only. Is that clear?"

"Perfectly." John is taken aback by the admonitory tone. "Is something wrong, Colonel?"

"Our ships carrying supplies of ammunition have been targeted by Japanese fighters and have had to abort their mission. We are *very* short. It makes my job *very* difficult. I have artillery and machine gun units in the north and west, but they cannot be mobilised in time." John senses the strain in the colonel's voice. Insufficient troop numbers, no artillery, lack of ammunition and the civilian evacuation in progress. No wonder the man is so terse.

"We will cooperate completely. Just tell me what you need us to do."

Chapter 7

Saturday, 14th February 1942

Looking up, John cannot quite believe his eyes. Filling the grey morning sky, small white patches appear like huge snowflakes gently dropping to earth.

They had worked through the previous night, setting charges around the installation under cover of darkness, hidden from the penetrating gaze of the Japanese reconnaissance planes. The work had not been completed, but they stopped at first light, confident they still had one more night before the Japanese landed.

Not long after sunrise, John had been woken from an hour of exhausted sleep on a makeshift bed in his office by the air raid siren. The Japanese bombers had targeted the airfield and town, keeping away from the refineries. After the all-clear, Fawcett had telephoned to confirm that P1 had been heavily bombed. Fortunately, no aircraft had been lost, as all the allied fighters were out, providing air cover for the Singapore evacuees trying to reach Java.

"All the bomber squadrons are still hidden at P2," Fawcett had explained. "The Japs haven't discovered it so far."

However, John's relief had been short-lived.

"What the devil…" John had heard the muttered swearing before Fawcett's suggestion that he should go outside and look up at the bloody sky.

"I see them too, Squadron Leader." The snowflakes were now discernible as parachutes, floating down towards the refinery.

"Bloody Jap paratroopers!" Fawcett bellows through the receiver. "My squadrons are all out of radio contact. They've caught us on the hop! Tell that Colonel Vogel to defend Pladjoe, and *not* to leave without destroying *everything*. We can't let the Japs get their hands on the oil." There is a momentary silence. "And John, get the hell out of there, *now*!"

The rattling blast of gunfire and clattering of boots on the refinery's metal walkways echoes through the installation as the invaders stream into Pladjoe – locating and disarming charges so carefully laid the previous night. In the smoke and chaos, despite the element of surprise, Vogel quickly organises his troops for a counter-attack. Outnumbering the Japanese, the Dutch begin to retake ground. Small fierce battles of hand-to-hand fighting break out between the storage tanks – the Dutch soldiers setting off the remaining charges, igniting the oil in the storage tanks – fiery steel dragons belching black smoke and flames. Choking fumes fill the shimmering air as each roaring blaze feeds on oil and oxygen. Sounds of gunfire, screams of dying men and the shriek of metal walkways buckling in the fierce heat, reverberate around Pladjoe as, doggedly, the Dutch drive the paratroopers back, out of the refinery and into the surrounding peat swamps – where they simply fade away into the undergrowth.

The close fighting takes its toll, the ground awash with the blood of dead and wounded soldiers. John and his unarmed volunteers had been ordered to take cover, away from the fighting, behind the anti-aircraft gun emplacements. Now, they emerge into the furnace and carnage, fashioning stretchers, carrying the wounded to their cars, driving the injured to the Charitas hospital, which soon becomes overwhelmed.

Peter and the nuns work tirelessly, patching men up as best they can, before loading them onto lorries bound for Oosthaven. The civilian volunteers, faces blackened with soot and covered in the combatants' blood, are given hot sweet tea for the shock, then despatched by train or lorry to safety.

"We're running out of supplies, John." Peter Janssen is mostly hidden behind his surgical mask. "Can you make it out to the Pladjoe hospital? It's been evacuated and we could use whatever they've left."

"On my way." John runs to his car, which is covered in mud, blood and the general detritus of battle. It is late afternoon, and the sky is filled with black smoke from the refinery fires. He sees the American installation at Sungei has been successfully destroyed by the allies – but at Pladjoe, only the tanks blaze while much of the machinery remains undamaged. He watches carefully for any sign of the Japanese paratroopers, but their job is complete: having successfully disrupted the plans to destroy Pladjoe, they are hiding in the swamps, awaiting reinforcements.

Reaching the abandoned hospital, so recently the well-stocked medical centre for the wealthy European community, John enters the eerily silent building, his footsteps echoing along the empty corridors. Much of use has been taken, but he raids every cupboard he can find and fills his car with medicines, syringes, bandages and blankets, before returning to the Charitas hospital. Noticing the petrol gauge is alarmingly low – he is struck, a real hammer blow, by the realisation he cannot return to P2 to be with Emily.

A white picket fence surrounds the garden entrance to the single-storey Charitas hospital, with its unbroken view down to the Musi river. Taking a break, Peter watches the last of the wounded being loaded onto ferries, heading inland with the remaining Dutch troops, away from the approaching invaders, to join their comrades further north.

John appears at his side, handing over a steaming mug of tea. The sun is an immense red orb, sinking towards the western horizon. Across the river, the storage tanks of Pladjoe burn brightly. A shiver runs through Peter's body as he stares at a world on fire.

They hear the deep rumble of approaching aircraft, looking up to see the returning allied fighters crossing the sky above them, heading into the setting sun.

"Where're they going?" asks Peter, not understanding why the planes are not landing at Palembang.

"There's another allied airbase half an hour from here, called P2. It's camouflaged so the Japs won't find it. I've been working out there for the past few months, which is why you haven't seen Emily or me lately. She's out there now. Our bomber squadrons are stationed there, ready to attack the Japs when they enter the Bangka Straits to come up the river."

"Will we be able to stop them?"

"I've no idea, Peter. P1 was taken completely by surprise this morning. Those fighters going over have been providing cover for thousands of Singapore evacuees heading our way. They'd already left P1 before this morning's air raid and surprise attack. It must've been a hell of a fight at the airbase. There's no word. I hope our boys made it over to P2."

"And Emily?"

"Under the watchful eye of Mike Harman. He'll get her out when the allies withdraw to Java.

"And us?"

"Absolutely no bloody idea!" and John raises his mug to Peter in mock salute.

They recall the last time they stood together, drinking beer, watching the children stroking Indah in the garden at John's bungalow. It seems a lifetime ago. Peter drains his mug and gives John's shoulder an affectionate pat.

"Come on," he says wearily, turning to re-enter the hospital. "Let's see what those nuns are up to." The smile does not quite reach his eyes. John gives the fires at Pladjoe a last lingering look before turning and following his friend back inside.

Over at P2, a despondent Squadron Leader Fawcett sits in the mess, preparing a report on the day's events.

He had been horrified by the sight of the paratroopers raining down on the airfield, hardly allowing the smoke to clear from the air raid. He had to admire the enemy's tactics. It was a masterstroke: the allies were expecting the invasion to come from the river the following day. The anti-aircraft guns had shot down a couple of the Japanese planes and killed a few of the descending paratroopers, but the ground staff had still been hard-pressed to keep the invading force from taking control of the airbase. By mid-afternoon, Fawcett's men had pushed the paratroopers back far enough from the base perimeter to begin the evacuation by lorry to P2. Fawcett had been one of the last to leave, by which time he had re-established radio contact with his fighters, ordering them to return directly to P2.

He sighs, rolling the pen between his fingers. In total, he has lost twenty men in the battle, but he is confident the Japanese paratroopers have sustained far greater losses. It is the only positive outcome to what has been a catastrophic day for the allies. The overwhelming feeling of responsibility for all the lost men is almost too much to bear, and he has to steel himself to face the pilots of the fighters he can hear approaching the runway. He stands, ready to go and count them in, knowing they will have lost many comrades.

In the fading light, beacons set along the runway guide the planes home. The ground staff move efficiently, checking for damage, ready to begin repairs immediately. Exhausted airmen weave their way between the mechanics, seeking sustenance and rest.

The de-brief is a grim affair, a catalogue of death and destruction: allied fighters shot down, reports describing the Japanese fleet encountering and destroying boats carrying Singapore evacuees, while dog fights played out in the skies above.

Now, Fawcett stands outside, needing to be alone in the dark, allowing his mind to grasp the enormity of the devastation he has witnessed today. He walks out of sight of the buildings, allowing silent tears to flow down his cheeks unchecked. He has lost friends, comrades, planes, the P1 airbase and the ability to defend Palembang. After his bombers have wrought vengeance on the Japanese fleet in the Bangka Straits tomorrow, he will order the withdrawal to Java, leaving Sumatra to its fate.

Surprised to find his distracted wanderings have brought him to the Crawfords' cabin, for the first time since their morning telephone call, he thinks about John and Pladjoe. Pulling himself together, he approaches the cabin. Another harrowing tale it may be, but Fawcett needs to find out what happened at the refinery while he had been dealing with the attack on the P1 airbase.

Knocking quietly, Fawcett is startled by the door immediately opening, finding himself face to face with a short stocky man he does not know. The man puts a finger to his lips, stepping outside, closing the door softly behind him.

"I'm looking for John Crawford?" Fawcett speaks in a low anxious voice.

"He's not here. I'm Mike Harman. I'm looking after John's daughter." Mike holds out a large calloused hand for Fawcett to shake. "I was hoping you'd be John. He didn't make it back yesterday and I'm getting worried. Emily got very upset tonight and I've only just managed to settle her down." Mike turns to face the small wooden structure, with its single mesh window and insubstantial wooden door – behind which, he hopes, its occupant now sleeps.

"Last night," explains Fawcett, "John was working with the Dutch troops at Pladjoe, preparing to destroy it rather than see it fall into Jap hands. I spoke with him this morning, but it was just as the paratroopers dropped down on us."

"I heard about the surprise attack. Anyone left at P1?"

"No. We've abandoned it and moved our HQ out here. As I said, I was speaking with John and he confirmed paratroopers were landing at Pladjoe too. I told him to get out. The Dutch troops were there to defend it, or blow it up if forced to retreat."

"So, what happened to John?" Mike's whispers become more apprehensive, gesturing to Fawcett to keep his voice down.

"He should've driven back here immediately, ready to depart for Java with the other civilians. The Dutch drove the Japs into the swamp, but I've heard reports they lost a lot of men, failed to destroy the refinery except for firing some storage tanks, and have retreated, leaving Palembang undefended. It's a bloody disaster."

"Maybe he's with the Dutch?"

"They've withdrawn completely, headed up river to join their units in the north. John wouldn't have gone with them, not without Emily. With the Dutch gone, the town and refinery are completely undefended, except for what little cover we can provide from the air."

Aware their voices have risen again, the two men stand silently in the darkness, listening for any sound of movement within the cabin. They can only hear Indah, restlessly pacing around her enclosure.

Finally, Mike breaks the silence. "What happens now?" His voice is barely audible, full of trepidation.

"In the morning, we send our squadrons over to bomb the hell out of the Jap fleet as it comes through the Bangka Straits. Once our men are airborne, we evacuate the base down to Oosthaven and cross to Java, where we'll rendezvous with the returning bombers."

"And Emily?"

"Goes to Oosthaven with you."

"And the tiger?"

"I'm not interested in the bloody tiger, Mike." Fawcett's voice betrays his frustration. "Let it go or shoot it. It's not my problem." Leaving an open-mouthed Mike Harman, the squadron leader strides away to hide the emotion he can no longer control. *He* had asked John to help the Dutch colonel, so *he* is responsible for whatever has happened to the man he has come to know as a friend. He may be responsible for leaving the child fatherless, but he will not take responsibility for a flaming tiger.

Still, silent, but very much awake, filled with anger and terror, Emily lies in her bed, having overheard most of the conversation. Why aren't they going to Pladjoe to find Daddy if he is there? With Daddy missing, there is only Indah. Indah, who she loves more than anyone except for Daddy. Indah, who the nasty officer wants Mike to shoot. Well, she is not going to allow that to happen. Emily waits until the cabin is completely silent before slipping out through the door and creeping round to the enclosure. Wrapping her small arms around the tiger's neck, she clings to Indah, desperately longing for Daddy and determined to keep Indah safe.

Chapter 8

Sunday, 15th February 1942

In the pre-dawn mist, the roar of engines reverberates around the P2 airbase as the Blenheim and Hudson bombers follow one another along the bumpy runway, launching themselves into the sky. Once in formation, they head due east, intent on unleashing their destructive cargo upon the Japanese fleet entering the Bangka Straits. At sunrise, the faster, more manoeuvrable Hurricane and Buffalo fighters follow as an escort, prepared to do acrobatic battle with the enemy's fighters intent on destroying the allied bombers.

Watching the insubstantial number of aircraft thunder away to attack a vast, well-armed invasion force, Squadron Leader Fawcett can only hope this final David and Goliath battle will inflict sufficient damage, delaying the invasion force long enough for any remaining civilians at Palembang and Pladjoe to escape. With a heavy heart – he knows many of his brave airmen will never reach Java – Fawcett forces his mind to focus on the evacuation of the base. There is still much to be done and he would like everyone en route to Oosthaven before nightfall.

By late morning, most of the ground crew and ancillary staff are ready to depart, so a final meal is served in the mess. Fawcett notes the absence of Mike Harman and Emily Crawford, assuming they are 'dealing' with the tiger. Ashamed of the previous evening's outburst, he hopes they are releasing Indah back into the jungle, rather than having to destroy the magnificent creature. There is still no word from John Crawford, and Fawcett is beginning to lose hope that his friend, if still alive, will get to P2 in time to join the evacuation.

Mike Harman is frantic with worry. Woken by the aircraft engines before dawn, he had been dismayed to find Emily's little bed and Indah's enclosure both empty. Despite attempts to keep their voices low, Mike is tormented by the thought that Emily may have overheard his conversation with the overwrought squadron leader.

For most of the day, Mike searches the jungle around the southern perimeter of the base. He knows Emily's camp is about a mile out, but not the exact direction, so there is far too much ground to cover for an effective search.

Now, with dusk approaching and only a handful of lorries remaining, there is still no sign of Emily. He spots Fawcett, who is checking that nothing of use to the enemy has been left behind. Taking a deep breath, he approaches the glowering officer.

"You and Emily should've been on one of the earlier civilian lorries. Why are you still here?"

"She's gone." Mike holds up his hands, palms open, a picture of misery. Fawcett immediately realises that 'gone' does not mean already left with the convoy. For a long moment, the two men simply stare at one another.

"She must've heard us last night," suggests Mike. "There was no sign of her or Indah this morning. I've been out searching all day."

There is another protracted silence while both men embrace the consequence of their indiscretion. The child, learning her father is missing and her beloved tiger may be shot, has fled.

"We *have* to go, Mike." To Mike, this softer, pitying tone, is unendurable.

"I can't go without her," is his simple response. "I can't. I promised her father I'd take care of her." Fawcett turns his back on Mike, striding away to the nearest lorry, where he opens the passenger door and speaks to the driver. Getting out, the driver and Fawcett move around to the tailgate, from where the silent ground crew watch the unfolding drama. Fawcett signals for two men to climb down from the rear of the truck. The four cross the compound to where Mike stands, still searching around for any sign of the girl.

"I'm sorry, Mike. I can't leave without you. The evacuation of everyone on this base is my responsibility." Fawcett nods to the three servicemen who take hold of Mike, wrestling him to the ground. Efficiently, they tie his hands behind his back, lift him and load him unceremoniously into the back of the lorry. Screaming obscenities, Mike struggles desperately to break free, before a well-placed punch to the temple renders him unconscious.

Fawcett takes a last look around the base.

"God forgive me," he mutters, "because John never will." As if in answer, a peal of thunder rumbles across the heavens and by the time he clambers up into the passenger seat, rain pounds the windscreen and forked lightning splits the darkening sky. Wordlessly, the driver puts the vehicle into gear, accelerating away along the Oosthaven road.

Just over a mile away, Emily listens to the tremendous storm, the rain thundering onto the flat rock above her head. Flashes of lightning illuminate the pool, and she is mesmerised by the raindrops bouncing on its glistening silver surface. Cuddled up beside Indah in their dry protected cave, Emily is not afraid of the savage storm – her fear is concentrated on the safety of her father.

Her thoughts return to the day she and Daddy had found the tiger cub, orphaned by poachers. It had been the last day he had time to spend with her. After that, the open grassland she had carefully sketched, had been transformed into the P2 airbase – the construction of which had taken up all Daddy's time. Moving out to P2 had been incredibly exciting, she adored the little cabin with its enclosure for Indah. Emily understood it would be too far from Pladjoe for Lai to come too and, although she missed the housekeeper's maternal presence, at least she no longer had to go to school but could spend her days in the jungle with Indah. Over time, she saw less and less of Daddy, often spending days with Mike while her father returned to work at Pladjoe. Adapting to her solitary existence, she only returned to the base at dusk, in time for the evening meal in the mess.

Emily pictures the last time she had seen Daddy – he hugged her tightly and waved from the car before driving back to Pladjoe, leaving her with Mike. Daddy had been distracted, not really listening as she told him how Indah's training was progressing – or not progressing, which was the real truth. He had insisted that, if he was not at the base when the order came to evacuate, she must go with Mike, releasing Indah to fend for herself. She had not believed that would ever happen. There were no air raids out here. Everyone said P2 was a secret from the Japanese. They were perfectly safe.

She replays the overheard conversation between Mike and the squadron leader: Daddy missing, the Dutch soldiers leaving, everyone leaving P2 the next day. She had been about to go outside to find out more about Daddy, to demand they help her search for him – but just as she rose from her bed, the officer had sworn and told Mike to shoot Indah. The shock, the anger, the terror, the determination. A faint smile crosses her face at the thought of the mess cook discovering his larder had been raided during the night. They had made their escape. Emily would take care of Indah until Daddy came back to find her.

Emily strokes Indah's soft fur. The tiger is restless, growling, unsettled by the storm. When the rain finally ceases, they emerge into the wet twilight, climbing up the slippery rock to avoid the squelching mud and mosquitoes surrounding the pool. In the weeks she has spent here with Indah, her confidence has grown: happy to pass hours foraging for wild fruit, digging up yams and collecting nuts. As for Indah, the supposed predator has caught nothing – relying on Emily to provide meat scraps begged from the mess.

Now, Emily watches Indah, hoping her tiger is finally learning to hunt, as the graceful cat stalks stealthily around nearby trees and bushes. Something has attracted Indah's attention, although she shows no sign of preparing to pounce, to make her first kill. Instead, Indah huffs and growls as she does at home when a stranger approaches her enclosure. Intrigued, Emily cautiously moves over to Indah, crouching down to look more closely.

"Oh!" She backs away in alarm, hand covering her mouth. A body lies in the bushes, face down, unmoving. Hand shaking, she presses gently on a shoulder. As there is no response, she tries again, more forcefully. A groan and, as the body rolls over, she sees it is a man, opening his eyes to stare up at her. He blinks rapidly as if to clear some hallucination.

"Water?" he croaks. Emily fetches her water bottle from the cave and holds it to his lips, allowing water to trickle into his open mouth. He coughs and splutters, trying to swallow.

"Can you sit up? It would be easier to drink." She takes the hand he raises, hauling him up to sitting. Grasping the proffered bottle, he drinks greedily.

"Not too quickly!" she admonishes. "You'll be sick! Can you walk? I've got food nearby and you need to get dry." He slowly shakes his head. "*Please* try, it's only a few yards. You're shivering. I can make tea for you." Again, he wearily shakes his head. "Crawl then," she pleads. "It's not far, just a little way. *Please!*" Eventually, he rolls forward, onto all fours, crawling with Emily supporting him under the arms, pulling, guiding him towards the cave.

Once inside, he collapses, breathing heavily from the exertion. In the dark, Emily finds the candles and matches – creating soft flickering light, casting shadows that dance on the cave walls. She lights a little camping stove, putting water on to boil. Once the tea is made, she adds a little cold water, then dunks a dry biscuit into the warm liquid and pushes it between his chattering teeth. With infinite patience, she feeds him tiny amounts of the soaked biscuit, supporting his head on her knees.

Indah pads into the cave, coming over to sniff both man and biscuit. She lowers her great head onto Emily's shoulder, clearly put out by all the attention being shown to this stranger. Emily offers her a biscuit, which she crunches noisily before settling down to wash herself.

How has he found her camp? He could be from the airbase, but in the weak candlelight, she cannot make out his features. Well, whoever he is, he has fallen asleep. Moving his head gently from her lap, she brings the candle closer, able to distinguish the flying jacket with the spread wings of the allied air forces. Satisfied she is in no danger from the sleeping man, Emily finally releases the tension keeping her alert. Exhausted, she wrestles the airman out of his sodden jacket, boots and muddy trousers, covering him with a blanket before curling up on the small picnic rug and instantly falling asleep.

All is dark and peaceful at the Charitas hospital. Ghostly white apparitions glide silently between beds as the nuns watch over the severely wounded and dying men.

Peter Janssen and John Crawford walk out into the night air, fresher after the ferocious storm, making their way down a muddy track to the river. The stress of the day's events drains away, leaving both men wrung out, exhausted. With no petrol or ferries remaining, there is no question of leaving now. John's thoughts are constantly with Emily, making her way to Java in the capable hands of Mike Harman. He feels a terrible sense of guilt – have his actions taken from his daughter the one parent she has left? Should he have abandoned the refinery, the Dutch troops, his volunteers and driven to P2 as soon as he saw the paratroopers?

"You did what you thought was right." Peter seems to read his mind. "You've made sure Emily is safe. That's all you can do."

"I should've stayed with my daughter and to hell with Pladjoe." John's guilt flares into anger.

"You helped save lives today, John," Peter soothes "Many lives."

The two men gaze up at the benign silver moon – ever dependable as she bestows her gentle light, a calming counterbalance to the harsh realities facing them with the new dawn.

Chapter 9

Monday, 16th February 1942

Unbidden sounds, images and emotions spiral through his mind, a kaleidoscope of flashing memories – claustrophobia, pressure in his ears, men's screams, tearing fuselage, impact, fire, green, heat, pain, thirst, fatigue, gunfire, running, rain, a tiger, a girl, water. He is too hot. He is so cold. He needs to run. Why has he stopped running?

P2 is eerily quiet as Emily and Indah pick their way through the abandoned base. In the mess, she discovers packets of dried soup, tinned spam and powdered milk – all forgotten in the rush to leave. She stuffs all she can find into her backpack while Indah licks the remnants of the final meal from the abandoned crockery left on rows of trestle tables.

Approaching the cabin, she pictures Daddy waiting there, experiencing a stab of disappointment at finding it empty. Packing a few clothes for herself and the airman into the bulging backpack, she drapes blankets and towels around her shoulders before stepping outside, closing the door for what she imagines is the final time.

Returning to the cave, she finds the airman semi-conscious, delirious. His head feels very hot but he is also shivering. Covering him with extra blankets, she soaks a towel in the pool to place around his head.

Outside, stripping off her dirty clothes, Emily wades out into the icy water of the pool. Indah follows, the partial webbing between her toes enabling the tiger to pull strongly through the clear water. No skulking crocodile will make a move on Emily with her swimming companion close by! Unexpectedly, Indah puts her head under the surface. Emily watches in amazement as water sprays into the air, igniting a myriad of sparkling droplets as the tiger's head bursts into view, a large struggling fish trapped between her mighty jaws. Indah swims back to shore, settling down with the fish between her front paws, ready to enjoy her fresh catch.

"You did it! You caught your own dinner! Hurrah for Indah!" Delighted, Emily turns somersaults in the water in celebration. Breathing heavily from the exertion, she doggy-paddles back to shore, clambering onto the rock to stretch out and dry off.

Closing her eyes, Emily listens to an array of birdsong. Each has its own melody and rhythm: high-pitched twittering vibrato and deep resonant long-held tones fill the air – accompanied by percussive crickets and the splashing stream, cascading over rocks, down into the pool.

Emily's thoughts settle on her father, a visceral yearning tightening her chest, forming its own tiny stream of tears, trickling down each side of her face, into her ears. Meal completed, Indah jumps up beside Emily, moving close to lick the salty tears. Her fishy breath is too much for the unhappy girl, who sits up, spell broken, leaning away from the rasping tongue.

Stoic, Emily dresses in clean clothes and takes the dirty pile to rinse out in the pool, spreading them out on the rock to dry. In the cave, she makes soup from a packet salvaged from the base, pouring it into two mugs. After drinking her own, she crouches beside the airman, hopeful he will be able to drink the soup. He seems calmer and has stopped shivering. Removing the damp towel, she gently rubs his arm until his eyes open.

"Do you remember where you are?" she asks. His eyes focus on her but he remains silent. "I'm going to support your head so you can drink this soup." He allows her to lift his head onto her lap, sipping cautiously as she tips the mug to his lips. It is a slow awkward process so Emily does what she does best – she talks to him.

"I found you after the storm last night. Actually, Indah found you. Indah's a tiger but she won't hurt you. At least, she hasn't hurt anyone before but she did kill her first fish today. We come from the airbase. Is that where you come from too? Why were you in the jungle? I thought all the planes had left for Java. I was supposed to go to Java but that horrible squadron leader told Mike to shoot Indah and I wasn't going to let him, so we came here, to my camp. I found this camp with Daddy when we found Indah. I'm Emily Crawford. Did I tell you that? Anyway, that's who I am. Who are you? Are you…"

He suddenly raises his hand – gesturing for her to be quiet.

"Sorry, Daddy says I can talk for England."

"He's right," smiles the man, pushing himself up to sitting, running fingers through cropped white-blond hair, studying the girl and his surroundings. "Give me a mo'?" he asks, "I'm not feelin' so great. A bit dizzy and that." Emily nods, taking the mugs out to wash in the pool. After a few minutes, he crawls out to sit beside her, shrinking back in terror as the tiger jumps down from a rock above their heads to flop down on Emily's other side.

"Jeez! Aren't y'fraid of that thing?"

She shakes her head, stroking Indah complacently.

"I've had her since she was a few weeks old," Emily explains. "Her mother was shot by poachers and she was all alone, so Daddy and I took her home."

"Y'know, now I come t' think of it, I remember some of the boys sayin' there was a girl with a tiger about the place. Must've been you! What did y' say her name was?"

"Indah. That's with an 'h' on the end. It means beautiful and I think she is." The statement brooks no argument. "What's your name? You sound Australian."

"Yep. Canberra born and bred. Flight Lieutenant Matt Connelly at your service!" He offers her a salute, making her giggle.

"How did you get here?"

Instantly, Matt's smile disappears, his voice quietening to a whisper. "Our plane crashed in the jungle. All m' mates are gone. I'm the only one left 'cause I was in the rear gun turret, which broke off in the trees. The rest burnt." He pauses, unwelcome images of the burnt-out fuselage pouring into his mind. "We'd blown a few Japs out the water but got hit by one of their fighters. Tried t' get back t' P2. Didn't make it." Matt shrugs, gazing bleakly into the distance. "When I came to, I just hurt everywhere. I *had* t' get goin' in the end 'cause I'd a terrible thirst on me. Then the bloody Japs started shootin' at me an' I had t' make a run for it. Lucky f' me, I lost'em in the storm. Thought I was a gonna when I heard that tiger of yours."

She grins up at him.

"Little did you know, Indah is the *worst* hunter in the world!"

"Well, that's all about me. D'you wanna tell me what on earth you're doin' out here all alone?"

"I'm not alone! Indah's with me. Anyway, Daddy brought me out to P2 when the air raids started. He said I could bring Indah back here to teach her how to hunt. But I can't teach her. I don't know how and Daddy is always too busy."

"What does y' dad do?"

"He works for Shell but the squadron leader asked him to help build P2. It was just a big field when we first came out here."

"Ah. I see now. Your dad's John Crawford, isn't he?"

Emily nods, looking away to hide the threatening tears. "He left me at P2 with Mike Harman. Mike works for Shell, too. Daddy made me promise to stay with Mike and I would've, but he was going to shoot Indah."

"Now why would he go an' do a thing like that?"

"That nasty squadron leader told him to. He didn't think I could hear, but I could, so Indah and I came out here. Mike doesn't know where the camp is. They've all gone now. I walked back to P2 this morning while you were asleep. Everyone's gone."

"So, what did y' plan t' do out here all by yourself?"

"Wait for Daddy, of course!" Indignant, she glares at Matt with absolute certainty.

"And where exactly is he now?"

"I don't know. They said he was at Pladjoe, but the Japanese came and the Dutch left, but Daddy wouldn't go with them. Mike and the squadron leader said he would come back for me."

Thoughtfully, Matt rubs the stubble on his chin. As far as he is aware, Pladjoe has been abandoned, the plan to destroy it having failed. If Crawford was out there when the attack came, he could easily have been killed or injured. If alive, he must be in danger of being captured by the Japanese landing at Palembang. If he did escape, he could be making his way back to his daughter. On foot, through the jungle, it could take a couple of days.

"Okay, Emily. Let's say your dad is makin' his way here from Pladjoe. On foot, it could take a few days."

"But he has a car!"

"I think if he still had a car, he'd be here by now. Let's give him a couple more days, eh? That'll give me time to feel better too."

"And what if he doesn't come?" Her voice is tremulous, full of dread.

"Well, then we'll make our way down to Oosthaven 'cause that's where we're all meant t' be headed, so we can get over to Java. What d'ya say? Is that a good plan?"

"I suppose so." Emily wraps her arms around her drawn in knees. She will not say anything to Matt, but she has no intention of going anywhere without Daddy and Indah.

John Crawford waits outside the hospital, gazing down to the river, watching the Japanese troop barges approach. He is terribly afraid, the contents of his stomach and bowels threatening to explode simultaneously from either end of his trembling body. In awe of Peter and the nuns, who continue administering to their patients with calm efficiency, he wishes he had a role to distract him from the rising fear.

The nightmare begins as the invasion force lands – staccato beats of marching boots with orders screamed in a language completely foreign to his ears. Black merciless eyes reveal contempt as soldiers arrive and he offers no resistance. John is pushed to the ground – kicked until he cries out in pain, folding himself into a foetal position to protect his head. As the invaders pour into the hospital, there is complete chaos. Peter roars, nuns scream, enemy soldiers shout – until a single shot rings out above the clamour, followed by an uneasy silence.

John lies still, unwilling to draw attention, afraid the kicking will begin again. Rough hands take hold of his arms, dragging him to his feet.

"Are you doctor?" a soldier – short, slight, in lightweight green tunic and trousers – shouts up at him, a fine spray of spittle covering John's face. Shaking his head, John is instantly pushed out of the hospital grounds, down to the quayside, to join other terrified Europeans – rounded up from the harbour or dragged off the barges.

"No talk! No talk!" The staccato mantra is repeated intermittently as sneering soldiers prod the terrified captives with bayonets, forcing the men apart from the women and children. John is fairly sure those dragged from the boats must be the unfortunate Singapore evacuees, taken prisoner in the Bangka Straits. The desperate wails of frightened children rise above the ineffectual hushing of distressed parents – unable to mask their own terror, leaving John grateful that Emily is not witness to this appalling scene.

At gunpoint, the men are marched off towards the town. Passing through abandoned streets, pitted with bomb craters and burnt out buildings, they are taken to Palembang jail, a whitewashed square stone building, enclosing a central exercise yard.

"No talk! No talk!" The dejected prisoners, in varying degrees of thirst, hunger, exhaustion, shuffle towards the unprepossessing building, with its sinister barred windows and iron gates. Like cattle, they are herded into empty cells, with tiny high-barred windows, which soon become ovens – airless and overcrowded. Slumped on the floor, men begin to break down: crying out in pain, fear, humiliation and utter desolation.

John finds a space where he can rest his back against a damp wall, stretching out his legs. Closing his eyes against the unfolding horror, he believes he has passed through the very gates of hell. A nauseating dread threatens his sanity. He attempts to slow and deepen his breathing, trying not to panic or give in to despair.

Chapter 10

Wednesday, 18th February 1942

From her vantage point on the rock, Emily admires Matt, gracefully carving his way through the water. Even Indah seems impressed as she sits by the pool, watching the airman swim back and forth, her head turning from side to side as if watching tennis. After a full day's rest, the Australian has regained some of his strength – is enjoying the exercise and the much-needed wash.

Becoming used to the tiger's presence, Matt allows her to sniff him. Despite Emily's encouragement, he cannot bring himself to stroke her, but at least his body now remains within its skin when she comes near. He remains amazed at how relaxed the girl is with Indah. She clearly loves the tiger and he worries about what will become of the big cat when they have to leave.

Wrapping a towel around his waist, Matt joins Emily on the rock.

"Tell me about Australia." Emily sits cross-legged, facing him, eager to hear about his life and country.

"Well now, I've lived all m' life in Canberra until the war, so I don't know much of anywhere else in Aus. Canberra is pretty small for a capital but there's a lot of construction goin' on, tho' it's stopped now there's a war on. Guess it'll get goin' again. I joined up when I was twenty, a couple of years ago, when the Aussie air force set up RAAF Station Canberra."

"Did you want to be a pilot?"

"I guess. I did m' basic trainin' but there was no time t' get m' wings. 'Cause of the war, we had t' learn real quick. I joined a Hudson crew and trained as the rear gunner. They're called 'Tail-end Charlies'. D'ya get it?"

"Of course!" Emily gives him a withering look. "The rear gunner is on the tail. I've seen the Hudson bombers at the base."

"Right, Miss Know-It-All," he leans forwards and ruffles her hair. Emily sticks out her tongue, making him chuckle.

"So, you're twenty-two. I'm eleven and a quarter. Carry on. Tell me more."

"Please?"

"Tell me more, *please*!"

"Well, I've got two brothers and a sister. Joe and Pete are both older, they joined the army. Gwen is fifteen and back in Canberra with m' folks – Alice and George. We've two dogs – Ricky and Beau, eight horses and ten thousand cattle."

"Ten *thousand*? Really? How do you count them all?"

"Slowly! Nah, it's a rough number but there or thereabouts."

"What does Gwen do?"

"She goes t' school mostly. She likes t' ride the horses 'n' she's a real good runner too."

"All those beastly brothers she needs to get away from!" Emily falls back on her elbows, giggling helplessly at her own joke, as Matt playfully cuffs the air in front of her head.

"Very funny," he pretends to be affronted. "How 'bout y' tell me who's in your family instead of taking the mickey outa mine?"

"There's just me and Daddy." He looks bewildered as the smile disappears and the huge brown eyes fill with tears. He waits, too awkward to probe further. "That's why we're in Sumatra. After Mummy and the baby died, Daddy wanted to get away from England. Granny and Grandpa wanted me to stay with them but I wanted to come with Daddy. They were really cross, but I think Daddy was pleased. I'm sure he wanted me to come with him."

"I'm sure he did, Emily." His heart breaks for this precocious little girl – so courageous and resilient. Deep inside this fierce little warrior is a fractured soul, unfledged, surviving alone in a hostile world.

Without thinking, he wraps his arms around her.

"We'll find him, okay?" She nods, clinging to him, comforted by the human contact. "Why don't you tell me about finding Indah?"

"When Daddy first came out to P2, I came with him and we found this pool. He wouldn't let me go into the cave because it was an animal's home." Successfully distracted, Emily begins to relax but Matt keeps his arms loosely around her waist as she leans back into his chest and they both face the pool.

"Was Indah in the cave?"

"No. We found her hiding under some tree roots. Then we found blood and Daddy swore and said poachers had shot Indah's mother. I carried her all the way home in the car but we didn't have any milk to feed her so Daddy stopped at the Charitas hospital to see Dr Peter."

"Is he the vet then?"

"No, silly. He's a proper doctor. He does operations and everything and he's Daddy's friend. Sister Catherina, she's a nun, was *really* scared and made a terrible fuss, which Dr Peter thought was very funny. Anyway, she got a baby's bottle and milk for Indah and we took her home."

Now Emily breaks away from Matt, turning to watch his reaction to her incredible tale.

"Dr Peter said it was my job to find a good name, so I searched through all my books. In the end, it was Lai, she's our housekeeper, who suggested Indah. Loads of people came to see her and the house Daddy and Dr Peter built. I brought her out and let them stroke her."

Matt can just imagine how Emily would have been in her element, showing off her exotic pet, impressing the local kids.

"She got so big, Daddy decided to bring her out to P2 and make a new enclosure by our cabin. It's been much more fun for her out here. She's even learnt to catch fish! She's so clever."

On cue, the tiger jumps up to join them and Emily rubs behind her ears, eliciting a loud purring which vibrates through the rock. They sit contentedly, these three unlikely companions – thrown together by the circumstances of war, weaving a bond of trust and friendship.

It is the casual brutality that shocks John Crawford. The Japanese may be the enemy, their countries at war with one another, but the savage treatment of the prisoners lacks any humanity.

After a night in the cells with no water, food or sanitation, the stink of unwashed bodies and human waste becomes intolerable, so the men are in a dreadful condition by the time they are ordered to the exercise yard. When a sallow middle-aged man finds he is no longer able to stand, a shot echoes around the closed-in yard: he is dead before he hits the ground. Instinctively, men attempt to support their weaker fellow captives – earning themselves slapped faces and vicious punches. Eyes down, John endures the clamour – animals being cruelly beaten, left whimpering in pain and confusion.

After standing in the hot sun for what seems hours, soldiers bring out several buckets of brackish water, allowing the men to drink using their cupped hands. Another soldier empties a sack of rice onto the ground. The hungry prisoners grab handfuls, chewing on the dry grains now covered in dirt from the yard.

Again, they are made to stand: more men collapse, shot where they fall. Sick with terror, John and a dozen other men are marched outside to what had once been a public garden in front of the jail. There, they are forced to dig shallow graves with their bare hands, carrying the dead bodies from the yard for burial. Their fingers become sore and grit from the sandy soil lodges deep under their nails. Sharp stones and rocks gouge fragile palms, their own blood mingling with that of the dead prisoners. Too dehydrated to shed tears, the gravediggers bow their heads in silent prayer before being manhandled back into the squalid cells.

In his mind, John erects a solid wall: brick by brick, encircling, rising to block the horror, protecting his sanity.

"I wish I'd been shot." The anguished words push their way through the cracked lips of a badly sunburned man lying on the floor beside John. "Then it would be over. I don't think I can take any more."

John reaches out to grip his shoulder. "Hold on." He hopes to keep the desperate man calm. "Try to hold on." For answer, the despairing soul begins to rock back and forth, quietly moaning. Others avert their eyes, unable to offer comfort – equally stranded in this waking nightmare. Each battles his own demons, struggling to stay afloat, above the threatening maelstrom of fear and madness.

Chapter 11

Thursday, 19th February 1942

Emily wakes from a dream of swimming with Indah in the Pladjoe club pool to the drier reality of the jungle cave. Aching from the hard floor, only slightly softened by a picnic rug and blanket, she checks both Matt and Indah are still asleep before crawling outside into the first cloudless sky she has seen for weeks.

She listens to the dawn song of gibbons: a long sweeping call, ascending to a stuttering high-pitched cry. Colourful birds perch among the trees, celebrating the new day with distinctive sweet melodies. Ever-present crickets and buzzing insects surround her, creating the rhythmic jungle heartbeat. Already baking hot and humid, Emily breathes in the earthy odour of damp foliage mixed with sweet floral blossom, giving her eyes time to adjust to the bright daylight.

Needing the lavatory, she pulls on her boots and picks up the trowel – kept just inside the cave entrance to dig the necessary hole. The 'dunny' as Matt calls it, is a small clearing about fifty yards from the cave, behind a row of bushes whose broad silky leaves have proved ideal in lieu of paper. A loud swish makes her jump. Looking up, she spies a huge orangutang, its immense orange arms pulling it gracefully through the canopy high above her.

"Can't a girl get a bit of privacy?" she laughs to herself.

Refusing to be alarmed by every forest creature, Emily digs her little hole, pulls down her lower clothing and squats, balancing carefully to avoid any unpleasant accidents.

The hand covers her mouth, cutting off Emily's scream as she is grabbed from behind and hoisted into the air. Held tightly against an unseen assailant, her eyes widen in terror as two Japanese soldiers appear before her, their predatory grins matching their malevolent black eyes. As urine streams onto her captor's trouser leg, he throws her to the ground, momentarily knocking the breath from her. Before Emily can cry out, cloth is forced deep into her mouth, making her gag. The taste is so revolting she retches, bile soaking into the cloth, burning her throat.

Pushed onto her back, shoulders pinioned, she kicks out wildly, shaking her head, desperate to disgorge the gag. The soldiers snicker, a pack of hyenas, eager to tear at her tender flesh.

One of her boots connects and the laughter ceases. Pain explodes in her head from a punch to her face. She experiences the sense of falling, images around her blur, sound is muffled. A sense of gazing up from the depths of a dark pool – struggling for breath, trapped, confused, frightened.

Rising back into full consciousness, rough hands grip her ankles. At the sight of the knife, she tries to scream, terrified, watery brown eyes pleading. The blade slashes through the clothing holding her legs together. Cruel hands slither up from her ankles to grip the insides of her knees, forcing them apart.

The solder pinning her shoulders covers Emily's face with his cap. She hears fumbling, heavy breathing. Shockingly, Emily's world turns white hot – an intolerable pain ripping her body apart. The detonation of unbearable agony deep within her rigid core, engulfs her whole being. A rising torrent, its unstoppable force splits into two: one crashing wave dislodging the gag, thrusting up and out in an ear-splitting scream – the other, a deadly tsunami, smashing through the delicate construct of every single thought and memory.

The terrible scream brings two hundred pounds of avenging teeth and claws down on the soldier kneeling between the girl's legs. His neck breaks, the windpipe crushed before he opens his mouth.

As Matt bursts into the clearing, Indah is at the second soldier, her murderous claws raking the man's chest, her jaws clamped around his throat. Before Matt can reach the third, the soldier draws a pistol and fires off three rounds at the snarling tiger. Wary of the gun, Matt gathers the dropped trowel and circles behind, knocking the last soldier out with the heavy wooden handle. As the man collapses, Matt smashes the trowel into his face, over and over, reducing it to a pulp of blood, bone and brain tissue.

As his uncontrolled fury ebbs, Matt confronts the macabre scene. Indah's lifeless body lies sprawled across one dead soldier, jaws still locked around his throat. Another lies dead in a pool of blood at Emily's feet, throat torn out. Matt crawls towards her, tears of impotent rage streaming down his face. Gently closing her bloodied legs, he searches for a pulse; overwhelmed with relief to feel a shallow irregular heartbeat.

Gathering the child's broken body into his trembling arms, Matt stares at Indah, fresh tears on his cheeks. The tiger had streaked away from the cave the instant Emily's scream had pierced the peaceful morning air – transformed from affectionate companion to ferocious killing machine in the few bounds it took her to reach Emily.

As he carries the girl back to the cave, Matt reflects on the magnificent cat. Without wishing to anthropomorphise the tiger, he concedes there had been a definite bond between Indah and Emily. Since he had been with them, Emily had never been wary or hesitant – nor had he ever heard Indah growl threateningly. Emily loved the tiger, no doubt about that, but what of Indah? A rational man would believe the cub had grown to depend on the human food provider, but there must be more to it – Indah had unhesitatingly killed to protect the child.

Matt washes Emily's face and body with infinite care, gently dressing her in clean underwear. She remains limp, unresponsive – increasing his anxiety. Her nose is no longer bleeding but bruises are darkening the swollen skin around her eyes, suggesting delicate facial bones may be fractured or broken. She still bleeds from the atrocious violation of her child's body and Matt experiences a renewed surge of rage, angered by the men's quick deaths – they deserved the same level of barbarity inflicted upon a helpless innocent. Unable to grasp the extent of Emily's trauma, he is consumed by guilt – he should have been with the girl when those bastards found her.

Matt goes to the pool to wash. His feet are cut and scratched from his dash to reach Emily, so he carefully bathes and dries them, before putting on John Crawford's socks. Matt quickly dresses, lacing his boots, preparing for the long walk to find help.

He fills Emily's rucksack with full water bottles, figs and nuts they have collected, and loosens the straps so it will fit on his back. Taking the largest blanket, Matt ties the opposing ends together, forming a large sling. He puts his head through and settles the sling on one shoulder – the knot behind the backpack so it will not rub while he walks. Gently, he places the inert child inside the protective pouch he has created, resting her head against his shoulder and wrapping the lower arm around his waist.

With his precious cargo in place, Matt returns to the clearing to retrieve the pistol. Sliding out the magazine, he finds three rounds remaining, so tucks it inside his shirt. He finds the knife used to cut Emily's clothing and sheathes it through his belt. Finally, Matt runs his hand through Indah's thick fur, silently thanking her for saving their lives.

Looking around the violent scene for one last time, knowing it will haunt his dreams for a lifetime, Matt strides off through the Japanese-infested jungle, beginning his forty-mile trek towards Palembang – in search of the Charitas hospital and Dr Peter.

PART THREE

Chapter 12

Doctor Peter Janssen and the Charitas nuns fall into an uneasy routine of care and prayer. With only a few patients remaining, they pass the time counting and organising supplies of medicines and food. Laundry is boil-washed and hung out to dry, sheets and robes bleaching white in the blazing sun. Floors and windows are scrubbed and mosquito nets repaired. The apparent industry forms a fragile dam, determinedly holding back a torrent of fear.

On the day of the landings, Japanese soldiers had stormed into the hospital, screaming orders, slapping and kicking both patients and staff. The European patients – mostly the injured from Pladjoe, unfit to be evacuated in time – had been dragged away, along with John Crawford. The few locals, with a variety of ailments from broken bones to malaria, after cursory interrogation, had been allowed to remain.

Now, Peter stands before the Japanese general, frightened nuns behind him, in enforced attendance. Grabbed by his hair, Peter is forced into a low bow. A kick to his lower legs drops him to his knees – a boot heel ground painfully into the hand he puts down to keep his balance. Hearing sharp intakes of breath and the rattle of wooden rosary beads, Peter sends up his own prayer that these gentle sisters will not be harmed.

The doctor looks up to meet the malevolent gaze of General Sato – small, slender, dressed in a double-breasted green tunic, his green trousers tucked into knee-length leather boots. An anxious-looking interpreter in uniform, clearly afraid of his superior, steps forwards to deliver the general's orders – unable to meet the prisoners' frightened eyes, focusing on a point above their heads.

"Hospital may continue. Only General Sato permit treatment for prisoners. Doctor and nuns stay at hospital all time. No leave."

With that short statement, the general, his henchmen and a relieved interpreter march out of the hospital – leaving behind a residual sense of evil, and two armed guards stationed outside the front entrance.

Reverend Mother Helena, the most senior of the nuns, moves forwards to help Peter back to his feet. Pulling a clean handkerchief from her robe and licking one corner, she gently wipes the dirt from the back of his bruised hand.

"Thank you, Mother, I'm fine."

"None of us is fine, Peter," Mother Helena's ashen face is drawn, anxious. "First, they take the poor injured men, including poor John, and now they attack you. It is too much. They go too far. It is barbaric!" Her voice rises with indignation in the aftermath of terror.

"Worse than the Nazis?" asks a pale Sister Catherina, coming forwards to inspect Peter's injury.

"Maybe so, Sister. Maybe so." Mother Helena's tone is one of defiance. "But we must still pray for them as we pray for all living souls."

Sister Catherina looks mutinous. "That's if they *have* souls."

Reverend Mother raises an admonitory finger, then pauses, the trace of a smile deepening the creases of her lined face. "All the more reason to pray for them, Sister." Sister Catherina bows her head in acquiescence, and to hide her own smile.

Reverend Mother claps her hands to gain the room's

attention.

"We must continue as we have always done, sisters, despite these difficult days. Our faith will be tested and we shall not be found wanting. We must open our hearts to all those suffering under this wicked oppression. We must care for the sick and bring comfort to the dying. We must trust in our Lord to bring us through this ordeal."

Peter looks round at the bowed heads and clasped hands of the nuns. He has become very fond of these selfless women and his admiration only grows at the courage they display in the face of such adversity. Struggling with his own faith after the death of his wife during the Nazi occupation of the Netherlands, Peter can still appreciate the comfort their belief brings. What he cannot understand, is why God, in whom these good souls place their entire trust, allows such torment to be inflicted upon his faithful servants.

At dusk, Matt Connelly seeks higher ground, away from the swamps and mosquitoes latching onto his exposed skin. Keeping the setting sun at his back, he moves cautiously towards Palembang, not allowing branches to swing back or thorns to become embedded in the blanket supporting Emily. Finding a small elevated area of grassland, he sets her down gently. After more than eight hours, his back aches and he is hungry and completely exhausted. Throughout the day, he has taken regular water breaks, pouring tiny amounts into Emily's mouth. Only once has she opened her eyes – empty, unfocused, they looked straight through him, no sign of recognition.

Matt empties the backpack, eating the figs and nuts. He will find more food in the morning. In the last of the day's light, he washes Emily's face and checks her over – relieved she is no longer bleeding. With darkness closing in, Matt wishes Indah were with them, picturing the young female tiger, alert to the slightest sound, confident in her natural dominion. At this thought of Indah, a deep sorrow builds inside his chest, imagining the devastation the tiger's death will bring to the child. He is desperate to reunite Emily with her father; terrified the man may no longer be alive.

Settling down next to Emily, Matt watches the motionless girl. It is as though she has withdrawn from life; only a shallow heartbeat anchoring her to this world. He hopes they will reach Palembang before dusk tomorrow, and that he can find the hospital without being caught by the Japanese.

He intends just to rest, keeping watch – but within moments, both Matt and Emily are asleep – lost to the rhythm of the night-time cicadas, low calls of nocturnal birds, and the rustle of living creatures scurrying through the undergrowth.

Through the high-barred window of his cell in Palembang jail, John Crawford watches the daylight fade, steadily erasing the appalling scene surrounding him. But darkness cannot mask the stench of human waste, the piteous cries of tormented men, the ache in his empty belly and continual thirst.

The prisoners had endured more long hours standing in the yard beneath the savage heat of an unforgiving sun. More had fallen and been shot; this time their bodies burnt – the prison guards creating a human pyre, fuelled by petrol, just yards from the ragged rows of horrified captives. Not all are dead when their bodies are thrown into the flames, their screams echoing around the prison walls. The sickly-sweet stink of human flesh cooking causes men to retch – dry painful heaving, lacking food or fluid to bring up.

Buckets provide little relief as many are unable to keep the brackish water down. Raw rice grains, rotting fish heads and spoiled fruit had been tipped onto the ground – starving men reduced to scavenging, stuffing the stinking muck into dry gaping mouths.

Inevitably, once prodded back inside airless calls, their stomachs reject the rotten food, in one or both directions, leaving wretched beings to lie in soiled clothing, in pools of their own vomit.

John has taken only rice and a couple of figs that seemed reasonably firm. Unlike those from Singapore who have spent days at sea, he is not yet starving, able to resist the rotten food. Closing his eyes, he forces his memory to recreate a healthier scene: a jungle pool, overlooked by a large flat rock, where he sits beside Emily. Recalling her smile, her innocence, her perfection, he concentrates on his reason to live – determining to survive, to be reunited with his beloved daughter.

Sitting on the reed-covered floor of her little home on stilts, Lai watches over the youngest of her grandchildren while their parents are put to work by the Japanese invaders. If her friends and family felt oppressed by the Europeans, their new masters are certainly no improvement. She is frightened by the strutting Japanese soldiers who treat everyone with such contempt and brutality.

According to her neighbours, the officers take young girls for their pleasure; the cruelty apparent on the bruised swollen faces as they stumble back to their homes. Daily, young violated bodies are pulled from the river – a watery grave preferable to continued torture and despair.

Lai fears for Mr John and Emily, having seen the fires at

Pladjoe, and the European prisoners in the Japanese river barges. Her children bring home dreadful tales of the prisoners' treatment: the beatings and shootings they witness daily while carrying out menial tasks for their new masters. At Lai's insistence, her family watches for any sign of the Crawfords, but so far, there has been no news, and she hopes they escaped south like so many of the Dutch civilians.

From her daughters, Lai learns of the camps where the women and children are imprisoned. The bungalows where her people previously kept house and garden are now surrounded by barbed wire. The European captives now exist like Lai's family – in overcrowded squalor, with little food or freedom. While this does not make her happy, the irony is not lost on her. For the first time, Lai feels she is their equal. The thought is comforting, providing her with a new level of self-respect.

A grandson enters, weighed down by two large fish he has caught upstream, well away from the jetties at Palembang. She smiles, noticing the small scar on his forearm, the burn from the oven in the club kitchen. The incident seems a lifetime ago. Lai feels a little ashamed of her harsh thoughts towards the Europeans, remembering the kindness of Mr John and the Dutch doctor. Perhaps the doctor will know what has happened to Mr John and Emily? Putting such thoughts aside, Lai hauls herself up. The world may have turned upside down, but the simple evening meal of smoked fish and rice must be ready for when the family returns, hungry and tired.

Chapter 13

Matt rests, hidden behind tall reeds flanking the Musi riverbank. He watches the wooden ferry making its way across – two local workers pulling hand over hand, guiding the primitive craft to the jetty, not thirty yards from where he hides.

For more than two hours, he has studied the ferry crossing back and forth, its cargo ranging from trucks carrying Japanese soldiers, to locals hauling sacks of rice and vegetables on their backs – under the constant scrutiny of their grim-faced armed guards. Now, as the light fades, the weary men secure their ferry to the jetty, ready to trudge home to their damp squalid shacks.

The evening is clear and still as Matt waits for sunset: the western sky melding from gold to blood red, fading to a rosy pink as the scarlet sun slips below the horizon. In the darkening sky, glittering stars gradually appear, mirrored diamonds in the still water of the river. The rising moon casts her silvery grey light, guiding Matt's stealthy feet towards the ferry – alert to any sound, still cradling the child, inert within the blanket.

Settling Emily down on the deck beside the backpack, Matt unties the knots securing the ferry and heaves on the thick rope, pulling the craft across the river. He turns in alarm at a swish of water behind, relieved to see a descending waterbird trail its feet across the surface of the river as it glides down to land. He marvels at nature's night beauty: the deep colours of sunset, the simple grace of birdlife on a quiet river, sparkling with reflected starlight – in contrast to the destructive ugliness of humanity, so apparent in daylight.

In the quiet night, the creaking of the pulling rope sounds deafening, increasing Matt's anxiety as they approach the far bank and the road to Palembang. Fingers fumbling in haste, he ties up, silently apologising to the ferrymen, one of whom may have to swim across to retrieve the craft. Replacing the backpack and gently draping the sling supporting Emily over his shoulder, Matt steps onto the riverbank, careful not to slip.

Instantly blinded by glaring headlights, he drops to the ground, rolling onto his back to protect Emily. A truck rumbles past, tail lights fading into the distance. Breathing heavily, he lies trembling for a few minutes, listening for more vehicles. As the road remains clear, he rises warily, keeping to the riverbank, stumbling over uneven ground, sliding on the treacherous mud in search of local workers who may be prepared to guide him to the hospital. After an hour of slow clumsy progress, Matt discerns the outline of a shack, weak light glimmering through the woven bamboo and palm leaves – building materials of the rudimentary riverside dwellings.

As Matt tentatively approaches, he hears low muttering voices. "Hello?" he calls softly. "I need help." Instantly, the voices inside the hut cease. Unmoving, silent, he senses their fear. "Please can you help me?" Matt entreats, his voice desperate, pleading.

A silent figure emerges, causing Matt to back away from a raised knife, moonlight reflecting on the deadly blade. Raising his own hands in supplication, Matt gestures to Emily, pulling back the edge of the blanket to reveal her ghostly pale, bruised face.

"Charitas? Hospital?" is his simple request.

The figure re-enters the shack; the muttering recommences.

Frustrated, Matt shakes out his tired leg muscles, impatient, willing someone to reappear. Finally, a far smaller figure steps out into the moonlight, beckoning for Matt to follow.

They traverse muddy tracks, keeping close to the river. After a few miles, Matt's aching back and tired legs protesting painfully, the small guide stops, hunkering down. Crouching just behind, Matt can now make out the features of a young boy with bright intelligent eyes – barefoot, wearing tatty shorts, his dark hair roughly cut and matted. The boy points at a large single-storey building; the front garden enclosed by a low picket fence.

"Hospital," whispers his young guide. "But guards." He gestures to where two Japanese soldiers stand on guard, one either side of the pathway leading to the front entrance.

"Can we get in at the back?" At the boy's shrug, Matt decides, "You stay with Emily and I'll take a look round the back. Okay?" The boy nods, studying the unmoving girl with undisguised curiosity.

Matt checks his knife and pistol, before moving furtively along the side fence, keeping low, out of sight of the guards. Rounding the back of the hospital, he finds it inaccessible, surrounded by barbed wire. Swearing under his breath, he turns back, noticing there is a small window, high on the side wall, covered with wire mesh to keep out insects. With no other option, Matt taps very gently on the mesh and waits – no response. Tapping repeatedly, he hears the scrape of chair legs, a shadow appearing behind the window.

"Who's there?" whispers a frightened female voice.

"Please, ma'am. I need help but the soldiers are out front."

"It's not safe here. You'll be caught."

"I've got a kid who needs help. She was attacked by the Japs. She's hurt bad. Emily Crawford. The doc knows her dad."

"Oh no! It can't be Emily! She evacuated to Java."

"She didn't. Long story. She's down by the river, wrapped in a blanket. She's in a bad way."

"Just a moment." Running footsteps clatter away. After what seems an age, another figure behind the mesh. This time, the deep tones of a man's whispered voice.

"Do you *really* have Emily with you?" The voice is incredulous.

"Yeah. I need t' get her in here, but there's guards out front and the back's all wired."

"Bring her to the back. There's a way in. I'll wait for you. Hurry, but be quiet. The guards are always alert."

Making his way carefully back to where Emily and the boy are hidden, Matt casts a wary eye across the garden to the guards. They smoke to keep insects at bay, apparently unaware of his presence.

The boy, watching over Emily, is delighted with Matt's gift of a water bottle. He slips away soundlessly, clutching his prize. With the last of his depleted strength, Matt shoulders the pack, gathering Emily to his chest. He retraces his steps, past the window to the rear of the building. A gap has appeared in the wire, presumably cut by the hospital staff, usually camouflaged from the suspicious eyes of the Japanese.

Gratefully passing Emily into the doctor's waiting arms, Matt follows the large man into the relative safety of the hospital. Once inside, he collapses to the floor, relieved to find the overwhelming burden of responsibility has literally been lifted from his shoulders.

Peter Janssen experiences a visceral rage so powerful, that he only clings on to his self-control by his fingertips. Trembling violently, hands shaking, unable to speak – his jaw clenched so tightly, it aches. He paces the office floor, allowing angry tears to flow, swallowing down the terrible scream of horror, grief, outrage, all threatening to overwhelm him.

Having examined and prepared Emily for the necessary stitches, also checking Matt over while listening to his incredible tale, Peter has left the traumatised pair under the gentle ministrations of the sisters, needing time to pull together his shattered emotions. That any man could carry out such an act of depraved violence is beyond his comprehension. But to do that to Emily? To any child? It is inconceivable, inhuman.

Peter recalls his last conversation with her father on the night before the Japanese landings. His friend, John Crawford, frightened yet comforted in his conviction that Emily would be safe. Instead, disastrously, she lies in this hospital: shocked, damaged both in body and mind – hovering somewhere between life and death, beyond Peter's reach.

Less than a year ago, Emily had sat in this very office, irrepressible, bottle-feeding a tiger cub.

"Ah, Indah," he sighs. "What a fateful day when they found you. So many ifs and buts. But I can't blame you. You saved her life at the cost of your own. If Emily recovers, she will be utterly heartbroken."

Stretching and flexing hands and fingers, the doctor takes deep breaths, exhaling the tension from his agitated body. He must be calm, focused, with steady hands, if he is to suture the deep vaginal tear without too much scarring. A normal procedure for women after childbirth – a travesty for an innocent child.

Sister Catherina cares for Matt – cleaning his cuts, removing deeply embedded thorns from his legs, gently rubbing salve on the many insect bites. The young man is very dehydrated, so she mixes a salt and glucose solution which he swallows gratefully. After a light meal of rice and baked fish, Matt feels more comfortable and is soon fast asleep on the ward.

"Mother," Sister Catherina calls over to Reverend Mother Helena, "I think we must pretend Matt's a civilian when the general comes to make his inspection."

Mother Helena nods in agreement, knowing the Japanese treat military prisoners with unimaginable cruelty. In their culture, surrender is dishonourable, so they have total contempt for men allowing themselves to be captured.

"Not that the civilian camp at the jail is very different," continues Sister Catherina. "We already have cases of dysentery coming in." The nun is appalled at the state of the men, doubled over in agony, permitted to visit the hospital for treatment.

"We will try to keep Matt here until he recovers his strength." Reverend Mother looks down at the sleeping Australian, thinking how his white-blond hair and relaxed features give him the face of an angel.

"How will we explain Matt and Emily appearing from nowhere?"

"Hmmm," Mother Helena taps a finger to her lips. "Let's say they've come in from a rubber plantation. Matt has brought Emily here following an accident. We'll say the girl has a serious head trauma and can't be moved. He has walked for days without food or sufficient water. We can say he has malaria."

"That sounds like a plan, sisters." Peter approaches, drying his hands on a cloth. "I've done what I can for Emily. There's no way of knowing the extent of the internal damage to her womb. She needs rest, nourishment and peace."

"Poor little mite," Sister Catherina's eyes glisten with the unshed tears she has striven to control all night.

"It's also the psychological damage that concerns me," explains the doctor. "She's unresponsive, completely withdrawn. We can treat her physical injuries but I feel she needs an environment both secure and familiar. We must contrive to bring John here. He may be able to reach her."

"Well, if we can convince the general that Matt is a plantation worker rather than an airman," offers Sister Catherina, "he'll be sent to the civilian jail and can try to make contact with John."

"Very good." Peter is a little more hopeful. "Burn anything of Matt's linking him to the air force. Let's hope he's convincing under interrogation."

The three are silent, contemplative for a few minutes. Peter sighs deeply.

"Let's try to get a few hours' rest." He turns to go, dejected, to lie down on the cot in his office. Physically exhausted, his mind cannot rest, images of the silent child's torn body tangle with those from the past – the girl cradling a tiger cub, chattering away, at peace with her world.

Matt wakes just before dawn. For a moment, he cannot remember where he is – only that he is comfortable. As recollection returns, he rises, padding around the ward until he finds Emily's bed. Asleep in a chair close by, Reverend Mother Helena snores gently, chin on her chest, hands clasped in her lap. He kneels at the bedside, taking Emily's limp hand. Her eyes open, she stares blankly at the ceiling, where a fan slowly rotates.

"Emily?" he whispers, close to her ear, not wanting to disturb the nun. There is no response – she does not move her eyes. "You're safe now," he tries to sound reassuring but she seems not to hear. "Squeeze my hand if y' can." Her hand remains limp in his own. He watches her for several minutes, rubbing her palm with his thumb. The only movement is the lightest flutter of her eyelids, just before they close. Sighing, Matt returns to his own bed and is soon asleep.

"Is Emily taking any food?" The doctor's deep frown the only sign of anxiety.

"Yes, Dr Peter," Sister Catherina replies from the chair recently relinquished by the Reverend Mother. "If I put a spoonful of broth into her mouth, she does swallow it." Emily is propped up on pillows, preventing her from choking while the nun feeds her with soup.

"Well, that's something positive," comments Peter, trying to sound cheerful. He and the two nuns have decided to speak in light confident voices around Emily, creating a reassuring atmosphere.

"Morning Doc." Matt, awake again, comes to stand beside Peter – looking down at Emily with concern. "Any change?" Peter shakes his head, taking Matt's arm to lead him out of earshot.

"Try to sound positive when you're within Emily's hearing, Matt. I want her to feel safe here. If her subconscious feels secure, it may help her."

"D'ya think she'll come out of it? Can she get better?"

"In time, her external injuries will heal, though there may be internal damage. Unfortunately, I have little experience with psychological conditions. She's in a deep state of shock. Sometimes the mind just shuts down when the trauma's too great to endure. I think this is what's happened to Emily."

"Poor kid. Indah was all she had left after her ma died and her pa went missin'."

"I didn't get a chance to tell you last night," Peter is

apologetic. "Emily's father isn't missing. He's in the civilian internment camp, at the town jail."

"So, he's alive?"

"He was when the Japanese marched him away from here on the day they landed. John had helped bring the injured Dutch troops here after the paratroopers attacked Pladjoe. Saving their lives and getting supplies from the Pladjoe hospital for me, cost him dearly. He'd no petrol to get back to P2 the night before the evacuation."

"I see. That's why Emily was with the bloke she called Mike?"

"Yes. She was supposed to go with him to Java. That's certainly where John thinks she is. Now Matt, when the Japanese come to the hospital, you must say you brought Emily in from a plantation. If they find out you're military, it will go badly for you. Treatment of allied forces is far worse than civilians. Not that the jail is much better, we've got cases of dysentery already."

Matt is silent for a while, taking this all in.

"Ya don't think I could make it on foot down to Oosthaven?"

"Not a chance. God knows how you got here at all. With every day that passes, the invasion force takes over more of Sumatra – south to Oosthaven, west to the mountains, even the north, are all cut off. I'm afraid none of us is going anywhere."

"So, I have to give myself up?"

"You must claim you're from a plantation. You're too fair to pass as a local worker, so they won't let you leave. You'll be interned, along with all the other civilians on this island."

"How often do the Japs show up? How long've I got?"

"There's no pattern. General Sato may come today. He may come in a week. With his guards posted out front and barbed wire securing the back," Peter gives Matt a brief conspiratorial smile, "he thinks he controls who comes in and goes out. It's going to be very unpleasant when he finds two unknowns in here. You *have* to stick to the plantation story – for Emily's sake as well as your own."

"Yeah, I get it. Just hope I've a few more nights in a comfortable bed with decent food."

"I sincerely hope so, Matt. I can't thank you enough for taking care of Emily, for bringing her here."

"I shouldn't have let her go to the dunny on her own."

"Emily was on her own before she found you, Matt. It's not your fault. You must believe that. If you hadn't been there, she'd probably be dead." Even Peter is a little shocked by his own pronouncement. "Come on, Matt," he pats the young man's shoulder, "No self-recriminations. We don't have that luxury. You've got to think on your feet when they interrogate you, get yourself into that civilian jail and get to John. Right?"

Matt nods, giving Peter a quick grin, to reassure the doctor he will play his part.

Floating, disembodied, in a beautiful blue aura. Silent. Safe. Bright colours, swirling, spiralling, revolving, merging. No memory, no boundary – only a vague sense of loss, of being lost. Searching, probing the colours – stirring, swishing, forming shapes. Circular, angular, regular, ambiguous, imperceptible, inconsequential. Nothing.

Chapter 14

After three days of rest, Matt sits quietly at Emily's bedside, watching dust particles float in the sun's rays flooding in through the open window behind her bed. Across the wide airy ward – liniment scented and spotlessly clean to prevent the spread of infection – white-robed nuns care for the men brought in with dysentery. Gentle soothing voices, a balm to their patients' traumatised minds, as effective as the medical treatment soothing their tortured bodies.

Shattering the peace, General Sato stomps into the ward, flanked by a brutish cohort of soldiers. Bringing up the rear – the runt of the litter – Matt spies an anxious-looking soldier wearing thick round spectacles, out of place amongst the military. Avoiding any eye contact, it is clear the discomforted man wishes to be elsewhere. From what he has been told, Matt realises this must be the interpreter.

Sato's steely eyes scour the room, coming to rest fixedly on Matt and Emily. The long slow blink sends a shiver of fear through Matt – the malevolent gaze boring into the depths of his soul; exposing every secret, every wrongdoing; facing Satan on the day of judgement.

All sound and movement ceases, except for the steady rhythmic rotation of the ceiling fan whirring above Emily's bed. The nuns and patients look on, paralysed by abject terror.

Impassive, Sato measuredly rotates his head from one side to the other, observing his men. Giving a single nod, he turns back to glare at Matt. At this, their master's signal, the soldiers surround Matt, grabbing his arms – dragging him from the chair, down onto his knees. Head forced down into a bow, he can smell the polish on the general's shiny leather boots.

A silence follows, broken by the groan of a patient leaning out of bed to vomit on the floor. Despite the splatter of fluid on wood, no one moves – until an ashen-faced nun, unable to ignore the retching man, heaves him back into bed, wiping tendrils of bile from his chin.

Sato angles his head to consider the little scene, lip rising in a sneer of disgust, eyes full of contempt. Quickly losing interest, his focus returns to Matt – the cat preparing to play with its mouse.

The ominous silence brings the doctor from his office. "General Sato," his tone is mild, soothing. "We haven't seen you for a few days."

The general regards Peter as an annoying interruption. Sato speaks to his interpreter, who steps forward, visibly shaking.

"General Sato say man on knees not permitted to be at hospital."

"He's come in from a plantation," replies Peter, allowing time for the translation between languages.

"General Sato want know how man get in hospital without permission."

"He arrived when the guards were checking the sick prisoners coming in from the jail. I need to speak to the general about the conditions there. Too many are falling sick."

"General Sato say no change subject. General Sato say man is soldier."

"No!" gasps Matt. "I'm from the plantation."

"General Sato say man not sick."

"He's recovering from malaria," interjects Peter. "He was also injured bringing a child here who had an accident."

Sato steps forward, placing his boot on Matt's shoulder. Without warning, he kicks out, sending the young man crashing into the chair and Emily's bed. Sato leans down, putting his face before Matt's. "Coward," the general hisses, spitting into Matt's face.

Straightening up, Sato again speaks with the interpreter.

"General Sato order man to camp at jail and child to woman camp at Pladjoe."

Peter moves to stand protectively beside Emily's bed, placing himself between her and the Japanese soldiers, Matt still sprawled at the general's feet.

"The child has a head injury. She's unconscious. We shouldn't move her."

The general pushes Peter aside, looming over Emily. Her eyes are open, unfocused. He clicks his fingers within inches of her eyes – no reaction. He pinches her nose closed – her mouth opens slightly and she continues to breathe. Still unconvinced, Sato slaps her face, leaving the red outline of his fingers across her cheek – she does not react. Peter lays a calming hand on Matt's head, sensing the young man's agitation. At Matt's glare, Peter gives a slight shake of his head – Matt looks away, face white with barely contained rage.

It is the interpreter who intervenes – coughing to attract Sato's attention, muttering a few words. The general grunts, examining his pocket watch. With a final venomous glare down at Matt, the devil marches out of the ward, followed by his stony-eyed accomplices. At the rear, the interpreter casts a frightened – but apologetic – glance back into the ward, before scurrying away, in the wake of his superior.

In the shocked silence, Matt rises to his feet, massaging his shoulder. He leans over Emily, a finger gently tracing the angry marks on her pale cheek.

"Was that the bastard's agreement t' let Emily stay?" Matt's anger flares.

"Sato can't be seen to change his mind without losing face. The best we can hope for is that he denies her existence and leaves her alone." Peter draws Matt away. "Come on, let's get a cup of tea to steady our nerves." As they depart, Peter calls over his shoulder – "A cup of tea all round, Reverend Mother? I think we *all* need one."

"I'm surprised they didn't drag me off with them," Matt follows Peter into the office.

"You can thank the interpreter for that. I don't know what he said, but the general couldn't get away fast enough. You must be ready, though. He's not one to forget."

"I know. What d'ya want me t' tell John Crawford, *if* I can find him?"

"I don't know if it would be best to tell him everything, or just say he's needed at the hospital," admits Peter.

"Well, if I get the chance t' tell him the whole story, he can get himself t'gether before comin' here. If I can't, I'll try t' get word t' him, tellin' him t' act like he's got dysentery, so he gets sent here t' see you."

"Mm. Just do what you think is right. There's no easy way for him to find out about Emily."

Within the hour, jail guards come for Matt – the devil's demons sent to drag the condemned soul down to hell.

Colours flicker. Beyond the aura, a danger, a fear. New shapes –

104

sinister, stable. Above, revolving light, rhythmic, gentle. Dark shapes, billowing, fragmenting. A silver flash pierces the aura, shattering the blue. White fog descends, envelopes, crushes, releases. A savage flame burns. A silent scream. Falling, sinking, back into the blue.

Leaning on the handle of his broom, John wipes his brow on the sleeve of his filthy shirt. As if content with the numbers eliminated by their human cull, the guards have set those still able to stand to clean out the cells with brooms and buckets of water. Weak from hunger, sweating profusely in the humid heat, John is flagging, ready to drop – even tempted to gulp down a few mouthfuls of the dirty water in the buckets. Resisting, he sweeps the brown stinking muck covering the floor towards the open door, and out into the yard.

To his relief, it starts to rain heavily. Stepping outside, he lifts his filthy face up to the dark clouds, opening his mouth wide to catch the precious drops. Other prisoners follow, relishing the unexpected shower. Completely drenched, they suck moisture from their clothes or cup their hands, drinking mouthfuls of collected rainwater. Eventually, like an angry rooster set amongst the hens, a guard emerges – gesticulating wildly, shrieking like a Celtic banshee, he chases them back inside.

Within minutes, the central yard is flooded, rainwater pouring into the cells. Spirits lifted, the prisoners sweep the remaining muck towards the door, against the flow – expelling the reeking sludge into the yard to be washed away in the deluge. Emptying their buckets, the men rinse them in the floodwater, then hold them up to the sky. This time, the guard leaves them to collect the rain: it will save him the daily onerous task of fetching water in the heavy wooden buckets.

Disappointed when the rain abruptly ceases, the men bring their half-filled buckets inside. In the ferocious heat, steam rises from saturated clothing – mother nature's way of reclaiming her cleansing tears. The smell of fresh damp earth permeates the cells, providing the exhausted captives with sweet moist air. Even the raw withered vegetables, thrown down for their meal, appear reasonably edible.

Contemplating possible reasons for the sudden alteration in conditions, John's brain does not immediately register someone is repeating his name. Avoiding the sun, he is resting on the floor of his cell, near the open door to the yard. Looking up, he sees a tall fair-haired young man, far too clean to be a fellow inmate, wandering around the yard asking for John Crawford. Unwilling to raise his voice, attracting unwanted attention, he waits until the young man passes his cell door.

"Over here," he croaks, his voice unused to speech.

The blond man comes to sit beside him, offering a hand for John to shake.

"G'day, John Crawford. I'm Matt Connelly. Recently arrived from the Charitas hospital."

John is startled, mind racing, desperate for news. "How is Peter? Peter Janssen? And the nuns? Are they okay?"

"They're fine but the doc's been worried about you. The dysentery. I hear it's bad here."

John nods, dejectedly. "Welcome to camp hell, Matt Connelly. Although you may've missed the worst. They've been killing off the weakest. Shooting those unable to stand. Giving out rotting food and dirty water. It's no wonder there's dysentery."

Matt studies John's gaunt, hollow-eyed face, the expressive

blue eyes revealing terrible suffering – a reflection of the horrors witnessed in this dreadful place.

"I'm sorry, mate. I'm real sorry, but we need t' talk." A screeching whistle interrupts, assaulting Matt's ears.

"It'll have to wait." John grimaces, getting to his feet. "It's time to line up and find out what these bastards have planned for us."

PART FOUR

Chapter 15

Thrown about in the back of the open truck, Australian Army Nurse Martha Kelly becomes aware that travel sickness compounds her burning fever and the agony of her infected leg. Concentrating on her breathing, she prays for the nightmare to end. Around her, fellow women and children sit silently; sliding into one another, flopping from side to side, following the motion of the rattling truck.

Finally, the vehicle comes to a skidding stop – the wheels unable to grip the muddy track. Flung to the driver's end, the prisoners begin to extricate themselves from the tangled mass of human bodies.

"Out! Out!" shrieks the Japanese guard. Untying the tail gate, he drags the sick women and children out, leaving them sprawled on the ground.

Almost immediately, Martha feels cool soothing hands rest gently on her bare sunburnt shoulders. Shocked, she looks up into the compassionate face of an angel – dressed in flowing white robes. This unexpected kindness is too much for Martha who begins to cry, great gut-wrenching sobs, burying her blistered face in the clean smooth fabric of the nun's white habit.

Along with the other captives, Martha is helped to her feet, supported as she limps past more Japanese guards, up a wide garden path and into a mirage of heaven: solid whitewashed walls, polished wooden floors, the smell of liniment, mosquito nets, beds with sheets. The events of the past weeks are stripped away – for a moment, Martha imagines herself back in the Singapore City hospital.

Guided to a bed, she runs her fingers along the top sheet, marvelling at the texture of the crisp white cotton. Behind a folding screen, the nun – introducing herself as Sister Catherina – helps Martha remove her filthy clothes, providing a bowl of warm water, soap and a sponge. Almost immediately, the water turns black and is frequently changed by the patient nun, until all the grime is completely washed away and she is handed a clean towel.

Sister Catherina's brow creases into a worried frown at the sight of Martha's infected leg. Despite her own attempts to remove shrapnel from just above the left knee, tiny shards of metal remain embedded in the red angry flesh, putrid dark yellow pus oozing from the wound.

"My goodness, it looks nasty. We'll need the doctor to deal with that!" The frown switches to a radiant smile. "I'll bring something for the pain, a clean nightgown and how about a nice cup of tea? I'll help you wash your hair tomorrow when you're feeling a little stronger."

Propped up on pillows, sipping hot sweet tea, Martha is comforted by the feel of a clean cotton nightgown, the low murmur of gentle voices, and the rhythmic whirring of the ceiling fans. A shot of morphine has taken the edge off her pain, so, for the first time since leaving Singapore, Martha allows herself to recall the events of her dreadful ordeal.

When news of the Japanese invasion reached them, panic had spread throughout the Singapore hospital. Within days, the wards had been overrun with wounded infantry – the Australian divisions decimated by the Japanese force unexpectedly landing on the northern coast. As the enemy advanced towards the city, the sick and injured had been evacuated to the harbour to board the waiting ships bound for Java.

Accompanying their patients, the Australian nurses found themselves aboard a Dutch liner, with about two hundred passengers and crew. There had been many ships, tugs, launches, sailing and rowing boats – all helping with the evacuation, all headed south in a trailing flotilla. Martha's ship had been basic, with little food or water – and no sanitation except for a bucket, the contents of which had been frequently thrown over the side rail. After thirty-six hours at sea, helping care for the rows of wounded men lying on the deck, Martha had fallen asleep on a pile of coiled rope, underneath a lifeboat.

During that second night, as the liner approached the Bangka Straits – the channel leading to Java between Sumatra and Bangka Island – their ill-fated flotilla had encountered a vast Japanese naval fleet, coming into the Straits from the east. Outlined in the glare of the Japanese searchlights, the allied vessels had come under heavy fire. The constant shelling had been terrifying: shrieking bombs exploding overhead, crashing into the sea, sending great plumes of water high into the air, flooding the decks. All too soon, Japanese aircraft carriers spewed their killing machines up into the sky and Martha had covered her ears to muffle the roar of fighter engines and the rattling of machine guns spraying the deck with bullets. In all the clamour and confusion, she had been unaware of the fire until the warning screams brought her scrabbling to her feet.

A sudden burning pain in her left thigh caused her to fall to the deck – almost trampled by the panic-stricken crowd surging towards the lifeboats. Lifted from behind, Martha had been roughly thrown into one of only two lifeboats lowered into the water before flames engulfed the deck. Paddling away to avoid being sucked down by the drag of the sinking liner, the survivors had watched in helpless horror as screaming human torches fell into the sea. They heard a tremendous creaking and the wrenching tear of metal as the ship broke apart – the two ends rising vertically before sinking out of sight. Overwhelmed by the sudden loss of so many lives, Martha had felt guilty, her random choice of sleeping place having saved her life – but why her? Why not another of the passengers who had as much right to survive but had been too far from the lifeboats to be saved?

They huddled together in their tiny boats, drifting between the giant metal structures of the Japanese ships. In the midst of the deafening battle – their blackened faces eerily lit by the flaming sky. Miraculously, they had floated away, unseen, unharmed.

After two dreadful days at sea, with no shade from the blistering heat of the sun, in the overcrowded boats – with barely enough water to survive – the miserable evacuees had finally sighted land and paddled to shore. Clambering out, the thirty or so women and children used small rocks to break into coconuts scattered around the palm trees – draining the milk and chewing hungrily on the firm white flesh.

Martha had been helped ashore by another nurse, who also found her a rock and coconut. After devouring its contents, Martha limped back to the shore and waded right in; ducking under to immerse herself in the cool refreshing water. As well as the terrible sunburn from the days at sea, the leg wound had become a constant pulsating torment – red and swollen, hot to the touch. The salt water stung both the leg and her blistered skin, but she endured the pain as the salt helped fight infection. Other women followed her, along with most of the children; the relief brought smiles to the reddened faces, though there had been little conversation – too many had left loved ones on the ship; dreadful images of burning bodies would forever haunt their dreams.

After an uncomfortable night in the open, the sight of a ship passing across the horizon had caused great excitement – the children jumping up and down, waving madly to attract attention. They knew they had been spotted when the thumping sound of diesel engines drifted across the water. Their elation had been short-lived – Japanese naval uniforms clearly visible in the approaching launches.

With nowhere to hide, nor energy to resist, the defeated evacuees climbed into the rescue boats. Taken to the ship, they had been locked in the dark airless hold. Trapped within the gloomy damp interior, time had been incalculable; it seemed to Martha they sat there for hours – hungry, thirsty, fretful children whimpering quietly.

When, eventually, they had been allowed up on deck, Martha needed help to climb the ladder – wincing at each tortuous step. Night had fallen, and she recalled how beautiful the sky had been – laden with glittering stars, reflected on the rippling black surface of the sea. The prisoners had each been given a handful of rice and a drink of metallic-tasting water. At dawn, the ship reached a harbour with an enormous jetty – which Martha guessed must be over five hundred yards long.

Two nurses had crossed arms and gripped one another's wrists to carry Martha the entire length, depositing her safely on the quayside from where they had all been marched to a nearby cinema. Throughout that day, more evacuees from Singapore had arrived, picked up from the wreckage of ships or from other beaches along the coast.

According to those seated nearby, they had been brought to Mumtok on Bangka Island and had become official prisoners of war. The nurses tried to care for the sick and injured, and Martha's leg had been roughly dressed with a scrap of cloth and wrapped tightly with a discarded stocking. By evening, the cinema had become crowded, the captives sat shoulder to shoulder; well over a thousand – with a single latrine and one lavatory cubicle between them.

Martha had spent an uncomfortable night seated on a bench – there being insufficient space to even lie on the floor. The hours dragged by in a confused half-sleep – each time she fell asleep, the loss of balance jerked her awake. In the morning, dizzy with exhaustion, Martha had been given a handful of rice with a few vegetable scraps and a cup of water from a shared bucket. After the inadequate meal, the men had been separated and sent to an internment camp – the women and children led to what had been a jail. Crowded into the gloomy building with damp crumbling walls, they had discovered a single dripping tap for water, an outdoor stinking trench for a lavatory and slabs of concrete on which they had to sleep.

Martha had no idea how long they had stayed in that appalling hovel, crawling with rats and beetles. The slightest infraction had been met with a beating – though acts of defiance became less frequent as the women grew weaker from hunger.

Under the tight stocking, larger pieces of shrapnel had risen to the surface of her leg, so Martha picked them out, biting down on a stick to stop herself from screaming. Discarding the stinking cloth, she replaced the dressing with a piece torn from her blouse and re-tied the stocking to keep it in place.

At first, they had taken turns telling stories to the children; even encouraging them to sing favourite songs. Martha passed many hours thinking up imaginary characters – creating a world of fantasy in which the children had undertaken dangerous missions, fought fire-breathing dragons and travelled to far flung kingdoms to rescue their friends. In fact, she created a rod for her own back – children continually pestering her for the next part of the story, eager to be part of her narrative, a valiant hero or heroine.

Despite their best efforts, the days had dragged by – monotonous, comfortless. Hunger and despair made them listless. In the first weeks, they attended to personal hygiene – queuing for the dripping tap to wash. Inevitably, sickness had struck their depleted bodies, and the first death had been very upsetting – a middle-aged woman with vomiting and diarrhoea had mercifully slipped into unconsciousness, dying after several hours. The nurses carried the body to the guards, insisting they be permitted to bury the woman. This had been allowed but as more and more died, no one had the strength to continue with the burials – the guards had simply dragged the corpses away.

Martha had all but given up hope of survival – the constant pulsating agony of her swollen leg wore down her spirits – when the remaining women and children had been taken without warning to line up in the yard. Stumbling out from the gloom, they had not only been hit by the fierce sunlight but by the force of cold seawater hoses, mercilessly pummelling their skin and stinging their eyes. Dripping with water, they had been marched back to the harbour, along the jetty and onto another ship. Martha had limped, her companions far too weak to be able to take her weight. Every step had been unbearable so when she finally reached the deck, Martha had collapsed, barely conscious throughout the long voyage across the Bangka Straits to Sumatra, up the Musi river to Palembang and the bumpy truck ride that had brought her to the hospital – to this sanctuary, and a bed with clean comfortable sheets.

As her recollections fall away, allowing Martha to appreciate her present feeling of comfort and security, she lets go, releasing the tension present since fleeing Singapore and drifts into an exhausted deep sleep.

Chapter 16

Doctor Peter Janssen is appalled by the state of the women and children brought to the hospital. In explanation, Sato's interpreter had described haltingly how the prisoners had been interned on Bangka Island following their capture from the ships fleeing Singapore. He had become distressed, admitting more than half had died from dysentery – clearly horrified by the inhumane treatment of these women and children at the hands of his countrymen.

Peter finds himself in sympathy with the poor man, wondering about his background. The interpreter is clearly uncomfortable with the bullying, violent Sato. More of an academic perhaps? In a different world, Peter considers they may have had much in common, may have even become friends. The interpreter, Peter decides, is as much a victim of this war as the European prisoners.

Now, making his way between the beds, the doctor examines his new patients: six Australian Army nurses, two civilian women and four children. One of the nurses, Martha Kelly – twenty-five years old and originally from Melbourne according to the notes left by Sister Catherina – has a seriously infected shrapnel wound in her left leg, just above the knee.

"I'm going to have to remove those fragments and cut away the infected flesh." Peter watches for the nurse's reaction. He can see she is very low. "We'll try to keep you here as long as possible, so you can build up your strength," he tries to sound reassuring.

"Thanks, doctor," Martha offers the trace of a smile. "I still can't believe I'm here, clean, in a proper bed. We've had an awful time." Her voice is hoarse from lack of use, filled with emotion.

"So I understand. I'm sorry for you all. I wish there was more I could do." Peter studies the exhausted woman – wide-set green eyes expressing such sadness, despair. He imagines that beneath the blistered red patches of burnt skin on her face, sore cracked lips and the lank matted hair, lies a dormant beauty, a vibrant spirit. With surgery, decent nutrition and gentle care, he hopes to one day meet the real Martha Kelly.

"Doctor Peter!" he turns to see the diminutive Sister Catherina, gripping her robes, revealing pale feet in white sandals, come running towards him as if the hounds of hell are on her heels. "Sato!" she wails. "Sato is here. He wants to take the women and children to Pladjoe camp."

"They've only just arrived, general." Peter is shaking with rage. "They're half-starved, dehydrated, have dysentery, beriberi from the lack of nutrition, head lice, infected rat bites." The doctor counts on his fingers. "Shall I go on?"

The two men face one another, eyes blazing with mutual hatred. The interpreter, having translated Peter's list of grievances, backs away, anticipating an explosion of violence. Terrified nuns, nurses, women and children, gaze at Peter in wide-eyed astonishment – never having seen *anyone* stand up to the Japanese officers.

Sato folds his arms and taps his foot, allowing the repetitive sound to increase the tension, filling the extended silence. He speaks to the petrified interpreter.

"General Sato say patients are nurses."

"That's right. Six are nurses." Peter confirms, wondering

where this is going.

"General Sato say if nurses stay at hospital, six nuns go to Pladjoe instead."

Peter covers his face with his hands, slowly dragging fingers around tired eyes and down sallow cheeks. He sighs deeply, shaking his head, having no idea how to respond.

"The nurses are sick, general. The nuns are nursing the nurses, so we need the nuns."

"General Sato say you have choice," the dejected interpreter lowers his voice, earning a glare from Sato. "You must choose six to go to Pladjoe. They must leave now."

Peter's beseeching eyes meet Reverend Mother Helena's. She comprehends he is unable to make such a decision. Stepping forwards, she turns to her sisters.

"I shall go to Pladjoe." Mother Helena's voice is firm. "Will any of you accompany me to see what help we may offer the prisoners in the camp?"

One by one, sisters step forward. Before Sister Catherina can move, Mother Helena shakes her head to signal she must remain at the hospital. When there are six volunteers, Sato and his men stride from the ward, followed by the nuns at a stately pace, Reverend Mother leading her sisters in prayer. In the shocked silence which follows their departure, Peter puts a protective arm around the weeping Sister Catherina, guiding her to a chair. He feels entirely responsible – burdened with an all-consuming guilt, threatening to engulf him.

The small stooped figure walks purposefully along the muddy track leading to the Charitas hospital. Taken for a local worker, she is ignored by the guards. Relieved, Lai nevertheless increases her pace until she reaches the hospital entrance.

Instantly, she knows something is wrong. Used to the calm welcoming nuns, she is surprised to find an empty hall. Mystified, Lai spots Mr John's friend, Dr Peter, coming out of the ward, looking pale and harassed.

"Lai!" the doctor almost screams her name. "Thank goodness. Have you come to help?"

"I come to see if you know of Mr John and Emily. I expect see Mother Helena and other nuns," she mimes searching. "They not here?"

"Sister Catherina and a couple of our younger nuns are here. The Japanese have taken Mother Helena and the others to the women's camp at Pladjoe. We do have nurses from Singapore but they're too sick to help."

"I bring help if you keep girls safe."

"Safe? Surely, the local girls are safe?" Peter looks bewildered.

"Not safe. Japanese officers do bad things to girls. Girls prefer die in river. Japanese very bad men." Lai's tiny hands ball into fists, her expressive eyes reflecting her impotent fury.

"I wish I could assure you they'd be safe here, Lai. As you see, the nuns weren't safe. They've been taken. The girls *may* be safer here, and we can certainly give them food. We really could use their help if they're willing."

"I bring girls, Dr Peter." Lai stands a little taller, feeling a sense of importance. "Mr John and Emily escape to Java?"

"Come to my office, Lai. I'll explain everything."

Lai sits by Emily's bed. Although the girl eats when spoon-fed, and uses a bed pan when it is placed beneath her, she remains totally withdrawn, unresponsive. The old housekeeper strokes Emily's forehead and whispers to her – reminding the child of her home at Pladjoe, of her father and Indah.

Lai had been distraught as Peter explained that John was in Palembang jail and Emily, having been attacked by Japanese soldiers, was here at the hospital. Hot angry tears had poured down her deeply lined face, where she sat moaning and muttering curses upon the entire Japanese nation, while Peter described Emily's injuries and his concern for the child's state of mind.

Peter had been so relieved when Lai kept her word – several local young women had arrived the following day to assist Sister Catherina and the remaining nuns. Lai appointed herself Emily's chief nurse and had spent every day at the child's bedside, sending one of the girls to watch over her grandchildren.

After several days' rest following her surgery, Martha feels better, becoming more interested in the daily routine of the hospital. Fascinated by Lai's devotion to Emily, Martha shares her concern for the silent girl. She dreads the arrival of General Sato – convinced he will pack her and the other evacuees off to the internment camp. She watches the four children – three girls and a boy, all under ten – playing a clapping game in a corner of the ward. As children do, they have recovered their physical strength quickly, romping around the ward, getting under everyone's feet. Their mothers and the Australian nurses look haunted, say little and often cry out in the night – all too aware that their time in the hospital is only a temporary respite.

"Have you put any weight on that leg yet?"

Martha looks up to see the doctor coming to her bedside. She offers an apologetic smile. "No, I haven't. I'm being terribly lazy."

Smiling, Peter wags a finger at her. "No excuses, Martha. Let's see how you manage."

Martha slides down off the bed onto her right foot, then gently puts down the left, gingerly transferring her weight. She nods, satisfied the leg can support her and takes a few tentative steps towards Peter. "It's very stiff, but not too painful, thanks."

"You must try not to limp or you'll hurt your back. Come and sit back down so I can take a look. I think we'll be able to remove the stitches in a day or two."

Martha moans, causing Peter to look up in alarm.

"Does it hurt?"

"No, doc. It's just that once I'm back on my feet, I'll be sent to the camp."

"Having taken my nuns, Sato should leave me with you nurses – but I think that may be too much to hope for." Peter smiles but Martha can see the exhaustion and strain in the dark circles under his eyes.

"I think you're doing a great job here, doc." She puts a hand on his arm, a gesture of support, reassurance. For a moment their eyes meet, then Martha drops her gaze in confusion, fussing over her bed linen.

"Thank you, Martha. That means a lot." Peter speaks quietly, also embarrassed by the moment of intimacy. "Right," he tries to make his voice light. "I'd best get on with my rounds."

The blue is calm, peaceful. Above, warm colours ripple – rising, lifting, welcoming, nurturing. Light shimmers, revolves, beckons, tempts. Recognition? Familiarity? Solace – beyond an impenetrable mist, an obstacle, barricade, protection, safety? Yearning, searching, probing, hearing? Sound? Whirring? Murmuring? Muffled, fading, far away. Back to blue – sheltered, secure, peaceful.

Chapter 17

Matt Connelly searches among sunburned faces for John Crawford. Separated since their first meeting, Matt is increasingly desperate to tell John about Emily. Now, he rests alongside fifty or so fellow prisoners, worn out from loading oil drums onto Japanese ships at Palembang. With the help of local workers, the Japanese are repairing the refinery and recommencing oil production. The working parties sent down from the jail at least receive increased rations of rice, as well as more water, during the long hot hours labouring in the sun.

Matt can feel he is losing weight. The waistband of his trousers is becoming looser and he is constantly tired. Sometimes, in the middle of the day, when the savage sun literally cooks his exposed skin, he feels dizzy and nauseous, stumbling over his own feet. When he can stand it no longer, he allows himself to trip and fall into the river, remaining submerged until his lungs almost burst. This little act of defiance earns him a few hard slaps, but he endures the beating – the cool water refreshes him enough to continue with his work. Others are starting to copy, more than one trying to swim away under water, in an attempt to escape into the jungle. Too weak to get far, they are simply shot – their bodies left floating in the reddening water – an example to all.

Arriving back at the jail at the end of each exhausting day, Matt continues his search for John as the men line up in the central yard. Dejected, heads bowed, it is difficult to identify any individual and he is increasingly frustrated. Only when the guards dismiss their prisoners for the night and the men flop down in small groups to eat their paltry rations is Matt free to continue searching, until the last of the daylight is entirely gone.

Gazing up at the night sky, wondering how such incredible beauty can exist above so much horror, Matt throws back his head, allowing his eyes to lose focus as if he might be absorbed into the glittering starlight.

"Where are you John Crawford," he calls out – causing muttered conversations to cease abruptly. Men stare in astonishment at the silhouetted outline of the man, standing alone in the centre of the yard, contemplating the heavens as though they can provide the answer. The scrape of a boot breaks the silence, a ragged man hauls himself from the ground and slowly, stiffly, crosses the yard.

"It's all right. Come over here and sit down with me." Matt is gently guided into the shadows, away from the intrigued guards. "I'm sorry, I've forgotten your name but I do remember you wanted to talk to me."

John leans his head back against the wall, completely stunned, unable to organise his thoughts. Dropping his head into his hands, he weeps silently for his beloved daughter. Belief in her safety has sustained him through the intolerable days of his captivity. A surge of burning rage engulfs his trembling body, leaving him keening – a soul in unbearable torment. Biting his knuckles, he rides the tempest, the maelstrom of emotion: guilt, fear, anger, love. Shaking uncontrollably, fingers tingling, he leans over and is violently sick.

Matt is frightened by John's visceral reaction, knowing his news has torn the man's world apart.

"Listen t' me, mate. Peter reckons you can see Emily if you pretend t' be real sick. If they think you've got dysentery, they'll send you t' the hospital." He looks into John's wild uncomprehending eyes. "John! You can see Emily," he entreats, "pretend you're sick so you can get t' the hospital." Matt shakes John by the shoulders until their eyes meet, comprehension dawns and John nods in agreement.

"Burst appendix."

"What?" Matt eyes John's resolute face.

"It'll be quicker if you tell the guard I've a ruptured appendix."

A slow smile of understanding crosses the young Australian's face.

"Go to it!" Matt grins, running off to find the guards.

Leaning against the door of the hospital entrance, breathing in the night air, Peter watches a truck's headlights bounce around as it manoeuvres along the muddy track. Relieved it is not a late visit from the general – it is a single truck, not the escorted staff car – he squints through the gloom, trying to make out what is happening. A groaning man, clutching his abdomen, is hauled out of the truck and dragged towards the guards stationed by the fence. At a gesture from one, Peter rushes forwards to offer assistance. Clearly in pain, the man remains doubled over, Peter helping him inside and closing the door.

Instantly, the moaning stops and John straightens up.

"Ruptured appendix!" He clasps the astonished doctor's hand. "Where's Emily?"

Dismayed, Peter regards his friend, seated at Emily's bedside. John is so thin, so fragile. Gently, Peter rests a reassuring hand

127

on his friend's shoulder, passing him a cup of tea.

"Thanks, Peter," croaks John, his voice tremulous, breaking. "And thank you for looking after Emily. Thank God Matt got her here. I… I can't believe…" his voice trails away. Bending over Emily, John places his lips on her cool forehead. "I'm here, Emily. Daddy's here." He strokes her cheek. "I love you." His voice cracks as he sits back up, sipping the tea in an attempt to mask his distress.

Peter pulls up a chair to sit quietly beside John, hoping his silent presence will be a comfort. Before morning, he will need to get John organised. Sato is no fool so Peter will have to operate – an appendectomy, but without removing the appendix. If he can convince the general that John's appendix burst, causing infection, he and Emily may have more time together.

"What's the prognosis?" John raises his eyebrows questioningly.

"Oh, you'll live."

"Be serious, Peter. I mean Emily. Will she recover, do you think?"

"Physically she's healing well, John, but I'm no psychologist. I think we must give her time. I believe that, on some level, she knows you're here and this will help. Lai talks to her every day and that's helpful too."

"Lai? You've seen her?"

"Yes. Lai comes here every day to be with Emily. She came here seeking news of you and helped me out by bringing local girls to work in the hospital after the Japanese took the Reverend Mother and five other nuns to the women's internment camp."

"I'm sorry, Peter. I've been so wrapped up in my own troubles I haven't thought about what you and the sisters have been through."

Peter shakes his head and squeezes John's shoulder.

"Don't apologise, John, not after what you've endured – what Emily's been through. It's too much to take in. There's only so much each of us can deal with. We all have our demons, our regrets, our burdens." Peter sighs and John recognises the anguish, the guilt over the nuns, burning in his friend's eyes – a mirror to his own sense of failure to protect his daughter.

From her bed, Martha witnesses the interaction between the two men. Her heart goes out to both, wishing she could offer comfort. This terrible war seems to have unmanned them, taken away their certainty, their self-belief. A doctor and a father – two men riddled with guilt, assuming responsibility for events over which neither has control. It is the helplessness, the impotence of their situation which is so heartbreaking, so sad it makes her cry. She knows they would not want her pity. These are men who need to feel relied upon, decision makers, protectors of those they love. They will never see themselves as victims, even though Martha knows that is what they all are – victims of man's inability to co-exist peacefully. She wonders if this is a paradox running through history – the desire to be real men, courageous, intrepid, drives them to war; while the same desire renders them incapable of accepting its inevitable outcomes.

Chapter 18

Margery Woods observes the six nuns climbing down from the back of a truck. She takes comfort in that they are allowed to climb down – rather than being dragged out and thrown on the ground as she had been. Not wishing to draw attention from the guards, she waits until the truck drives away, leaving the nuns in the middle of a muddy courtyard, lifting their robes clear of the foul-smelling effluent – the result of a drain flooding during the last torrential downpour.

"Good morning, sisters." Margery holds out a welcoming hand. "Welcome to our camp. Aren't you the nursing sisters from the Charitas hospital?" Margery has heard of the white-robed nuns at the hospital – already famous for their small acts of defiance against the Japanese oppressors: the sisters' kindness in arranging emergency appointments so separated wives and husbands are able to meet for a precious hour; the regular smuggling of personal letters between the men's jail and the women's camp – selflessly risking their own lives in order to bring comfort to the suffering prisoners.

"Good morning, dear. Yes, we're from the hospital. I'm Reverend Mother Helena." Mother Helena introduces each of the anxious-looking nuns. "The Japanese commander, General Sato, has sent us here in place of six Australian nurses, too ill to be moved from the hospital. We wish to offer ourselves to assist you in any way we can."

The appearance of the nuns brings women and children from

all over the camp; eager for any distraction to the monotony of their long dreary days.

Mother Helena becomes aware that Margery is a person of importance here. Her voice carries authority; the women and children appear to wait for her to speak, to provide guidance. Tall for a woman, at five feet ten, Margery has a strong jawline, grey hair tied back in a loose ponytail and intelligent blue eyes. A teacher perhaps? Definitely one to issue orders rather than receive them. The Reverend Mother senses Margery may be much like herself – confident, a natural leader, prepared to shoulder the burden of responsibility.

"As you see," Margery gestures around the camp, "We live in these houses, about thirty of us to each and ten to each garage. We divide the chores between us and have formed groups to be responsible for cooking, clothing, cleaning and entertainment. I'm responsible for musical entertainment. We have a vocal orchestra and are always delighted to welcome new members." Margery smiles at Mother Helena, hopeful that the nuns will have good singing voices.

"This is Nora Palmer." Margery beckons to a much shorter, frail-looking woman, wearing a peculiar red hat resembling a short-spoked umbrella. "Nora, come and meet Reverend Mother Helena and the Charitas sisters. We'll need to find them accommodation – I'm sure they'll wish to be together. Can we manage that?"

"Of course, ladies!" Nora bustles over, giving a beatific smile. "It's all first-class accommodation here!" Margery guffaws, Mother Helena frowns anxiously – wondering if their ordeal has sent these women slightly mad.

"Well now," Margery spreads her arms wide. "As you see, we're encircled by this magnificent barbed wire fence so you won't be bothered by tigers. I can't say you won't be bothered by animals; many's the night I've woken to find one of our guards peeking under my blankets. There's nothing to be done – just pretend to be asleep and they eventually go away."

The nuns' eyes widen in alarm and disbelief. "Are you serious?" asks the Reverend Mother.

"I'm afraid so, Mother." Margery suddenly looks less confident and vulnerable. "They've no respect for us, for our dignity. They watch us wash, use the lavatory – they enjoy our discomfort." She sighs, staring into space, lost in some dreadful recollection.

"These houses were built by the Dutch colonists." Nora takes over, giving Margery time to gather her thoughts. "We share eight houses and three garages. That one, over by the gates," Nora points towards a house beside the large gates which form the entrance to the camp, "is the Japanese barracks and they've four guards posted around the perimeter." She waves in the general direction of each sentry post, none of which is visible, tucked away behind the houses.

At a gesture from Margery, the group moves towards an area of jungle, within the fence boundary but away from the houses. The dreadful smell enlightens the nuns before Margery explains about the trench, which serves as the camp lavatory.

"Those of us with a strong constitution take turns to clean out the trench. Despite our best efforts, it floods if we have heavy rain." Margery takes hold of a coconut shell, miming the act of scooping. "We scoop the contents into buckets, which the guards allow us to bury outside the gates."

"Further into this area," Nora explains, walking beyond the trench to where the vegetation becomes thicker, "we collect edible ferns and other vegetation we can use to supplement the awful food we're given."

"It's a far more popular job," smiles Margery. "We get the opportunity to search for passion flower blooms or other flora to brighten up birthdays or anniversaries of any kind—"

"And firewood," interjects Nora, pointing out a tree stump. "This is where we chop the wood for the cooking fires."

"You have an axe?" asks an incredulous Mother Helena.

"The guards have an axe. They stand over us with a rifle while we chop the wood." Margery looks wistful. "What I could do with that axe if I wasn't at gunpoint." She grins wickedly.

A young woman with loose, fair hair, in a ragged sleeveless dress, her feet bare, calls out as she crosses to where they stand. "Margery! Nora!" The two women look around questioningly. "We've cleared house five for the sisters." The girl smiles shyly at Reverend Mother.

"Thanks, Susan." Margery drapes an arm around Susan's shoulder, bringing her into their circle. "Reverend Mother Helena, this is Susan, the youngest of our wonderful Australian nurses who came here from Singapore."

"Lovely to meet you, Susan." Mother Helena shakes the young woman's hand, noticing protruding collar bones, wasted muscles and haunted eyes. The nun is reminded of Martha and the other nurses arriving at the hospital, similarly malnourished. "Thank you for finding us somewhere to stay, but we couldn't possibly take over your house. We're happy to share, or to find a garage or something else."

"It's fine, Mother Helena," insists the young nurse. "House five is very small. We only had to move a few people around to make room for you. Shall I show you?" Susan looks to Margery for confirmation.

Looking up at the small dwelling, Mother Helena sees Susan has not exaggerated – the house is far smaller than the others. She wonders if it had been used by the servants to one of the larger houses. With wooden shutters rather than glass windows, the tiny house has a total of four small rooms, no bathroom or kitchen facilities, not even a tap. Margery appears to read Mother Helena's mind.

"None of us has running water, Reverend Mother. We all use the well. I'll show you where it is. You mustn't drink the water before boiling it, though. We all have containers to put outside when it rains, as that's fine to drink.

"The original residents left sleeping mats," explains Susan. "We've put blankets in for you and a couple of metal pans. One's so you don't have to go to the trench at night, the other's for collecting rainwater."

Mother Helena is overwhelmed by the kindness and generosity of these remarkable women. They have so little and yet they share what they have.

"God will bless you for all you have given us," Mother Helena's eyes glisten. "We can't thank you enough. We'll strive to follow your example and contribute in any way we can."

As Margery returns to her own house, she inwardly admonishes Mother Helena's God for allowing his most devoted servants, the nuns, to be sent to this intolerable place. If he does intend to send his blessing, please could it be in the form of sufficient food for them all?

Chapter 19

Emily dreams she is swimming through a thick blue liquid. Her arms and legs feel heavy, tired, but the blue is buoyant, pleasantly warm. Above her whirrs a ceiling fan, like the one in Daddy's office. In the distance, Emily sees her father talking to Doctor Peter. She tries to wave, but her arm is too heavy. She calls out, but they do not hear. Emily feels a soft touch on her forehead. She knows this is Lai, but like Daddy and Peter, Lai does not hear her.

"I'm here," Emily shouts. "Can't you hear me?" She waits, frustrated, but there is no reaction. She tries to swim to them, to make them see her, listen to her. Confused, she cannot understand why she cannot leave the comforting blue. Why it will not release her, why it keeps her from Daddy. Daddy? His image fades, her memory fades; she is drawn back into the protective cocoon of blue.

"I just think you should go back to the camp for a few days, John. I can pre-arrange an appointment for you to come back and have the stitches removed. If we wait any longer and the general shows up, getting you back here may prove impossible. It's hard to explain, but the general has a way of obstructing everything I try to do. It's like a game to him. He's no fool and if he senses we're up to something, well, he's capable of anything. He's an absolute monster." Peter and John sit beside Emily, speaking in low voices, not wishing to disturb the other patients.

"You're right, of course, but I don't want to leave Emily. I want to be here when she wakes up." John holds his daughter's hand, caressing her palm with his thumb. He is beginning to regain his strength after three days of regular meals. The shave and haircut after a long hot bath had felt so good – he had been so grateful to Sister Catherina; she had even provided clean clothes to replace his filthy tattered ones.

"We've no idea when that'll happen, John, and the longer you remain, the more danger you and Emily are in. I'll get word to you somehow if there's any change."

"What'll happen to her, Peter?"

"I imagine she'll have to go to the women's camp. Mother Helena's there. I'm sure she'll take care of Emily."

"I'd like to help." John turns, noticing the Australian accent, as a young woman with chestnut brown hair framing gentle green eyes crosses the ward, coming to stand beside Peter.

"John, meet Martha, an Australian Army nurse, an evacuee from Singapore." The radiant smile Peter bestows upon Martha is not lost on his friend.

"How d'you do, John." Martha holds out a hand, giving John's a firm shake. "I'll be sent to the same camp so can help take care of Emily."

"Thank you, Martha. That's very kind. Peter's trying to get rid of me, as you probably heard."

"He's right, though. The general is a vicious, cruel devil. If he thought you'd any connection with Emily, he'd do something awful to one or both of you."

"Okay!" John raises his hands in surrender. "I'll go, just give me a little more time." Peter and Martha step away, leaving John to be alone with Emily for a few minutes longer.

"She's been very restless," Martha whispers to Peter. "I've

been watching her. D'you think that's a good sign?"

"I just don't know." Peter grimaces, shaking his head. "It could be increased brain activity – memories, dreams. I just don't know." Together, they watch John lean forwards to hug his daughter, holding her tightly as if he will never let go. Eventually, he straightens up, blows her a kiss and walks quickly from the ward. Peter follows him out, Martha remaining to watch over the silent child.

"Good man." Peter pats John's back. Through the rough cloth, he feels the tension, the repressed emotion. "Give my best to Matt, won't you?" John nods, pressing the heels of his palms against his eyes, holding back the tears. "Wait there, while I write an appointment slip." Peter goes into his office, returning with a slip of paper. "The stitches will come out in four days. Okay?" John nods again, the lump burning the back of his throat making it impossible to reply. Impulsively, John turns to embrace Peter, clasping him tightly.

"Look after her," he croaks – releasing the doctor and heading out of the door. Stumbling into drizzle falling from a grey overcast sky, it is all he can do to stop from turning around and running back to Emily. Walking slowly towards the guards, John feels an acute sense of loss, as though his soul, unable to leave, is being ripped from his treacherous body. His heart, he knows, will remain at the hospital, at Emily's bedside. As one of the guards escorts him on the long march back to the jail, John allows a lethargy to spread throughout his body, numbing his mind, allowing him to cope, to return to the hell that is the jail.

Matt waits patiently for John's return to the camp. It has been a few days, during which time he has been forced to toil at the refinery. Each day, the jail becomes more overcrowded as the

137

invaders round up all the civilians from the oil fields and rubber plantations throughout southern Sumatra. News of brutal treatment exacted upon these colonists quickly spreads through the jail: executions, beatings, starvation – it comes as no surprise. The battered state of new arrivals appears unremarkable to those already imprisoned.

Finally, John returns and Matt is relieved to see a physical improvement – less haggard, now clean-shaven and more decently clothed, John still looks haunted, dejected, a man weighed down by his sorrow and regrets.

"Well?" Matt's eyebrows raise questioningly.

"She looks so delicate," John flops down next to Matt, they lean against a shaded courtyard wall. "So small, fragile, perfect… just not there." John turns agonised eyes to Matt. "She's not there, Matt. It's as if she's left her body, empty but living. But Emily, whatever makes her Emily, is missing." His halting voice peters out, leaving him broken, staring at the ground. Matt's heart sinks. Like the doctor, he had hoped being with her father would bring Emily round.

"Maybe she just needs more time, mate. I'm sure she knew you were with her. She'll come back, mate. I'm sure she'll come back."

"If she does," John's voice is low, almost a growl. "What future does she have? Life in an internment camp, at the mercy of these utter bastards. Starved, humiliated. That's what we'll all become, Matt. Animals. Ill-treated, underfed work-horses." John finishes with a deep breath and a shuddering sigh.

"Will ya see her again soon?"

"Four days. I've an appointment to have the stitches removed."

"You've had an operation?" Matt is astonished.

"An appendectomy without removal of the appendix to be precise. Peter said it had to be convincing in case the general showed up."

"Christ, mate. He's a livin' nightmare, all right."

"So I hear. Fortunately, I haven't had the pleasure. Peter made me leave."

Matt offers a silent thank you to the doctor. He remembers Sato slapping Emily's face. John would have gone berserk, prisoner or not. Resting his head back against the wall, Matt wonders about his reaction to John's words. Something about the essence of the girl being absent resonates, but he cannot identify the sensation. For now, he just acknowledges that something of her is present within him, and closes his eyes.

"Doctor?" Sister Catherina knocks gently on the office door, entering to find Peter gazing out of the window, deep in thought. She studies his profile: the new grey hairs at his temples; deepening lines around his haunted eyes; tension in his clenched jaw, lips pressed together. She notices he fidgets, constantly rubbing the quick around his fingernails with his thumb.

"Doctor?" Peter jumps at the sound of her voice.

"What's wrong?" his eyes plead for her not to impart more dreadful news.

"Nothing's wrong," she reassures, noticing his shoulders slump in relief. "I just wanted to talk to you about the Australian nurses and the civilian mothers and children. We can't keep them much longer. We're running out of excuses. If the general comes and finds them still here..." she does not need to finish the sentence – Peter can imagine Sato's explosive reaction.

"You're quite right, Sister," his bleak expression confirming his understanding. "I'll talk to them. Get them ready. Can you see what we can give them to take? It'd be good if we can send something to Mother Helena too."

"Thank you, Doctor. I'll see to everything." Sister Catherina backs out of the office, gently closing the door, leaving Peter to his introspection.

An image of Martha, her beautiful green eyes, so vivid, expressive, fills Peter's mind. He has been dreading her departure. From the day the nurses had arrived, so battered, filthy, starving and he had examined her infected leg, something had stirred within him. A connection, a simple release of a hormone into his bloodstream – not looked for, completely unexpected. As Martha had recovered, a lovely young woman had emerged from the tormented patient. He senses she, too, feels an awkward attraction – so inappropriate in this time of suffering and horror. Will Sato allow the nurses to remain at the hospital? After all, he has taken the nuns in their place. Dare he make this suggestion? He knows he must not hold out any hope. Hope makes him vulnerable to Sato's cruelty. As long as Peter has no expectations, Sato cannot crush them. Peter shakes his head in frustration. He knows what he *should* feel, how he *should* act. But he cannot deny himself the tiniest hope she will not be sent away.

Chapter 20

Before dawn, the indomitable figure of Margery Woods strides up to house number five, where the nuns have spent their first night in the camp. From within, she hears the murmur of chanting voices – gentle, rhythmic, peaceful. Mesmerised, Margery waits until there is quiet, then gently knocks on the door.

"It's Margery, Mother Helena. I'm sorry to disturb you so early, but I forgot to warn you about Tenko." The door opens, revealing Reverend Mother and a circle of kneeling nuns, hands clasped in prayer.

"Do come in, Margery. We have Lauds, our morning prayers before dawn, so you aren't too early." Mother Helena smiles warmly at a relieved Margery.

"It occurred to me in the middle of the night – as these things always do! They wake you up, a light comes on inside your head," Margery points to her temple, "and ping, you remember!" Completely baffled, the sisters simply gape at her. "Well, that's what happens to *me*." Margery shrugs, her tone dismissive, a little embarrassed. "*Anyway*, what came to me was that I hadn't warned you about Tenko." The nuns' expressions remain confused and Margery realises they have no idea what she is talking about. Clearly, Tenko is not observed at the hospital.

"Tenko," she explains, "is roll call. Every day at dawn, we're summoned by the guards to line up in the courtyard, for the officer – usually the colonel – to inspect us. As he's driven in through the gates, we put our hands together and bow very low.

After that, we just stand there, sometimes for hours, until we're dismissed."

"I see," Mother Helena's lips press together in disapproval. "We're made to stand in the sun for hours?"

"I'm afraid so, Mother. It's important to wear a hat – though your wimples will do. Make sure you drink water before going out, as that helps too. Also, try not to attract attention from the guards." Margery rests her chin on her thumb and folded fingers, looking thoughtful. "That'll do for now. You'll soon discover the games they play. I always imagine we're little mice, trapped, at the mercy of a great... fat... ginger... *cat!*" The nuns' look startled, making Margery grin ruefully. "But then, I 've always had an over-active imagination. Mostly, I harmonise."

"You harmonise?" Mother Helena raises a questioning eyebrow.

"To pass the time, I create four-part harmonies inside my head. If they're any good, I transcribe them later."

"Well, Margery, we shall pray." Mother Helena gestures to her fellow sisters. "We shall pray to God, who sent his only son to die on the cross in order to save our souls. As Jesus prayed to his father in heaven, so shall we pray to our Lord God – asking him to relieve the suffering of the women and children imprisoned within this camp."

Margery is touched deeply by the total sincerity of Mother Helena's words. Her absolute faith and trust in God clearly brings her great comfort. Unfortunately for Margery, her faith in divine intervention had been lost somewhere between Singapore and Sumatra – while clinging to the wreckage of a bombed-out ship, about to be taken prisoner aboard a Japanese destroyer. Only music soothes Margery's troubled soul and, rather than pray, she still intends to harmonise during Tenko.

Within the hour, a shrill whistle assaults the prisoners' eardrums as they emerge from their houses to line up for Tenko. The cloud cover offers some respite from the sun, but the still air is hot, humid, difficult to breathe. The nuns join the rows of women and children – all eyes focused on the entrance gate, anticipating the Japanese officer's arrival.

As the gates open, the prisoners all bow low, remaining obeisant as the car draws up, disgorging a short stocky Japanese officer – in a double-breasted tunic, pantaloon trousers and long leather boots. Slapping a riding whip against one boot, he struts up and down the lines of prisoners in malevolent silence. With the slow stealthy steps of a stalking predator, he walks to the front of the lines, turning to face his prey.

"*Tachiagaru*!" As he barks out the order, the internees instantly straighten, obediently keeping their eyes fixed on the ground. The confused nuns hesitate, then copy the others – but the momentary delay catches his attention. For several seconds, he glares at them, sucking in his lower lip. Finally, he turns back to the car and shouts in rapid Japanese. On the far side, the rear door opens, a soldier scrambles out, straightening his uniform as he runs over to the colonel. Mother Helena immediately recognises General Sato's interpreter – bespectacled, anxious, unhappy.

The two men speak before the interpreter crosses the courtyard to face the nuns, his eyes widening in recognition at the sight of Mother Helena.

"Colonel Kimuru say *tachiagaru* mean you rise. He say you must rise when he order, not keep him waiting." His back to the colonel, the interpreter grimaces, his eyes apologetic as they meet Mother Helena's. "Colonel Kimuru say you stand all day for punishment." There are a few gasps amongst the prisoners, the angry colonel searching their faces for the culprits. He allows the tense silence to continue for a couple of minutes, the tap of the leather whip against his boot marking out time. Mother Helena notices the interpreter's eyes are shut tightly, his face screwed up, anticipating a violent outburst. When nothing awful happens, his face relaxes and he rushes back to join the colonel – both men returning to the car.

As the rumble of the engine fades away, there is a collective sigh of relief – the internees turning towards the nuns in pity; looking away before meeting the bewildered sisters' eyes. All too often, the prisoners have witnessed terrible punishments for the slightest infraction. For too many hours, they have been forced to stand beneath the blazing sun, sick and dizzy from the intense glare and heat.

"Cheer up!" Margery calls out to no one in particular. "At least he forgot to order no food or water this time!"

Rumour spreads through Palembang jail – a move, a new camp.

"Thank Christ," Matt wipes sweat from his eyes. "Any more in here and we'll be stacked on top of each other." He and John stand side by side with the rest of the prisoners, lined up in the jail courtyard, waiting to be dismissed by the guards.

John replies quietly, keeping his eyes straight ahead.

"I hear the new camp's a half hour's walk and we'll be building it ourselves."

Both men volunteer for the working party set up to build the new camp. The work will be a change from loading oil drums and being in the jungle may provide the possibility of scavenging for extra food.

The ragged line of ragged men marches through the deserted

town of Palembang. Most of its buildings have been destroyed by the air raids – leaving streets covered in rubble, strewn with debris from the bomb blasts. The European inhabitants have all gone – fled to Oosthaven, interned in the camps or killed by the invaders. John is filled with a mixture of rage at the wanton destruction and sorrow for the town's displaced citizens. He imagines the abandoned buildings full of ghosts – wandering in the wreckage, haunting the ruined houses, unable to find peace.

The fifty or so men eventually leave the town behind, crossing the Musi on the old wooden ferry. As they trudge along muddy tracks, splash through the knee-deep murky water of the peat swamps and tramp over grassland, Matt is reminded of his arduous trek to bring Emily to Palembang – his terror that she might die or that they would be captured. He recalls their time spent at the cave, Emily's vivacity, the certainty that her father would come. He pictures Indah, who had frightened him half to death, trying to protect her. The images of the dead soldiers and tiger, Emily on the ground broken and bleeding, are still too raw and salty tears sting his sunburned cheeks.

"Look!" Matt is jerked from his painful recollections by John, pointing to a group of houses surrounded by a barbed wire fence. "That must be where the women are!" The other men gradually become aware of the camp, amazed as women and children appear on the top of a high wall, shouting and waving.

"Gracie!" a man screams out, dropping to his knees; smiling despite tears pouring down his mud-streaked cheeks. "My Grace is alive! Can you see her, Bob? There she is! On the wall! I'm not dreaming, am I?" Another prisoner, presumably Bob, pats the kneeling man's shoulder reassuringly.

"No, Frank, you're not dreaming. That's Grace all right."

"No stop! No stop!" the Japanese guards shout at the men,

who have all stopped to wave enthusiastically. Pulled roughly to his feet and forced to march on, the shocked Frank continues to cry out.

"My Gracie's *alive*! She's not dead! Thank God! Thank God! Gracie! Bob! Gracie's alive! You saw her, Bob, didn't you? I thought she'd drowned when our ship went down. I thought I'd lost her. Gracie! Gracie! I love you!" As the women disappear from sight, he begins to sob, great howls of relief racking his entire body. The realisation that they will see the women every morning and evening, lifts the men's spirits, instils a new optimism, a reason to go on living.

"It's just a bloody field!" an incredulous Matt swats at the flies, swarming out of tiny holes in the earth disturbed by the men's heavy tread. John's memory flashes back to another empty field, Emily quietly sketching, while he made plans for the P2 airbase. His thoughts jump to Mike Harman. John would have staked his life on Mike's reliability, his absolute certainty that Mike would get Emily safely out of Sumatra.

"Matt?" John attracts the other man's attention. "You said Emily ran away from Mike Harman because he was going to shoot Indah?"

"Yeah, that's what she said."

"It doesn't make any sense. He'd never have done that. He certainly wouldn't have let Emily know if he'd planned it – if he'd had no other choice."

"Emily told me she'd overheard Mike talking to an officer, but I've no idea who it was, or exactly who said what. Anyway, what made you think of that now?"

"This big empty field. It's how P2 looked when Emily and I first saw it."

"As I remember, P2 ended up with comfortable wooden

barracks. Not luxury exactly, but good enough."

"Well, don't expect much here. I imagine we're going to make use of all this bamboo." John spreads an arm to indicate the wealth of trees surrounding them. "I expect we'll thatch the roofs with coconut palm leaves woven together, just as the local workers do when building their huts."

"Proper bloody boy scout, aren't ya!" Grinning, Matt watches a group of local Malay workmen tramp into the field, bearing axes and saws. "Now these boys'll know what's to be done, I reckon."

By midday, the Europeans are wilting: blistered from the saws used to cut bamboo, fatigued from the sun and lack of food, and very dehydrated. At first, the guards had prodded, slapped and shouted – but their efforts had little effect on the exhausted men. Now, collapsed under shady palm trees, the prisoners gulp down their inadequate water ration, watching the apparently indefatigable local men continue with the work.

"Fresh water's going to be a problem out here," remarks John. His shoulders ache and his blisters have burst, leaving open red sores which attract the flies. Carefully, he tears a huge palm leaf into long strips; wrapping them around his palms and thumbs, gesturing for Matt to tuck in the ends, to keep them secure. "Matt, what are you doing?"

"Shush, mate!" Matt looks around to make sure they are unobserved, his guilty expression switching to a wry grin. "I slipped away for a minute or two and found these beauties." Fishing in his pocket, eyes still darting around, Matt retrieves half a dozen squashed figs, which he quickly hands to John. Savouring the sweet flesh, John cannot imagine food ever tasting so good.

"How're the stitches, mate?"

"Itchy." John absently rubs at his side. "They're coming out tomorrow."

"Say hi to Emily and the doc for me. Wish I'd an excuse."

"I could saw off a finger or two if you like?"

"Nah! You're all good. I'm rather fond of my digits."

In the orange glow of the setting sun, the weary men set off on the long march back to the jail. The guards are relentless – trying to force the pace as they pass the women's camp. Despite the sting of bamboo canes on their backs, the stubborn prisoners slow, taking time to wave and shout greetings to the women and children gathered on the wall.

In the fading light, they emerge from the forest – the sad silent ruins of the town casting long sinister shadows. The exhausted men stumble along the dark streets of Palembang – now the domain of hungry rats as well as John's restless ghosts.

As the sun sets behind the camp, silhouetting the barbed wire, symbolising imprisonment, the guards finally dismiss the exhausted nuns. Margery and Susan help the sisters back to their house. Nora arrives with steaming bowls of rice and vegetable scraps for their evening meal. Throughout the day, Margery has defied the glowering guards by taking water and cold sticky rice balls to the nuns. To help pass the intolerable hours standing in the heat, she has been teaching them harmonies to the Christmas carols she is arranging – encouraging the children to join in with the main soprano melodies. Margery has great plans for a Christmas concert and is determined to make use of the nuns' singing abilities. As she suspected, they have beautiful voices.

The appearance of the men passing their camp that morning and evening had provided another distraction – Grace Fielding, having seen her husband for the first time since their ship had been sunk near the Sumatran coast, spends hours on her knees, begging the nuns to say prayers of thanksgiving to God for saving his life.

After the empty bowls have been removed, Susan gets the nuns to lie flat on the floor with their legs elevated, feet resting against the room's walls.

"It'll help the blood flow," she explains. "Where you've been standing all day, the blood sort of pools around your ankles. By lifting your legs, the blood flows back to the heart, sending fresh blood down to your feet."

"Not very elegant," laughs Margery, "But very effective. You shouldn't feel too stiff in the morning. The colonel will be watching for you to rise when he gives the order. Please don't hesitate. I wish I'd warned you, but I never thought…" her distressed voice trails away.

"Please, Margery," Mother Helena assures her, "it's not your fault. You've done so much for us already. You couldn't have known what would happen. Anyway, it's been quite a day – finding missing husbands and preparing for Christmas. The time passed constructively with prayer and song. Now, I think we can forgo evening prayers as we're all too tired to get up again. Thank you, Susan, for your kind advice. I'm sure we'll be fine in the morning and you can rest assured, we will rise as the order is given!" The Reverend Mother nods decisively, emphasising her point.

The women leave the nuns to sleep, hoping they will be all right in the morning, able to stand for Tenko.

"When this bloody war is over," Margery scowls at the guards as they pass. "I want to be there. I want to wipe that self-satisfied smirk from the colonel's nasty face. Give him a taste of his own medicine. Stand him out bareheaded with no water, for a day or two in the sun, and see how he likes it!" Her hands form claws. "I want to throttle his scraggy neck with my bare hands!"

"Oh, let me be there too!" Susan grins. "I want to see you do your worst."

Nora chuckles, keeping her own counsel. Deep inside, she is frightened there will never be an end to this suffering; to the privations, indignities, fear. She feels herself weakening, both physically and in her mind. Nora Palmer is not at all sure she will live long enough to regain her freedom.

In the silvery light of the moonlit ward, Emily wakes, wondering where she is. Her surroundings seem familiar – the whirring ceiling fan, the smell of disinfectant and the gentle swish of nuns' robes as they pass around the patients' beds. These familiar sounds and smells are comforting – she feels secure, relaxed in the bed. Turning her head, Emily makes out the ghostly figure of Sister Catherina, washing her hands at a sink. The trickle of water stimulates a feeling in her bladder, creating the need to visit the lavatory. Sitting up, Emily swings her legs out of the bed. The movement makes her feel sick and dizzy; she is not sure she can stand.

"Sister," Emily's voice comes out as a croak, so she clears her throat to try again. The sound brings the nun running, leaving Emily confused by the look of astonishment on Sister Catherina's face.

"I need the lavatory," Emily explains, her voice still very hoarse. For a moment, Sister Catherina just stares at her, open-mouthed. "I *really* need to go, Sister," she pleads.

"Of course, Emily. Hang on a minute." To Emily's frustration, the nun takes off at a run, disappearing from the ward. Really, why the fuss? She only needs to spend a penny. Emily decides to find the lavatory herself – but when her feet touch the floor, she finds her legs will not support her, and ends up in a heap.

"Emily!" Doctor Peter charges onto the ward, skidding to a halt at her side. Emily thinks he looks rather excited, like a child at Christmas, finding a new bicycle under the tree. It is all very peculiar.

"I just need to go to the lavatory, but my legs won't hold me up. Can you help me?"

"Let's get you back into bed." Effortlessly, he lifts her onto the bed. "I'll get Sister to bring a bedpan."

"Urgh! Do I have to?" groans Emily, her expression mutinous.

"Just until you feel stronger. Are you hungry?"

Emily considers – she cannot remember when she last ate. "Yes, I think so. Why am I here, Dr Peter?"

"You've been ill, Emily. Do you remember anything?"

"No. Where's Daddy? I remember dreaming about Daddy and Lai."

"They'll both be here tomorrow to see you."

"Oh good. Then we can go home."

Peter is amazed. Emily is behaving as if she can wait for Lai and her father to take her home – as if none of the recent events ever happened. A worried frown crosses his haggard face.

"What's the matter?" Emily asks, pausing to look up, before dunking her biscuit into the cup of tea provided by Sister Catherina.

"Everything's fine, Emily. Can you tell me the last thing you remember?" The doctor's voice is gentle, encouraging.

Emily shakes her head as if trying to clear her mind of cobwebs.

"Honestly, Doctor Peter, I can't remember *anything*. I know I'm Emily. I know you and Sister Catherina, Daddy and Lai. I know this is the Charitas hospital but I've no idea why I'm here. Why can't I remember anything? I mean, if you asked me what I've been doing, I just can't remember. It's all very odd. Is it because I've been ill?"

"That's exactly it, Emily," the doctor nods slowly. "But you're not to worry about anything, you're safe."

"Why wouldn't I be safe?"

"Emily, it's the middle of the night. Do you think you can go back to sleep? You may remember more in the morning and we can talk about everything then."

"Okay. I'm feeling tired anyway. See you in the morning." Peter waits as the child snuggles down and drifts back into sleep. He is very worried. She is going to get a terrible shock when she sees the state of her father. How are they going to explain what has been happening? Should they tell her or wait to see which, if any, of her memories return? He looks across to see where Martha is sleeping – or perhaps pretending to be asleep. She and the other evacuees will probably be sent to the camp in the next few days. Will Emily have to go too? He is torn between wanting to watch over her recovery and getting her away before Sato's next visit. Peter's mind races with all that needs consideration and the arrangements to be made – yet he is consumed by a dreadful premonition that events may well spiral out of his control.

Chapter 21

John watches the work party heading off through the town. At a questioning look from a guard, he lifts his shirt to point at his stitches, then makes a scissor-cutting motion with his fingers. Understanding, the guard gestures for John to climb onto the back of a truck; ten minutes later, he is roughly pulled off, and dumped unceremoniously outside the hospital.

Peter is anxiously waiting for John by the main entrance. Putting a finger to his lips, he beckons John to follow him and the two men go into Peter's office.

"How's Emily?"

"She's fine – that's why I brought you in here first."

"Go on." John's eyes focus intensely on the doctor.

"In the night, she woke up. It was so unexpected, John. Emily woke up and demanded to go to the lavatory. She can't remember why she's here. She tried to get up but fell on the floor."

"What? Is she okay?"

"Yes. More frustrated than hurt, and none too pleased to have to use a bedpan."

John's expression softens. "That sounds like her."

"Exactly. Everything about her is normal – her mannerisms, her personality, all the same. It's just she doesn't remember anything."

"Does she know who you are?"

"Yes. She named me and said she'd dreamed about you and

Lai. I told her you'd both be in today and she was happy, saying she wanted to go home."

"So, what did you tell her? I mean, how did you explain her being here?"

"I was evasive – told her it's the middle of the night, go back to sleep and we'll talk in the morning. She didn't object. She was asleep again in moments."

"Is she awake now?"

"Not yet. It's still early. I hoped to see you first. We have to decide what to tell her. Come and have a wash first, I'll remove the stitches and find you a clean shirt. You look terrible and that'll be a shock for her."

"Does Lai still visit?"

"Yes. I think that's why Emily dreams. Lai speaks to her about you all the time. She doesn't mention anything that's happened, just general talk about your house, school and the club."

"What do you think we should tell her, Peter? If she's not even aware of the war, that I'm a prisoner..." tears glisten in John's eyes. He cannot imagine how he can possibly describe what has happened to him, let alone speak of the appalling things that have been done to her during the past weeks.

"There's no need to talk about her being in the jungle if she doesn't remember, but she'll have to know about the war." Peter looks thoughtful. "Perhaps we could say she was hurt in an air raid, knocked out by the blast? That could explain why she's here and why she can't remember."

"What'll happen now she's awake? Will you be able to keep her here?"

"I doubt it. She'll be sent to the women's camp. Martha and the others have to go too – I haven't told them yet. Perhaps Emily can go with them? Martha will look after her, I'm sure."

Peter notices the way John fidgets – continually running his hands through his hair, rubbing his chin, shifting uncomfortably on his chair. He recognises the signs of nervous exhaustion. Hopefully, seeing Emily awake and back to her usual self, will help John's state of mind. Peter tries to distract him.

"Have you seen Matt?"

"We're on the same work party – building a new men's camp, not far from the women."

"How's he bearing up?"

"Pretty good. He slipped away and found us some figs yesterday. He wanted to come today and sends his regards, by the way. Has Emily mentioned him or Indah?"

"No. I'm not sure if she remembers either of them. It's probably best if we don't mention Indah – better for her not to remember at present."

After washing, having his stitches removed and putting on a clean, if rather large, short-sleeved shirt of Peter's, the two men nervously enter the ward.

"Daddy!" Emily calls out, her voice still hoarse, but her smile radiant. "Doctor Peter said you'd be here today. You need a haircut and a shave. What've you been doing?"

"Hello, Em," John leans over, bestowing a kiss on her forehead, taking hold of her hand.

"You're shaking, Daddy." Emily looks bewildered. "Are you ill?" Her voice rises in alarm. "You really don't look very well."

"I'm fine, darling. You've been unconscious for quite a long time and a few things have happened." Emily looks from her father to Peter, their sombre expressions making her anxious, churning her stomach. Somewhere deep within, just out of reach, she senses the fear – she has been very frightened but has no idea why. Peter comes to her bedside, taking her other hand, speaking gently.

"Do you remember the air raids, Emily? The Japanese planes bombing the town?"

Emily screws up her face in concentration, desperately trying to remember. Heaving a great sigh, she slowly shakes her head.

"Don't worry, darling." John squeezes her hand. "D'you remember we live on Sumatra, with Lai?"

"Yes. I know we live here and you work at Platjoe, I go to school and swim at the club. I know Lai helps us at home. I know we came here because Mummy and the baby died." Her tears start to flow, breaking John's heart.

On the other side of the ward, Martha covers her mouth with her hand. She had no idea Emily's mother had died. She wants to reach out to the child, to comfort her, to lift these terrible burdens from her. Sister Catherina notices the nurse's distress, coming to sit on Martha's bed, offering her own silent support.

Lai comes through the door. A look of sheer astonishment on her face as she is met by the sight of Mr John and Emily sitting together. Giving a little cry, she runs over to them, looking from one to the other, putting her hands to her face, repeating their names. The unexpected scene is too much for her and Lai bursts into tears. Putting a comforting arm around her shoulders, Peter draws her towards Emily's bed, including her within the intimate circle.

Emily, completely unused to Lai expressing emotion, becomes more fearful. Nothing is as it should be – Lai crying and Daddy looking ill. She shakes her head again, trying to comprehend; unhappy, frustrated, desperate to remember and needing to understand.

"Listen to me, Emily. I know how brave you are, so I'm going to explain what's happened to us all. Okay?" Emily nods at her father, swallowing the lump rising in her throat.

"While you've been unconscious, the Japanese army has invaded Sumatra, taken over at Pladjoe and we are all now called prisoners of war."

"What does that mean, Daddy? Am I a prisoner too?"

"Yes, darling. We *all* are." John extends his arm to bring Emily's notice to the other people in the ward – Martha, Sister Catherina, the other nurses, civilian women and children.

"I thought they were just patients. I thought they were sick."

"They have been sick, Emily, but they're better now and will be leaving the hospital to go to a camp."

"A camp with tents?"

"No. The women and children live in houses assigned by the Japanese. The houses are surrounded by a big fence and they're not allowed to leave. The houses inside the fence are their camp. Do you see?"

"I think so. But why can't they leave when they want to?"

"Because the Japanese soldiers, who're now in charge, won't allow it."

"If we have to be prisoners, can we still stay in *our* house? You, me and Lai?"

"I'm sorry, Emily, but the men are separated from the women and children. I have to stay in a different camp, with the other men. Lai stays at her own house by the river. The locals are not made to stay in camps but they have to work for the Japanese."

"But I want to be with *you*, Daddy."

"I know, I know. I'm helping to build a new men's camp and it isn't too far from where the women and children live."

"Can I come and see you there?"

John sighs, trying to hold himself together. "I don't think so. Not at the moment."

"Then I'm not going. I'm staying here with Dr Peter and Lai."

Peter rests his hands on Emily's shoulders, making her look at him. "I'll keep you here as long as I can, but only sick people are allowed to be here and you're getting better. When the Japanese think you're well enough, they'll take you to the camp. Look," he gestures to Martha and the other evacuees, "they'll be going to the camp too. Reverend Mother Helena is already there. Do you remember her?"

Emily tilts her head to one side, thoughtful. "Yes. Yes, I do remember Mother Helena. She's very kind. I remember Sister Catherina as well." Emily points at the nun, giving a little wave. Sister Catherina smiles, then turns away to hide her distress. "Daddy?"

"Yes, darling."

"I don't think I want to be brave. I just want to be with you. Can't we go back to England and not be prisoners?"

"Not right now, but one day, Emily. One day, we can go back to England. It may take a long time and you have to be brave. We have to stay in our camps until the war ends and we are free."

"When will that be?"

"I honestly don't know." John wraps his arms around his daughter and they cling to one another. "We will get through this. You're so brave and clever, you'll be fine."

The ward falls silent while its occupants become lost in their own thoughts. Memories of better times, worries for the present and fear for the future. The children scan the adults' faces, unsettled by their sad expressions. Martha exchanges a lingering look with Peter, understanding passes between them – separation is inevitable, but they will try to survive, to be reunited.

The heavy tread of approaching boots shatters the peace. The door to the ward is thrown open, crashing against the wall, shattering the glass in its window. General Sato strides in, surrounded by armed soldiers, the terrified interpreter scuttling in behind. Sato takes up a position in the centre of the room, scowling round at the ward's occupants – suspicious, enraged, rising to the balls of his feet, a deadly snake preparing to strike.

The sight of John holding Emily and Sister Catherina sitting on Martha's bed increases his anger – blazing eyes darting, selecting a victim. Sato screams in his own language, ordering the shaking interpreter to step forwards and translate.

"General Sato say you run holiday camp not hospital." His voice is ragged and hollow, the voice of doom.

Peter takes a single step towards Sato, raising his hands in a calming gesture. He cannot find words to explain, he is transfixed by the expression of pure hatred in the general's eyes.

"P-p-please," Peter stammers, "we're making arrangements for the patients to leave for the camps." The general's expression is cynical, disbelieving.

"General Sato say you have a party. You dishonour him, you disobey orders."

Peter is frozen with terror as Sato unholsters a revolver and releases the safety catch. As if in slow motion, he watches the arc of the gun rising to point straight at his chest.

"You don't need to do this." Peter's voice is quiet, placating, trying to find a way through Sato's maddened rage – hoping to avert disaster. A malevolent grin crosses the man's features and Peter realises this is the opportunity for which the general has been waiting – finally, he has his victim in his sights. The weeks of stalking over, he intends to kill.

Peter closes his eyes and is knocked off his feet as the room resounds with the explosion – the acrid smell of sulphur filling his nostrils. Confused that he feels no pain, Peter opens his eyes and jumps up, gasping in horror as dark red blossoms through brilliant white fabric.

With sightless eyes staring up to the heavens, Sister Catherina lies on the floor. As she is much shorter than Peter, the bullet intended for his chest has passed clean through her throat, shattering the carotid artery – the final beats of her heart pumping out a torrent of bright blood, drenching her white habit. Peter drops to his knees beside her, but he can do nothing: she is already dead. Overcome with grief and rage, he staggers to his feet. Abandoning all reason, he hurls himself at the general. Peter feels the impact, an agonising pain in his skull, before his whole world turns black.

Having fainted, Lai is also on the floor, leaving John and Emily still clutching one another, eyes wide in terror. Martha looks on in horror at the unfolding scene – Sister Catherina lies in an ever-increasing pool of blood, while Peter lies prone at the general's feet.

All eyes focus on the gun in his hand.

Something rises from deep within Emily; the unstoppable force of recollection. Her body stiffens in her father's arms as she begins to scream – a continuous high-pitched remorseless howl; knowledge of her own pain echoing the cries of thousands of prisoners – their unendurable suffering at the hands of these evil oppressors.

The scream continues, wave after wave, bringing the general to a heightened level of rage. He hisses in her direction.

"General Sato say she be quiet or he shoot her too."

But John is helpless to stop his daughter. She fights to be released from his hold. Her eyes are unfocused. She has retreated, he cannot reach her.

Sato raises the gun, aiming it directly at the still screaming girl when the interpreter, with new-found determination, places himself in the line of fire. The general lowers the gun, a look of surprise quickly turning to annoyance. He turns away for a moment, as if considering his next move – giving the interpreter time to regret his bravery. With a slow shake of his head – a seemingly benign gesture of disappointment – Sato carefully raises the gun, pauses, a cat toying with its mouse, then calmly shoots the interpreter between the eyes. The shot silences Emily – though her mouth stays open wide, in a silent scream of terror.

Sato shrugs, indicating his indifference, before turning maniacal eyes upon his own men – shouting, gesticulating to the dead interpreter. One of his escort steps forwards, giving a respectful bow as more words are exchanged.

"General Sato say," the soldier pauses, trying to summon the English words he needs to translate the general's orders. "General Sato say hospital finish. Leave now. Five minutes." He holds up his hand, indicating five fingers. Satisfied, the general holsters his gun and marches out of the room, followed by his obedient retinue.

Martha leaps out of bed and is at Peter's side in an instant. He groans, screwing up his eyes in pain as she strokes his hair, moving it away from his temple, and the deep cut caused by the impact of the solid pistol. The other nurses surround Sister Catherina, helpless, distraught.

With the general's departure, Emily's mouth closes. Tears pour down her cheeks as the memories continue to flood in: her beautiful Indah; the cave and flat rock overlooking the pool; finding Matt. Now, she recalls the Japanese soldiers with their wicked expressions, grinning hyenas and the absolute terror of being gagged, seeing the knife and her eyes being covered. Finally, she relives the moment of intolerable all-consuming pain, of her body being ripped apart. Emily looks down at her body which appears to be whole under the nightdress. Closing her eyes, she tentatively runs her hands over her stomach and down her legs, amazed to find she is still in one piece. Opening her eyes again, Emily meets the distraught expression in her father's tear-filled eyes. Hugging him close, she buries her face in the warmth of his chest, releasing her grief – for Indah, for Daddy, for Sister Catherina, for herself.

Slowly, using the bed frame for support, Lai pulls herself to her feet – surveying the macabre scene. The dead sister, arms extended where she pushed the doctor aside, lies on her back – an open red maw where her delicate throat had once been. Her face is slack, spattered with bright arterial blood – now reduced to a trickle, seeping through the white robes, spreading on the floor. The young nuns and Australian nurses stand like statues around the nun's body, motionless, impotent – silent witnesses to a violent sacrifice.

Martha – ashen-faced, skeletally thin in a white cotton nightgown – sits on the floor, cradling Peter's head in her lap; rocking and whispering endearments – oblivious to the red streaks from Peter's cut, forming gruesome patterns on her white gown.

Beside Lai, John holds his sobbing daughter – his face sorrowful as he stares down at the dead interpreter, splayed on the floor on the other side of Emily's bed, blood oozing from the hole between his eyes.

Across the ward, four whimpering children crawl out from underneath the hospital beds, averting their eyes from the dreadful scene, rushing into the arms of the frightened and shocked women.

As Lai's tears blur her vision, the haunting tableau loses its stark clarity. Dominated by the blood and white habit, her traumatised mind sees only red on white; the Japanese flag, a circular stain of blood on a pure white background.

Reverend Mother Helena sits silently in the darkness, gazing out of the window at the full moon – radiating pure light, allowing the world to appear in monochrome. She wishes life were black and white, simple, more comprehensible. Her faith is being tested to its limits; the loss of Sister Catherina is a raw open wound, her appalling death abhorrent. Beside Mother Helena, Emily sleeps restlessly on a mat, exhausted from crying.

As the truck had driven into camp, dumping its shocked silent prisoners, Margery and Mother Helena had come running, sensing the terrible distress. Martha, still wearing the blood-streaked white nightgown clinging damply to her thin frame, assisted by the two nuns who remained at the hospital with Sister Catherina, carried a sobbing Emily up to house number five – to be placed in the care of Mother Helena. Margery had taken charge of the Australian nurses and the civilian women with the four children – handing them over to the capable Nora and Susan, before rushing up to the nuns' house to find out what had happened.

Martha had explained about Emily's unexpected recovery, how John had faked appendicitis to be with his daughter and why he had come back that morning. Once Margery arrived, Martha described how General Sato had marched into the ward, threatening, enraged. Listening to the terrible tale, the stunned sisters had begun to pray, clutching their rosaries, as Martha told them how Sister Catherina had bravely flung herself across the ward, pushing the doctor out of the bullet's path. They wept as they pictured little Sister Catherina dead and Doctor Peter unconscious from the blow to his temple. All the nuns, except for Mother Helena, had been surprised by the interpreter's sacrifice – she had recognised his humanity, his loathing of the cruelty displayed by his superiors.

Emily had become increasingly distressed as Martha described General Sato marching out, giving orders for them to be removed in five minutes. Soldiers had returned, ripping John from his daughter's arms, before dragging both him and Peter off to the men's camp. All the women and children had been rounded up, bundled into the back of a truck and brought to the women's camp. They had been given no time to grieve; no time to bury their dead.

The two young nuns then revealed the medicines, dressings and disinfectant they had managed to secrete in their robes. Martha thought the Australian nurses had also grabbed what they could but doubted it would be much.

A stunned silence had followed Martha's explanation, finally broken by Mother Helena, suggesting they pray together.

"Our prayers are offered to God the Almighty – Father, Son and Holy Ghost – asking him to take into his heart, the soul of our beloved sister, Catherina, who willingly gave her life to protect that of our dear friend, Doctor Peter. May she be welcomed into heaven, leaving her mortal suffering, to rest in eternal peace. We also pray for the Japanese interpreter, who sacrificed his own life to save that of our beloved daughter,

164

Emily. May his soul rest in everlasting peace."

They had all chorused, "Amen."

The rest of the day had been spent finding accommodation and clothing for the new arrivals. Emily had clung to Mother Helena, begging to be taken to her father. With infinite patience, the Reverend Mother soothed her, helped her to wash and eat before settling beside her – stroking her forehead, waiting for the child to cry herself to sleep.

Now, in the pale moonlight flowing gently through the window, she watches the sleeping child – knowing this brief respite will end when Emily wakes. In the morning, they will face the colonel, and the possible reprisals resulting from the appalling events at the hospital.

As well as enduring the deep sorrow, Mother Helena's heart swells with pride at the selfless action of Sister Catherina – the diminutive nun with the heart of a lioness. Mother Helena wonders if she could have done the same. With a wry smile, she accepts she would never have been quick enough. Only Catherina – perceptive, spontaneous – could have made such a brave unhesitating decision. Had God's hand guided Mother Helena to insist Sister Catherina remain at the hospital?

Overwhelmed by the burden of responsibility, Reverend Mother believes God wishes her to become the spiritual mother – not just for her sisters, but for the entire camp. She believes God is testing her resolve – asking her to provide understanding, comfort and hope to all the nuns, nurses, women and children, in their time of need.

For the first time in years, she is truly frightened; afraid to fail her ultimate test. Trembling, she raises her eyes to the moon. In her moment of epiphany, Mother Helena sees a face, smiling, encouraging. The pale glow soothes her, calming her thundering heart. She believes the full white moon represents the communion host, the small circular wafer, transformed into the body of Christ. She experiences a connection, a joining: her face becomes serene as she receives God's grace through the moonlight, filling her heart, bringing her strength.

Bowing her head, Mother Helena weeps silent tears of joy. She has seen God, received his love and his blessing. Full of a new courage, renewed confidence and faith, she prepares herself for sleep, knowing she will have the strength to face the new day.

From his usual position – seated on the ground in the shade of the inner courtyard wall – Matt looks up to see John helping Peter navigate a path through the throng of male prisoners.

"Over here, John!" he calls out, waving his arms. Surprised to see Peter, Matt notices the blood trickling down the doctor's face from a cut on his temple. "What the hell's happened?" he demands worriedly, looking from one to the other.

"Sato. That bastard Sato is what's happened!" John's face is a mask of fury and distress.

"I'm guessing he's responsible for that?" Matt points to Peter's cut.

"Much worse, Matt. So much worse." John shakes his head, defeated, distraught.

"Sato killed Sister Catherina." Peter's words come slowly, as if he is struggling to force them out. "He was going to shoot *me* but she pushed me out the way. It should be *me*, not *her*." His voice cracks, trailing away. Peter focuses his eyes – full of intolerable pain – on Matt's. "*I* should be dead, not brave little Sister Catherina. It's all my fault."

"Peter hurled himself at Sato who knocked him out with the butt of his gun." John continues, relating the details. "It was all too much for Emily. I think seeing the soldiers, hearing the shot, it brought back her memory."

"Jeez. Poor Emily." Matt looks down until a sudden, terrible thought occurs to him. "What happened to her? Is she okay?"

"She started screaming the place down. It was like a volcanic eruption. I could do nothing to stop her. Sato threatened to shoot if she didn't stop, but it made no difference. I watched him raise the gun – I thought it was all over." John stops, picturing the awful scene in his mind: Emily struggling out of his arms, out of his protection, into terrible danger.

"And?" Matt cannot hide his impatience.

"Incredibly, the interpreter put himself between the gun and Emily. At first, Sato lowered the gun and looked away, as if annoyed. Then, he turned and calmly shot the poor chap straight between the eyes."

"Christ!" Matt can think of no other word.

"Sato seemed indifferent, and found another of his men to translate. He said the hospital was finished and we had to leave within five minutes. We were all too shocked to move, so when the soldiers came back, they just dragged Emily away from me and brought us here. I could hear her screaming for me. It was unbearable." John puts his head in his hands, hiding his distress.

"We'll need to stop that bleeding, doc." Matt attempts to distract the two men.

Slowly, Peter starts to pull items from his pockets – dressings, disinfectant spray and aspirin.

"The bare essentials." Peter offers a weak smile. "Will you do the honours, Matt?" He hands over a dressing for Matt to unwrap, while he sprays the cut on his head with the disinfectant.

"D'ya think the Japs'll let us get more supplies?" Matt asks.

"Not a chance," replies Peter.

"Don't forget Lai and the other local girls weren't dragged off." John looks a little more hopeful. "I'm sure they'll grab what they can and get it to us somehow."

"Won't they keep it for themselves?" Matt is cynical.

"You'd think so, wouldn't you?" John replies. "But they've little faith in Western medicine so we may get some back."

"So," Matt looks thoughtful, "if you're back on the camp building, mate, you should be able t' keep an eye on Emily if she climbs onto the wall."

Peter looks confused, raising his eyebrows questioningly.

"He's right, Peter. I told you we're building a camp near the women. We pass them on our way out and back. If they climb up on the wall and wave, you can make out who's who. You'll be able to see Martha."

"Who's Martha?" Matt asks.

"Ah, now that'd be telling!" John grins. "I'll leave that for Peter to explain."

Chapter 22

"I really don't think we can take the risk, Mother Helena." An agitated Margery paces up and down outside the nuns' house in the pre-dawn grey light. "Word's bound to have reached the colonel. He'll know Emily's here and she's the reason his interpreter's dead."

"But the child is in no fit state to line up this morning." Mother Helena grimly faces Margery, determined to have her way.

"He'll want his revenge, Mother. It's not safe giving Kimuru the opportunity to take his anger out on Emily. You've seen him in action. Surely, the girl's suffered enough?"

Margery is beginning to lose her temper. Up to now, the nuns – including the Reverend Mother – have deferred to her experience. Margery is unsettled by Mother Helena's new-found self-confidence, sensing a challenge to her own authority.

"I'll explain to the colonel. Emily's unwell, Margery. She's traumatised by what's happened. She'll be terrified of the colonel, so goodness knows how she'll react if he approaches her."

"I *do* understand, Mother. We'll have to explain to her what to do. I think it'll be far worse if she's absent altogether."

"Please stop arguing!" the small ethereal figure demands, standing in the shadow of the doorway – hair loose, dark eyes huge, clad in an overlarge white nightgown.

"Hello, Emily." Margery holds out her hand. "It's Margery.

We met yesterday but you may not remember. We're not really arguing, we just want what's best for you and everyone in the camp."

Emily steps forwards briefly shaking the extended hand, before moving closer to Mother Helena, clasping the nun's arm.

"Daddy said I must be brave. I don't want any more trouble, so I'll do whatever you want." Resigned, Emily stares down at her bare feet, scuffing the dirt with her toes. "What do I have to do?"

"Every morning the whole camp has to line up in the courtyard, to be inspected by a Japanese officer, Colonel Kimuru. He's a nasty little man, who struts up and down like a peacock." Margery does her best impersonation of the colonel – hands clasped behind her back, taking long, slow strides and pulling ridiculous faces. "He wants us to make mistakes so he can hand out punishments. His favourite is to make us stand in the sun all day. Mother Helena will explain what to do, but if you can manage not to attract his attention, he may leave you alone. D'you think you can manage?"

Emily nods, amused by Margery's antics – her hands releasing Mother Helena's arm.

"Once we're all dismissed," Margery continues, "we can go to the high garden wall – on the other side of the camp – and wave to the men who pass by each morning and evening, on their way to build their new camp. If you're lucky, Emily, your Daddy may be amongst them."

At this news, Emily's brown eyes brighten and more colour comes into her cheeks. Mother Helena looks singularly unimpressed – concerned with how Emily will react if her father is not one of the workers.

"I can do it, if I can see Daddy," Emily confirms, gazing up at Margery – her eyes eager, hopeful. Catching sight of Mother Helena's expression of displeasure, Margery heaves an inward sigh. After all, she is only trying to keep the peace and keep Emily away from the colonel's notice. Surely, Emily's father will manage to get onto the work party if he can? He will want to see his daughter as much as she does him. Margery decides a change of subject is needed.

"How would you like to join my vocal orchestra, Emily?"

"What's a vocal orchestra?" The girl looks confused.

"Well, as we don't have any musical instruments, we sing the orchestral parts. Our children are the woodwind – soprano voices are perfect for the flutes, oboes and clarinets. The nuns' beautiful voices form the string section – ranging from the high sweet violins to the low melodious cellos." Margery glances at Mother Helena, hoping to regain her favour. "The rest love to bellow out the brass – strident trumpets, horns and trombones. We don't leave anyone out. Those who choose not to sing," Margery lowers her voice to a whisper, her eyes darting around, over-exaggerating the need for secrecy, making Emily giggle, "those who sound more like screeching cats," Margery covers her ears, giving Emily a conspiratorial grimace, "they're the percussion!"

"I think I'm better than a screeching cat!" Emily grins. "May I be in the woodwind section?"

"Indeed, you may. I'm planning a carol concert for Christmas and we'll be rehearsing every day. I'll introduce you to the others and you can get started right away. I've all the parts written down if you read music, otherwise I teach by ear – you know, I sing a line and you repeat it, until you know the whole thing. We leave the difficult harmonies to the experts," Margery gestures towards Mother Helena, "so it'll all sound beautiful in the end."

Mother Helena is now smiling, though Margery suspects it has more to do with the change of subject than her flattery. Still, it has diffused the tension, so Margery makes her excuses, hurriedly leaving before she and the Reverend Mother can argue further.

Emily observes Margery as the woman strides away. Tall, forceful yet friendly, Margery reminds her of Peter. A little afraid of him at first, Emily found Peter very funny, as well as kind, especially when they had taken Indah to him. He had made her laugh by teasing Sister Catherina – who had been so frightened. Emily pictures two Sister Catherinas: one, standing in the doorway to the hospital treatment room, too frightened of the cub to come in; the other, dead on the floor, blood spurting from a hole in her throat. Having realised Sister Catherina must have pushed Peter out of the way, without hesitation or fear, Emily understands that, in reality, Sister Catherina had been incredibly brave.

No one has mentioned Indah and Emily is too afraid to ask. She thinks Daddy would have told her if Indah had still been alive. There had been gunshots – but she and Matt had not been killed. One day, if she ever sees him again, she will ask Matt to tell her. For now, Emily imagines Indah is beside her, protecting her – invisible to everyone else. If she feels frightened by the colonel, she will imagine herself on the flat rock, overlooking the pool, hugging Indah.

The shrill whistle startles Emily, cutting through her thoughts. Mother Helena takes her hand, pulling her towards the courtyard.

"No time to dress," Mother Helena's voice is urgent, anxious. "You'll stand next to me. When the main gate opens, join your hands and bow low. Stay there, don't move or look up. The colonel will get out of the car and walk around – just as Margery described. You *must* stay bowed until he shouts a single word in Japanese. It means rise – then you instantly straighten up, keeping your eyes on the ground. Don't hesitate when you hear the order. Keep your eyes on the ground all the time, Emily. Do you understand?"

"Yes – join hands, bow, stay still. Rise when he shouts a word but keep looking down. Whatever happens, don't move or look up."

"That's it!" Mother Helena sounds relieved. "And let's pray he leaves you alone."

Martha – reunited with a few of her fellow nurses from Singapore – stands in the courtyard, waiting for the gates to open. Briefed by the others, she understands exactly what is required to avoid notice. She scans the faces until she finds the nuns and Emily. Catching her eye, Martha raises crossed fingers – Emily gives a nod, smiling nervously in return.

At the sound of the car's engine, the camp falls silent. The women and children all bow as the gates open, listening to the tyres crunch across the rough earth. Martha hears the slam of the car door, then the steady tread of the colonel's boots as he makes his way between the lines of terrified internees. Unlikely to be recognised, Martha is fearful for Emily's safety. She would have put the girl with other children, making her less conspicuous.

"*Tachiagaru!*" Martha straightens up at the command, taking a quick look in Emily's direction to make sure she has done the same, before fixing her eyes back on the ground. Another car door slams. Reflexively, Martha looks up, her eyes widening in horror as General Sato walks around the car; coming to stand at the colonel's side. Glancing across at Emily again, she is relieved to see the girl still looking down – giving no indication she is aware of Sato's presence.

Martha listens to the low muttered exchange between the two officers. They sound relaxed and she is sure they are enjoying tormenting the prisoners. Their conversation peters out – leaving the camp silent; heightening the tension. Martha becomes aware of ragged breathing around her – the palpable fear, the dreadful suspense. The air is oppressive, dark clouds gathering above them: ominous, portentous.

When the colonel coughs unexpectedly, they all flinch. Sato gives a derisive laugh; amused by their terror. The two men speak again, this time in whispers. Martha senses their excitement; the gratification derived from the absolute terror instilled in these helpless half-starved women and children. She is sickened by their behaviour. In their position of power, they have lost their humanity – every thought allowing them to see the prisoners as people has gone. To these evil men, the prisoners of war are mere playthings – there to be abused and tormented for their pleasure.

A young boy in the front line loses control – urine splattering onto the ground at his feet. Disgusted, the colonel grabs the boy's hair, forcing his head to the ground, grinding his face into the puddled earth. One of the women, probably the boy's mother, begins to cry – receiving a lash of the leather whip across her face. Once more, Martha glances across at Emily – still ramrod straight, staring at her feet, lips pressed determinedly together. Switching her gaze to Sato – Martha sees he is also watching Emily through narrowed eyes. Looking down quickly, not wishing to be caught staring – Martha closes her eyes for a moment, breathing deeply, impressed by Emily's stoicism, her strength of character.

Above them, the laden clouds finally burst; torrential rain drenching them all in moments. The Japanese officers seek shelter in their car – which eventually makes its way out of the gates, disappearing into the murkiness of the heavy downpour.

The women and children look up to the sky, thankful for the rain which has ended their torment. The downpour douses their terror, mingling with their tears. Stinking mud is washed away from the boy's face. Cool rain eases the stinging welt on the woman's cheek. Emily feels closer to Indah – imagining they are swimming together in the jungle pool. Mother Helena offers prayers of thanks to God for his timely intervention. Martha raises her face, opening her mouth wide to drink the refreshing water, marvelling at their good luck – knowing the rain is only a reprieve.

The male prisoners squelch through the mud, drenched in the torrential downpour.

"At least it's washed the swamp muck from my legs," Matt remarks, wringing the water from his saturated shirt straight into his mouth. "In fact," he continues, grinning, "it's the cleanest I've been for weeks!" His grin disappears at the sight of his two sombre friends. "I'm sure they'll be up there. It'll be good to see Emily – and get a look at your Martha." He nudges Peter, trying to be cheerful, knowing how worried they are.

"Emily was in a terrible state when I left her, Matt." John's face is drawn. Peter remains silent as they all trudge on towards the camp they are building.

Finally, the houses surrounded by barbed wire come into view and figures appear on top of the wall. In the general hubbub of waving and shouting, the three men search desperately, slowing down to get a better look.

"There!" shouts John. "There she is!" He waves at the small figure, bouncing up and down on the wall, waving and yelling. Tears of relief pour down his face. "And there's Martha!" John points her out to Peter, indicating where Martha stands, holding on to Emily – preventing her from falling off, straight into the barbed wire.

Peter's face lights up. Overwhelmed with relief, he waves enthusiastically to Martha and Emily, speechless but elated.

"No stop! No stop!" Peter hardly feels the bite of the bamboo cane on his back. Attempting to walk and wave over his shoulder, Peter stumbles – falling to his knees. John and Matt drag him up, warding off the guard's blows. They hold on, keeping him moving, the smile still stretched wide across his face.

General Sato looks out of the window, down to the Musi river. The hospital building will make fine offices for the senior officers. He has had a brilliant idea. He will form an officers' club in what had been the ward – set up a bar and bring in the local girls; one or two of the younger prisoners too. The corners of his mouth rise, but his eyes remain cold – merciless, deadly.

Chapter 23

Lai approaches the barbed wire fence surrounding the women's camp, keeping to the shadows cast by the trees. She waits, watching carefully, as the women and children move about, undertaking their daily chores. Squinting in the glare, she can just see where the fence runs behind an area of jungle. Edging around, constantly checking for patrolling guards, she follows the fence into the trees, screwing up her face as the smell of the latrine trench grows stronger.

Under the jungle canopy, the air is more humid. The long wait produces a dull ache in her back and hips. Lai looks longingly at a tree stump, inside the perimeter fence – the perfect place to sit and rest. These days, she is constantly tired: food is scarce at home and Lai gives most of her portion to the family members working long hours for the Japanese. Even her young grandsons are forced to load oil barrels onto the ships on the quayside. If not for the fish she catches in the nets slung below their house on the river, they would not be able to survive on the paltry rations of rice provided by their new masters.

A burst of conversation alerts Lai to approaching women. Scanning their faces, she is disappointed not to recognise anyone. She moves away from the fence to hide in the trees – not wishing to be seen. Lai watches four women pick up coconut shells and begin scooping human waste from a trench into large wooden buckets. She fervently hopes Emily will never have to do such an awful task. More women appear, heading into the trees – Lai immediately recognises the nuns' wimples.

Moving silently up to the fence, checking around for guards, Lai edges closer to where the nuns are collecting various plants. Recognising the sound of Mother Helena's voice, Lai's heart starts to race. She picks up a broken twig and runs it across the wire. The unusual sound makes the nuns look up, Lai quickly raising a finger to her lips.

"Lai!" A whispering Mother Helena rushes to the fence, reaching through to touch the old woman's arm. "Emily's fine, Lai. She's staying with me and spends most of her time with Martha and the other nurses."

"That good news." Lai smiles, pushing a cloth-wrapped bundle through the wire into the Reverend Mother's hand. "We take from hospital. I bring to you." Lai nods towards the package – a tacit invitation for the nun to look inside.

"Oh! Thank you, Lai. This is wonderful! You've all taken such a risk. We can't thank you enough." Within the bundle, Mother Helena finds dressings, disinfectant, quinine and vitamin tablets, even a small pair of scissors. "I'll give everything to Martha and the other nurses, to distribute where needed. These will be a huge help. You really are so very kind." The Reverend Mother is quite overcome – though she has the presence of mind to hand out the supplies for the other nuns to secrete in their robes. A guard could appear at any time. "Thank you again, Lai. You really must go. It's not safe. You could be caught. I'll tell Emily you were here. She'll be so pleased to hear we've seen you. Take care. God bless."

After waving to the nuns, Lai moves deeper into the trees. Stiff and painful limbs hamper her movement, but she is too pleased to care. She has done what she can for Mr John and Emily. Now she must concentrate all her efforts on caring for her own family.

"The camp must be nearly finished. I reckon we'll be moving here soon – finally leaving that God-awful jail." Matt surveys the rows of bamboo and palm leaf huts; while he waits in line, ready for the long march back to Palembang.

"Mm." John is unsure. "There's still the guard house and barbed wire perimeter to be done. I wouldn't get your hopes up, Matt. As I've said before, we may have more room here, but there's no water supply. So I guess we're going to have to dig a well. We're close to the peat swamp so the water will be brackish and it'll have to be boiled before drinking."

"I hope the fence goes outside the fig trees, mate. I've got used to a little fruit in my diet."

"Always thinking of your stomach, Matt!" Peter teases, binding his blistered fingers with torn strips of palm leaf.

Matt lifts his shirt, revealing protruding ribs.

"I need it, mate. My stomach thinks m' throat's bin cut!"

"Go! Go! Go!" the guards shout, beating the men to get them moving.

"Thankfully there's been no rain today." John wipes the sweat from his brow on his sleeve. "The swamp shouldn't be too deep. I'm so bloody tired."

"I don't think our guards realise you have to put food in to get energy out of the workers." Peter looks at John with concern. "We've burnt off all our body fat. Everyone's just skin and bone. Eventually, we won't be able to do this work." He shakes his head despondently.

All the men are exhausted so there is little talk as they tramp along the rutted track, towards the swamp. With insufficient food and water, they are becoming progressively weaker – work on the camp slowing down. Their heads bowed, concentrating on putting one foot in front of the other, it takes time for them to react to the sound. Gradually, they stop and look up. Even the guards stand, staring open-mouthed.

Women and children are gathered on the high wall; singing the Christmas carol, "Silent Night." The hauntingly beautiful melody, rich and harmonious, floats across the grassland – caressing, comforting, full of love. The men weep openly, overwhelmed by the purity of the voices, the emotive words of the carol – the kindness of the women and children in offering such a glorious gift. They had all forgotten it is Christmas Eve. As the last notes fade in the dwindling light, the men cheer and clap, yelling their thanks – spiritually revived.

As the guards start to wave their canes – urging the men to march on – the choir begins to sing, "Deck the halls with boughs of holly…" and the men join in – filling the evening air with a multitude of voices, lifting their feet with renewed vigour, marching in time to the music.

PART FIVE

September 1943

Chapter 24

In the stifling mid-afternoon heat, John rests in the shade of the trees closest to the hut he now shares with Peter, Matt and several other men. Since finishing the huts and moving to the camp, there is little work to occupy them. Rations are gradually diminishing as the Japanese lose interest in their idle prisoners and the jungle within the perimeter fence has been stripped of anything remotely edible.

As John had predicted, the prisoners had been forced to dig a deep well. The peaty water is not fit to drink, so a communal fire is kept alight for boiling water and cooking the meagre rations.

At first, efforts had been made to keep fit and cheerful: a cloth ball, made from an old shirt stuffed with leaves, had been kicked around until it accidentally ended up in the fire. Singing, story-telling and staging humorous sketches had been welcome distractions to the monotonous days.

As the months had passed, and the rations reduced, the men had lost their energy and enthusiasm. Now, they barely exist; sleeping whenever possible, conserving their energy for the essential chores – repairing the leaking roofs of the palm leaf huts, digging fresh latrines, cooking and keeping the fire going.

The rain had been their ally – providing fresh water. It had become their enemy – the torrential downpours flooding the camp with effluent and extinguishing their fire.

Resting his head back against the tree trunk, John's mind wanders – finding it difficult to focus on individual thoughts. Images of Emily, unseen for months, swirl in his fretful mind: waving from the high wall, lying motionless in the hospital bed, playing with Indah in their garden. He tries to hold on to the pre-war images when she had been happy, but they drift away – replaced by the blood-spattered hospital ward with Emily being dragged from his arms. He remembers her screaming for him – he can still hear her calling.

"John! John!" Why is she using his Christian name? "John! Wake up!"

Peter stands breathless before him, eyes full of concern.

"John? Are you all right?" John looks up – dizzy, confused and struggling to focus his blurred vision.

Peter crouches down, putting a tin mug of water to John's lips. The doctor frowns, his concern increasing day by day as he helplessly watches his friend weaken.

"Listen, John. I've got news. We're moving again. We're going back to Palembang then downriver on boats. No one knows why or where we're going. Some say Java, or even Australia. Imagine, John! Australia! Perhaps the war's over!"

John blinks, hardly able to take in the meaning of Peter's words. He drinks more of the water offered – cooling his head, easing the pressure.

Having collected firewood and stoked the communal fire, Matt joins them in the shade.

"What's goin' on, mate? The whole camp's buzzin' like a swarm of angry bees."

"We're leaving Sumatra," Peter replies, helping John to his feet.

"Is the war over?" Matt takes hold of Peter's arm – his fingers easily encircling the fleshless limb.

"It's all rumour. I don't know where we're going – Singapore, Java, Australia maybe?"

Matt's agitation is infectious as the men eat their pathetic meal – a handful of cooked rice, flavoured with scraps of unidentifiable vegetables. A sense of anticipation envelops the camp – could the nightmare finally be coming to an end?

The long march back to Palembang is slow and arduous. Breathing heavily, John shambles along, supported between Peter and Matt. The relief of walking at night – guided by the gentle moonlight, eluding the raging sun's burning rays – is tempered by the disappointment that they will not see their loved ones; the women's camp is dark and silent, unaware of the passing men. There is comfort in the hope that the women and children will soon follow – there will be tearful reunions, they will hold one another again.

By the time they reach Palembang quayside, the exhausted men flop down in small groups – warily eyeing the dilapidated flat-bottomed river boats tied up along the bank.

"They don't look very seaworthy," Matt remarks before a movement above attracts his attention. "Oh, look who it is – our ol' mate, the general. D'ya think he's come to wave us off?"

Stalking down the rough track from the hospital to the river, General Sato glares at the prisoners; sneering at the ragged starving men. His malevolent eyes search the gaunt faces, coming to rest on Peter. As their eyes meet, Peter shudders under the baleful gaze. As Sato's mouth gradually reforms into a sinister smile, his glittering eyes seeming to convey satisfaction, triumph. Peter looks away, no longer so sure they are destined for freedom.

In slow convoy, the overcrowded boats move down the wide black river. With barely enough room to sit, the men wriggle uncomfortably – legs entangled, soaked in the stinking bilge water. Despite the dreadful conditions, they remain alert – hoping they have seen the last of the mosquito-infested peat swamps, the appalling camps and their cruel captors.

After many hours of heading east along the Musi river, the boats finally reach the Bangka Straits. The endless sea is calm and welcoming, reflecting the changing colours of a brilliant dawn. In hopeful anticipation, they wait for the boats to turn north towards Singapore, or south towards Java. Forgetting their thirst, their hunger, their discomfort, they breathe in the salty fresh air – a cool sea breeze caressing each man's sallow sweaty skin.

When Sumatra disappears over the horizon behind them, the muttering begins. Why have they not changed course? Why are they heading for Bangka Island?

For one prisoner, evacuated from Singapore – taken to Bangka Island after being captured from the wreckage of his shelled boat, it is intolerable, too much to bear. When the guard's back is turned, he hauls himself up onto the gunwale, closes his eyes and simply drops back into the calm clear water with hardly a splash – silently sinking beneath the sunlit surface. Men stare in horrified fascination, but John understands – if not for his daughter, he would gladly follow the man into the watery grave – the brief torment, before a merciful release.

Miserably, Peter stares at the long jetty – a sinister beckoning arm. Remembering Martha's tale of her incarceration on Bangka Island, he is full of foreboding and self-loathing. Why had he encouraged John to hope? How stupid that had been. What would become of them now?

As night descends, rough hands grab John, dragging him from the boat onto the jetty. Before he can fall, Matt is beside him, offering support. In his confused half-consciousness, John imagines himself on a swaying rope bridge, high above a canyon full of glittering diamonds. His head aches, his body aches and he is unable to stop shaking. When Peter catches up to help support him, John lets his head drop, closing his burning eyes – allowing himself to be led before finally losing consciousness. The ragged line of prisoners snakes its way along the jetty, the starlit sky reflected in the rippling water.

Peter passes through the narrow passageway – enclosed in barbed wire – that runs between Tinwinning hospital and the island's Muntok Jail. Scratching his lice-ridden scalp, he follows the damp labyrinthian corridors to reach the cell he shares with Matt and twenty or so other men. The stench of human waste and disease is ever-present – no longer bothering him. A tiny window provides sufficient light to reveal Matt: corpse-like, laying on the concrete platform they share in the bare room, its damp crumbling walls mottled with mould. Comfortless though it is, at least the raised platform stays reasonably dry when the rain storms flood the cells, circulating the diseased stinking debris throughout the jail.

"How's John?" enquires a listless Matt.

"His fever's down but there's no quinine here. There's nothing at all in that so-called hospital – but at least he has a quiet place to lie down and rest."

"That's good he has a bed then." Matt tries to sound encouraging.

"Not a bed, Matt. A raised concrete platform like these. Still, it's an improvement to this place. It's staffed by monks, Singapore evacuees brought here after their boat was hit. They do their best to keep the place clean and care for the men. I've offered my services as there's no doctor; not that I can do much with no medical supplies. There's water at least, and it's okay to drink. I was able to sponge John down until the fever broke."

"How many's in the hospital?"

"About a hundred. It's full already. There're different wards – the monks keep the infectious patients apart, so John shouldn't catch TB or dysentery. They're all malaria cases on his ward."

"What's his chances, Doc?"

"Well, he's come through this bout, but last week's long journey hasn't helped – he's very weak. The problem is that he needs nutrition. We all do. Without nutrition, our bodies can't fight infection. It seems to me that the men in this prison go from here to the hospital, then up the hill to the cemetery. The Japs don't care. The white rice we're given has no nutritional value – no vitamins or minerals. We're all showing signs of beriberi – that's why John's having trouble with his vision – it's a clear symptom."

It seemed that, having marched from the jetty to Mumtok Jail, the clang of the iron gates closing behind the prisoners from Sumatra had signalled the beginning of a harsh new regime. An overcrowded jail with no sanitation: in the oppressive heat, it had become the perfect breeding ground for infectious diseases, its starving occupants offering little resistance.

John stares up at the crumbling ceiling. Originally whitewashed, rain has leaked through in places, giving it the mottled look of unhealthy skin. Finally free of the fever, his mind feels clearer, more focused. His memory of the journey from Sumatra is vague – except for the stark image of a man drowning himself.

In the solitary hours of reflection, John finds it easier to believe he had wished to ease his burning head in the cool seawater, rather than face the actual desire to end his own life by drowning. In any case, he had put Emily first. Despite his pain and confusion, he had remained in the boat, tethered to life by the love for his daughter.

The train of thought takes him back, to the days following the deaths of his wife and son. His only reason then, as now, for continuing to live had been Emily. Precocious, funny little Emily – his beautiful and courageous daughter. She had suffered the same loss – the deaths of her mother and brother. She had survived the dreadful ordeal in the jungle. There would be scars – fine cracks in her psyche needing care, reassurance – most of all, love. John needs to survive, to be reunited – he only hopes his failing body will not betray him.

Exhausted from being on his feet all day, Peter nevertheless remains on the ward the monks have assigned to prisoners suffering with severe beriberi. Sam Johnson, an Australian rubber plantation worker from southern Sumatra, is nearing the end. His legs are swollen to the size of tree trunks and he is having difficulty breathing. Demanding water, Sam vomits up the few drops Peter offers, tossing and turning on the unyielding concrete slab. Through Sam's sweat-soaked shirt, Peter feels the palpitating heart. Sam shrieks in agony and his breathing becomes fast and shallow.

In the fading light of evening, a monk glides silently into the ward, lighting a single candle. As Peter tries to calm the dying man, Brother Thomas kneels, clasping his hands in prayer. Sam's breathing becomes more laboured as his lungs fill with fluid – his shriek now a wet rattle. In his panic, Sam claws at Peter, his eyes pleading and his pupils dilated. Peter holds Sam's hands, gripping them tightly in a gesture of reassurance.

Sam's mouth opens wide in a last silent scream of distress. His torso writhes in its last throes of agony. Suddenly, he is still – the life gone from his eyes. The suffering is over – Sam is finally free. Brother Thomas continues to pray while Peter stares down at the dead man – relieved he will no longer have to witness the continued suffering, guilty for wishing any man dead.

Chapter 25

October 1944

Unaware they are following the route taken by the male prisoners a year earlier, the women and children fill the same dilapidated boats at Palembang. In the early dawn, Emily – squashed between Martha and Margery – looks ahead to where the wide silver river reaches the red glow of the rising sun. Disturbed by the boats, waterfowl explode like sneezes from the tall reeds bordering the riverbank; beating their wings to gain height before soaring away, majestically riding the warm air currents.

"Free as a bird," sighs Emily. "I wish I could fly away."

"And if you could," Martha asks, "where would you go?"

"Somewhere there's no war. A country where I can eat meat and potatoes – anything but rice!"

"I've always wanted to go to Africa." Margery's gaze follows the birds as they fade into the distance. "I'm told that in the south, on the Cape Peninsula, there's a mountain with a flat top. It's called Table Mountain and when the clouds settle on top of it, the people say it has its tablecloth on. There's a local myth, handed down through generations, that the clouds are formed from a smoking contest between the devil and a pirate king called Van Hunks. I'd love to see it. On a clear day, they say you can stand on top and see for miles and miles. That'd be a bird's eye view, Emily."

"I'd love to go home to Australia." Martha looks wistful,

clasping her hands around her knees. "Home to Melbourne. It's a huge place. It was the capital until parliament moved to Canberra. There's this place called the Shrine of Remembrance on St Kilda's Road. It was built to honour those killed in the last war."

"The *Great* War. How can war be considered great? The war to end all wars. What a load of rubbish that turned out to be!" Margery shakes her head. "Why do we have to fight one another? Why can't we all try to get along?"

"Tell me about the Shrine of Remembrance," asks Emily, forestalling the lecture she has heard before from Margery – man's inhumanity to man.

"It's built of granite. It's one of Australia's largest war memorials. Inside, is a marble stone which has an engraving. It says 'Greater love hath no man'. There's an aperture – that's a deliberate hole in the roof – so that at eleven o'clock in the morning – the eleventh hour, when the war ended – the sunlight shines directly onto the word 'love'. Isn't that wonderful?" Martha squeezes Emily's hand. "Maybe you can come to Australia to see it one day?"

"I'd like that, Martha. I'd love to see koalas and kangaroos too."

"It's from John, chapter fifteen." Margery nods her head sagely.

"Sorry?" frowns Emily.

"Greater love hath no man than this, that a man lay down his life for his friends."

"Not just men. It's what Sister Catherina did for Doctor Peter." Emily shudders, recalling the dreadful sight of Sister Catherina lying dead on the floor of the ward, covered in the blood pouring from her throat.

"Yes, Emily. She did." Martha smiles, admiring the girl's maturity.

"Daddy said the Japanese soldier who spoke English died to save me. I don't know why, though. He wasn't my friend. He didn't even *know* me."

"He was a good man, Emily," Martha explains. "He knew it was very wrong of the general to shoot anyone, let alone a child. I'm not sure he expected Sato to actually kill him, though. He just wanted to make sure the general didn't shoot you. It was instinctive and very brave of him to stand between you and the gun."

"I remember that interpreter coming to the camp with Colonel Kimuru." Margery grimaces at the recollection. "He wasn't happy having to tell Mother Helena she had to stand in the sun all day – but he was so terrified of the Colonel, he had to tell her. I think she understood, though. She knew he was only translating orders. She told me he used to interpret at the hospital so had recognised her. I think she felt sorry for him – said he always looked frightened."

The two women and Emily sit quietly, lost in their own thoughts. Martha recalls the constantly terrified expression of the unfortunate interpreter; how he used to hang back –miserable, retreating, disassociating from his countrymen's cruelty. He had been so different from the other soldiers who all seemed to take delight in Sato's sadistic antics. In her mind, Martha conjures an image of a gentle dove, surrounded by a flock of murderous crows. Her thoughts turn to Peter, wondering where he might be, hoping he still lives. If not for Sister Catherina, he would have been killed. Emily had not known her saviour, but Peter had, and the guilt of surviving must torment him. She recalls his appalled expression as the nun lay dead on the floor. His rage had been frightening. He would have murdered Sato with his bare hands, had he been able.

Conscious they are nearing the Bangka Straits, Martha worries, wondering where they are going – remembering the horrors of the island across the narrow sea. Shuddering, she puts her arm around Emily, suddenly needing human contact, the comfort of knowing she is not alone.

As the long hours slowly pass and the sun crests its daily arc, the relentless heat and glare become intolerable. As the afternoon drags, leaving them sweltering in the open boats, Martha's dread increases as they travel inexorably towards Bangka Island – her mind filling with horrific images of the jail at Mumtok. Trapped in the waking nightmare, her stomach plummets at the sight of the huge jetty, confirming her worst fears.

"I can't," she whimpers. "I can't face it again."

Emily looks up in concern as Martha and some of the boat's other occupants begin to moan and cry.

"Come on, Martha," Margery encourages. "It won't be as bad this time. It can't be. They'll be more organised. We'll be in a proper camp, I'm sure." Margery is not sure who she is trying to convince – Martha's description of her imprisonment on Bangka Island had been harrowing.

Attempting to keep her fear under control, Martha takes in long deep breaths, not wishing to frighten Emily. "I'm all right," she smiles weakly at the anxious girl. "Just a bit sea-sick, that's all."

The sun is setting as the last of the prisoners disembarks; exhausted women and children stumble along the six-hundred-yard jetty. Reverend Mother Helena and her nuns are helped from the last boat by the older boys; the sisters' long robes making it difficult to climb over the gunwale.

After only a few yards, they come to a sudden stop – almost tripping over one another. One of the boys leans out over the railings, trying to see what is causing the hold-up. "We're all on the jetty," he shouts, "no one's getting off. Those at the front are sitting down so I think we'll be here for a while."

"Let's all sit," suggests Mother Helena. "My balance is off – my body thinks it's still on the boat."

The uneven wooden planks are damp and uncomfortable, but they are able to lean back against the vertical wooden struts supporting the handrail. After an hour or so, word trickles back that they are staying on the jetty for the night. There is no food or water, so it is hours before the last of the hungry children cries themselves to sleep.

Mother Helena rests her head against a wooden strut, looking up into the clear night sky, whose starlight is reflected in the gently lapping water buffeting the jetty. She winces at the abdominal pain that has racked her wasted body for weeks. The bouts of vomiting and diarrhoea are increasing in their frequency and severity. Despite her acute discomfort, she feels blessed to witness such natural splendour. The stars appear so very close, enveloping her in their radiant beauty. The crescent moon casts an ethereal silver pathway across the flowing black surface of the sea. Bowing her head in prayer, she is convinced the silver path is a sign that God is calling her, welcoming her home. With a profound sense of peace, she closes her eyes and sleeps.

"Go! Go! Go!" Guards move among the prisoners, prodding them with bamboo canes to get them moving. Despite the sting of the cane, Mother Helena cannot move. Her limbs will not cooperate with her attempts to rise. Word reaches Margery, who tries to restrain the guards' cruel efforts to make the nun stand. After much shouting and gesticulating, Martha manages to insist they cannot go on without food or water. Eventually, a sack of rice is emptied on the quayside for the women and children to grab handfuls as they pass. A few buckets of brackish water are provided for them to drink. With cheeks smarting from the guards' repeated slaps, a nonetheless triumphant Margery organises two groups of prisoners still strong enough to help take turns carrying Mother Helena as they are marched away.

Entering the camp, Martha exhales in relief. Instead of the concrete mausoleum she has been dreading, they are led into a barbed wire enclosure, with six, long accommodation blocks built from bamboo and woven palm leaves. There are smaller huts to function as cooking and washing areas, and a hospital block set back from the others.

Martha and the nurses take charge of the hospital – new and clean, it is completely empty of furniture and medical supplies. Mother Helena becomes their first patient – fussed over by the anguished nuns. They lie her on an old blanket, folded on the earthen floor.

"I'm going to look around to see what we've got here," Margery addresses the nurses and nuns. "I'll be back once I've got a general idea and let you know where everything is. How's Mother Helena?"

"Not good." Martha draws Margery away, out of earshot. "The nuns tell me she's not been well for some time. She's kept it hidden and never complained. Now, she can't keep food or water down. As fast as we put fluid into her, it just pours out from both ends. All we can do is try to keep her comfortable. Can you try to break it gently to Emily? I really don't think Mother will be with us for much longer."

"I'll take Emily with me and do my best. I'll bring back anything of use I can find but I suspect we'll be starting from scratch."

"Here's the water, Margery!" Emily calls out, pointing to the freshly dug well. "There's the trenches for the lavatory over there by those trees. It's all new and clean. It's better here than on Sumatra, isn't it?"

Margery nods, standing with her hands on her hips, surveying the camp facilities. "I think you're right, young lady. There's even a breeze as we're near the coast. I imagine the poor locals were forced into building this camp. Still, we must make the best of it. Let's see what's to be found in those trees."

"There's no fruit here, Margery. Lots of bamboo. The palm trees aren't coconut either, so there's no extra food."

"No, but we can use the palm leaves to weave sleeping mats and make things with the bamboo if the guards let us have tools. We may be able to grow our own vegetables if we can find any seeds. It'll be all right, Emily. We'll manage."

"I wish I could weave a new dress from the palm leaves, Margery. This one's all torn where it's got too tight and it's so short, it's embarrassing."

"Mm. You're still managing to grow despite the lack of food. I'm sure we can find you something to replace your tunic. Thirteen now, aren't you? Have you had any bleeding?"

Emily looks down, shaking her head – cheeks flushing red under Margery's scrutiny.

"I'm not surprised. Most of us have stopped menstruating. Our bodies know we can't afford to lose the little nourishment we have. Don't worry about it, Emily. It's one less thing to bother about."

"Is Mother Helena going to get better?" The girl is desperate to distract Margery from asking such personal questions.

Stepping forwards, Margery places a reassuring arm around Emily's shoulders – her voice low and gentle.

"Mother Helena's very weak. Martha doesn't think she'll be with us for much longer. She's been in terrible pain for a long time, Emily. You wouldn't want her to suffer any more, would you?" Margery wraps her arms around the sobbing girl. "It's all right, Emily. Mother Helena will go straight up to heaven. She'll be with Sister Catherina, won't she? They'll never be hungry or in pain ever again. I'll miss her from my vocal orchestra, but she'll be singing with choirs of angels this Christmas."

Wiping her eyes, Emily offers a bleak smile. "I don't want her to be in pain any more. I'm not sure about heaven and God. I don't know if I believe in angels. I know they don't sit on clouds and play harps but if they do exist, where are they? If God exists, then why are we all in prison? Why doesn't he help us?"

Margery stares down in astonishment at the tear-streaked face, unusually lost for words.

"If there's a God," rages Emily, "he must *hate* me! He let my mummy and baby brother die. He's taken Daddy away, too, and now he wants Mother Helena. Why's he left me all on my own?"

Margery opens her mouth, but no words come out.

"Why would God make men like General Sato and Colonel Kimuru? Horrible, cruel men who kill other people. They're bad, aren't they? So, why do they live with lots of food while we have nothing, even though we've done nothing wrong?"

Margery looks around, desperately seeking inspiration.

"That's a lot of questions, Emily, and I have no answers for you. Mother Helena would tell you that God loves us all so much, he sent his son to earth to die on the cross for us – to save us from our sins."

"But why? What good did it do? Men still commit the same sins they did before Jesus came here."

"Oh, Emily, I teach music, not religion. I'm so sorry, but I'm the wrong person to ask."

"Do *you* believe in God, Margery?"

"I think so – but not in the way the nuns do. They believe in everything written in the Bible. They follow rules, pray at certain times. They live their whole lives dedicated to God. I'm not saying they're wrong – it's a matter of belief. For one thing, at least Mother Helena will die happy because she believes she will go straight to God and to everlasting life in heaven."

"Is that what you think too?"

"I'm not sure, Emily. There must be a creator for us to be here at all, but whether they're called 'God', who knows? There are other religions with other names for God. No one can say for sure who's right." Margery wipes Emily's fresh tears away with her thumbs. "Listen to me, Emily. You have to believe in something to give you hope. Whether it's in God or something more abstract – such as good will always triumph over evil so we'll win the war – you *have* to believe in something positive. I believe you're courageous and will one day be free to live a happy life. I believe that one day I'll go to Africa to see Table Mountain. I believe Martha will go home to Melbourne."

Emily presses her lips together, contemplating Margery's words. Unknowingly, Mother Helena's certainty that God is in all things – watching everything, omnipotent – has made Emily feel anxious, afraid her own doubts are responsible for all the things that have gone wrong in her life. She had never known she had a choice in what to believe. She had not understood that she could believe in something less defined than Mother Helena's God, without fear of punishment for her lack of faith.

"Are you sure, Margery? Are you sure God won't mind if I don't believe everything I've been taught? I mean, doesn't he hate me because I don't believe everything? Didn't he take Mummy and the baby, and Daddy, because of me not believing properly?"

"Absolutely not! If there *is* a God, Emily, I can assure you he wouldn't punish you for not believing everything you've been told. Remember, the Bible's written by men, adding their own interpretation. Every religion has its scripture – the word of its God. They're all written by men. I like to think that any God would prefer to be associated with love and kindness, not punishment and retribution. Take strength from your beliefs, Emily. They're your own, and just as valid as anyone else's. Remember that, please!"

Emily nods, feeling lighter, less anxious – a little wiser, perhaps even a little more grown-up.

Closing her eyes, Emily listens to the melodious voices of the nuns singing the Ave Maria. The music takes her back to the cold church: the deep woody odour of incense, the hard wooden pews and the tears running down Daddy's face. She had gripped his hand tightly, watching as the priest sprinkled holy water over the coffins of Mummy and the baby brother she had never known.

As the hymn ends, she opens her eyes to release the painful memory, looking on impassively as the nuns throw handfuls of earth into Mother Helena's shallow grave. Dappled sunlight finds its way through the trees, softening the tableau of grieving sisters; giving a sense of peace to the Reverend Mother's final resting place.

Breaking the uncomfortable silence, Margery leads her singers into the opening bars of "All Things Bright and Beautiful." During the final refrain, she waves her arms, dispersing the women and children, giving the nuns the opportunity to mourn at the graveside in relative privacy. Looking back to where they stand, Margery wonders how many more graves will be needed before the war ends and they are released. Perhaps they will all rot here – abandoned and forgotten by the outside world.

"Wake up, Margery! Wake up!" Emily shakes Margery's shoulder until she opens one bleary eye.

"The guards are here! They're taking the boys away!" Margery sits up, becoming aware of the shouting and wailing. Pulling on her dress, she runs into the yard, closely followed by Emily.

In the flat light of a cloud-covered dawn, a Japanese officer she has not seen before is inspecting the terrified boys; pulling down the front of their shorts while outraged mothers are held back by the guards.

"What's going on?" Margery demands as she strides towards the officer. A guard blocks her path, slapping her hard as she tries to sidestep him. "What are you doing?" she calls out, raising a hand to rub her stinging cheek.

The officer gives her a baleful stare then continues his inspection – dividing the boys into two groups. The prisoners look on in horror as the oldest boys are separated from the rest.

"Of course!" Margery cries out to the other women, "they're looking to see if the boys have reached puberty. They're checking them like farm animals – looking at the genitals to determine maturity. Oh, it's so barbaric!" Her distress is echoed by the shrieking mothers, held back while their sons are herded towards a waiting truck.

"Where are you taking them?" pleads Margery, breaking free of the guard's grip and running towards the truck – where the officer now waits for the boys to be loaded.

"Men camp." The two words stop her in her tracks, mouth open in horror.

"No!" a screaming woman passes Margery at a run, flinging herself at the officer, raking his face with her nails. "You can't take my son! You'll have to kill me first!"

Margery steps forwards to pull her away – aware of the officer wiping his face with his hand; inspecting the blood on his fingertips.

Slowly, he walks towards the two women – the deep angry tracks clawed into his angular face adding to his malevolence. They back away, the mother covering her face with her hands, whimpering in terror. Pushing Margery hard in the chest with sufficient force to send her sprawling to the ground, he grabs the woman's arm, dragging her to her knees.

From the back of the truck, her son sobs uncontrollably. Helpless, he watches the officer kick his mother repeatedly; only stopping when her cries cease and she lies bleeding and unconscious on the ground.

At the back of the onlookers, the young Australian nurse, Susan, collapses into Nora's arms. "I remember him," she sobs. "That officer. I've seen him before."

Nora puts a supportive arm around Susan, drawing her away from the shocked crowd, back to their accommodation block.

As Margery rises stiffly to her feet, the truck pulls away. The boys cry out in terror – young frightened calves, destined for the slaughterhouse.

Martha rushes forwards to help the mother, feeling for her pulse – but as Margery looks around questioningly, Martha shakes her head. Within a week of their arrival, a second grave must be dug.

"Margery, can I have a word?" Nora approaches the woman, sitting alone in the shade of the trees, deep in thought,

"What? Oh, sorry, Nora. I was miles away."

"It's Susan. I'm really worried about her. She recognised the officer who took the boys. She's so distressed. She's in our sleeping block – just sitting, staring into space. It's very disturbing, especially as everyone's so upset already. Please could you come?"

Without a word, Margery rises and follows Nora over to the block. Inside, she finds Susan – pale as a ghost, trembling.

"Susan?" Margery squats beside her, speaking very gently. "Susan, can you hear me? Tell me what's wrong. You'll feel better if you tell someone what's upsetting you."

"I can't," wails the nurse. "He'll kill me if he knows I'm here, still alive."

"D'you mean the Japanese officer who came here this morning?"

Susan nods, burying her face in her hands.

"Well, telling me won't make any difference to his recognising you or not. Perhaps I can help? I won't breathe a word to anyone if that's what you want."

"I need to tell someone, in case I die. I'm the only one who knows what happened. But if I do tell you and he finds out, he'll kill us both. He won't want *anyone* to know what he did." Susan shudders, tears falling unchecked.

"Let's go outside," suggests Margery. "We can find

somewhere more private – how about under the trees? No one will bother us there and we'll be able to see if anyone does come along."

Helping Susan to her feet, Margery leads her out into the yard. Susan focuses on the ground, and Margery avoids making eye contact with the women casting questioning looks in their direction. They settle down on the ground beside Mother Helena's grave, marked with a little wooden cross.

Margery waits patiently for Susan to gather her thoughts. Shaded from the sun's glare and cooled by a fresh sea breeze, she has chosen a setting that is quiet and peaceful. Upwind of the trenches, they breathe in the earthy pungent scent of the rainforest.

Susan draws in her knees, wrapping her arms tightly around them – literally holding herself together. In a shaky voice which grows stronger, she begins her tale. "When the Japanese invaded, I was evacuated from Singapore with other Australian Army nurses and some civilians. There were no children on our ship, thank goodness. During the second night, we ran into a Japanese convoy and were shelled. Those of us who made it to the lifeboats before the ship went down were washed up on a beach. We could see a long jetty in the distance, so knew we weren't too far from a port. Us nurses stayed to patch up the injured, while a few of the men walked to what turned out to be Mumtok to find help."

Susan hesitates. Filling in the background had been straightforward. The evacuation and shelling, although frightening, held no terror in the retelling. Putting into words What had followed on the beach after the Japanese arrived is altogether different. Taking a deep breath and gripping her knees more tightly, she continues.

"After some hours, they returned with the Japanese officer

who was here this morning and several soldiers. We thought they'd come to help us. We knew we were surrendering, but there was nothing else we could do. We couldn't stay on the beach indefinitely and one or two of the more severely injured needed more medical care than we could give."

"I would've done the same, Susan. You were quite right to seek help. You'd no other choice. What happened when the Japanese officer arrived?"

Susan hesitates, closing her eyes tightly – fighting the emotion threatening to overwhelm her.

"They took half the men around the cove, out of sight of where we were camped. We couldn't hear anything, but when the soldiers came back, they were wiping blood from their bayonets. We were becoming more and more frightened, especially when they marched the rest of the men away. This time, we heard the cries and the sound of gunfire. We didn't try to run. We just sat there, petrified, as the soldiers walked back towards us, grinning. They were actually *grinning*, Margery."

Tears course down Susan's cheeks at the recollection of the soldiers' wolfish grins as they calmly walked back towards the terrified women cringing on the sand.

"We didn't kn… know what to do," she sobs. "They just st… stood there grinning. It was so awful." Susan rubs her eyes, trying to wipe away the dreadful image: the armed men spattered with blood, sated by their killing spree, facing the women, feeding off their terror – a pack of cackling hyenas, circling their hapless prey.

"Take your time, Susan. You're doing really well. I know this must be difficult." Margery rubs Susan's back, soothingly – appalled by the story, bracing herself for more.

"We weren't sure what to do. They pointed at us, then

pointed to the sea. At first, we thought they were asking if we'd come to the beach from the sea – so we nodded. This made them angry and they pointed their guns at us. We raised our hands, shrugging to show we didn't understand. They gestured for us to get up, so we stood. Then, they started shoving us towards the sea, making us go into the water and wade out. I tripped on a rock, falling right under the water. As I came up, I heard the guns and someone fell on top of me. She'd been shot in the back of the head, there was a lot of blood. I hid underneath her – lying on my back, breathing where her hair fanned out around her face. I could smell the blood. My ears were underwater, so the screams and gunfire sounded muffled. It went on and on for ages. When the shooting finally stopped, I lay completely still – under the dead woman's body, taking shallow breaths. I could only see the sky, not the soldiers on the beach, so I didn't know if they'd gone. I thought I'd be sick. I tried not to think about the dead body lying on top of me, but I couldn't help it. Everything inside me screamed to push her away, but I was too scared of being shot, so I stayed where I was. Then I got a cramp in my leg. In the end, the pain got so bad I had to stand up – to stretch out the muscle. All around me were dead bodies, face down, shot in the back as they waded out. Nurses I'd trained with – we'd travelled to Singapore together, excited by the adventure. Even when we were evacuated, we thought we'd get to Java, to safety. We were invincible – or so we thought."

For a few precious moments of respite, Susan pictures the voyage to Singapore. How excited they had all been. Young women, eager to start a new life abroad, talking of the doctors and soldiers they would meet. War had been an adventure, from which they would all return – regaling stories of their exploits and love affairs.

"I shook so badly when I made it back to shore, I collapsed on the sand. For a moment, I wondered if I'd drowned and it was my spirit lying on the beach. I know it sounds silly, but I was completely numb, so thought I might be dead. In a way, it was very peaceful – just the gentle swish of the sea on the shoreline, and the cries of a few distant seabirds. The sea was so calm, the floating bodies hardly moved. But it *wasn't* peaceful at all, was it? Just the quiet aftermath that follows violence. These punctured bodies had been people I'd known – friends, colleagues. They'd been butchered – picked off like sitting ducks at a fairground target range. Left there, to be washed out with the tide. Lost to families who would never know their fate. Forever hidden from the world."

Susan's voice peters out. Her eyes lose focus and Margery understands she has drifted away to the isolated beach – forever haunted, the only living witness to a senseless bloody massacre.

"I went to look for the men," Susan continues unexpectedly. "I've never seen anything so… so horrific in my life. Two piles of blood-soaked corpses. Eyes open. Mouths open in silenced screams. Bodies torn and disfigured with entangled limbs at unnatural angles. So much blood, Margery. I've never seen so much blood. I retched and retched until my throat was dry and burning with acid. I couldn't do anything – they were all dead. Nothing moved except for the flies. A carpet of black flies, feasting on those innocent men. Men who'd never go home, nor have the dignity of a decent burial."

Suddenly, Susan looks up, eyes bright and intense.

"As I walked away, Margery, I was overcome with rage. I was the single surviving witness. I owed these people. I owed them the truth. I had to tell the world what had happened. I had to make sure those Japanese soldiers paid for their crimes." She drops her head just as suddenly – the intensity draining away. "Then I saw him this morning. The officer from the beach. I watched as he murdered that poor woman – and I did nothing. I was afraid that if he saw me, he'd see the truth in my eyes. He'd kill me to make sure I'd never reveal what he'd done. Oh, Margery, I'm too afraid to confront him. Anyway, what's the use? We'll probably die here and the world will never find out what happened to all those poor people."

Exhausted, Susan lets her head fall against Margery's shoulder, closing her eyes. She has carried the terrible secret for more than two years. Relieved to have unburdened herself, she wishes only for sleep.

"I doubt he'll recognise you, Susan, but it's best to keep your eyes on the ground if he comes again. If one of us dies, then another must be told. That way, we ensure the world will learn of this atrocity when we are finally free."

"Thank you, Margery. You're right. I couldn't carry this burden alone any more. I'd like to go and lie down now. You stay here if you like. I need to sleep."

"Before you go, Susan. What happened to you afterwards?"

"I hid in the jungle for the night, eating coconut and drinking the milk. I knew I couldn't survive on my own, so the next evening I walked to Mumtok. In the dark, I managed to get to the harbour without being seen. After hanging around for a few hours, I slipped into a line of prisoners being led towards the jetty. I ended up on a boat to Palembang and was sent to your camp."

"Well, Susan. Never under-estimate your bravery and resourcefulness. I'm certain you'll survive to tell your own tale."

Margery watches the exhausted young nurse walk unsteadily away. Recalling her conversation with Emily about belief, she wonders how Mother Helena's God could allow such brutality.

Had it been God's will or just luck that had saved Susan? Margery shakes her head in bewilderment – having lived a life untroubled by doubt, confident in her own opinions, since her captivity, she finds herself plagued by more questions than answers. It is all very unsettling.

Chapter 26

Matt helps John through the jail and onto the raised concrete slab in their cell. Exhausted by the walk from the hospital, John collapses back, gasping for air.

"Here, drink this." Matt offers the tin cup he has brought from the ward, which still contains a few mouthfuls of water.

Rising to one elbow, John drains the cup thirstily, before lying back down and closing his eyes.

"Thanks, Matt. I thought I'd never leave the hospital alive. It's terrible in there. Men dying all around you." He falls silent, overcome by unwanted images of suffering men, enduring the final agonies of disease.

"Peter's told me, mate. You're a real survivor. Welcome back to the Mumtok Jail – firm beds without bathroom facilities. Starvation rations and unfriendly staff. What more can you ask for?"

"How about a gin and tonic on the rocks?"

"Sorry, mate. We're right out of ice. We can offer water, contaminated with dysentery, on the house!" Matt lies beside John, one arm folded back, supporting his head. "Seriously, it's bloody awful. I don't know how we'll survive. As Peter says, without nutrition, we can't resist infection. The place is swimmin' in effluent. We're just lyin' here, waitin' t' die."

"We're *not* going to die, Matt. At least, you're not. One of us *must* survive to take care of Emily. Promise me, Matt. If I don't make it, you'll look after Emily? My body won't stand up to another bout of malaria."

"If I survive, of course I'll find Emily and take care of her. I promise. But you've got to live, John. It's you she'll want."

"I know – it's my blasted body that needs convincing. How long have we been here?"

"A couple of months, maybe? Not really sure. I just lie here, sometimes sleepin', but mostly contemplatin' my eventual demise. Oh, hello, Peter. What's up, mate?"

A thunderous-looking Peter stomps into the cell, throwing himself down to join the others on the platform.

"Here we are, all starving to death," his furious voice echoes around the concrete walls, "and the camp commander decides to send flowers to the burial of a man who died yesterday. *Flowers*! We need food, not bloody flowers! What's wrong with these bastards? They do their best to kill us all, then mourn us with flowers." For a few moments, the three men lie in silence. "Come on. I came back to tell you it's raining. Let's go outside for a shower and some fresh water. Bring that tin cup, Matt. We need to get out of this fetid air for a while. Here you go, John. Lean on me. You're still rather weak."

Heavy rain clouds rumble across the leaden sky, releasing great torrents of cleansing water. The men stand – heads back, mouths open to drink. Completely drenched within seconds, they pull off their filthy clothes – rubbing and wringing them to remove most of the grime. Many of the other prisoners emerge, following their example. These downpours provide the only opportunity to wash and drink fresh water. John is reminded of the early days in the Palembang jail. There, too, the rain had cleansed them, lifting their spirits. As they had done then, the men open all the doors wide, allowing the corridors to flood – flushing away much of the contaminated human waste and the appalling stench. Anything that holds water – buckets, clothes, coconut shells – is brought out to catch and store the lifesaving rain.

While they wash, Matt studies John closely. Malaria has taken its toll – John's body is just skin stretched over bone – no fat reserves remaining, all muscle wasted away. Matt had not hesitated in promising to take care of Emily should John not survive. Since carrying her through the jungle, he senses her within him – as if her soul had fled her traumatised body, seeking refuge, burying itself deep within him for protection. It is a belief he will never reveal. A belief that Emily has unknowingly entrusted the damaged essence of herself to his safekeeping.

Throughout the long hours sat by her hospital bed, Matt had held her hand – offering to restore her spirit to her body. Where she had withdrawn so completely, he felt no flow of energy. Her spirit could not return to her, remaining safely hidden within his heart. Only when he had seen her up on the high wall of the women's camp, had he felt the tug. Instantly, he had vowed to find her – to return her essence, to make her whole.

As the months pass, rations are further reduced, leaving the men barely able to rise – doing so only to eat the watery gruel, visit the outdoor latrines if they can make it in time, and stand or sit in the rain. They lie inert: living corpses, trying to sleep – seeking oblivion for as much time as possible. Torn and filthy clothing hangs from their skeletal forms, as one by one, they succumb to privation and disease.

Exhausted, Peter moves around the overcrowded hospital wards – a walking skeleton himself – offering only water and a few words of comfort. More than half of the monks have contracted their patients' diseases and died. Despite his own poor health, Peter feels duty bound to help where he can – unable to abandon the dying men.

A dull depression paralyses the living prisoners – certain their own deaths are at hand. Hopelessness is etched on the deep lines of every gaunt face; hollowed-out sockets contain sunken eyes, dulled by despair.

When the guards appear without warning, prodding the men until they leave their cells to stumble into the yard, there is no curiosity or resistance. Scooping water from the buckets and chewing grains of rice picked up from where a sack has been emptied on the ground, they wait, expressionless, blinking in the sunlight.

Without explanation, they are marched down to the harbour and along the jetty. Too weak to help one another, those who fall are left to die, drowning if they fall into the sea. Like cattle, the survivors are loaded into the hold of a cargo ship – squashed in so tightly, they are forced to stand in total darkness, enduring the stifling heat and lack of air. Sandwiched together in the stinking hold, those who faint or die are held up by the living.

"Peter? Are you here?" John whispers, barely able to take in sufficient breath to speak.

"I'm here and Matt's with us too. Just let go if you have to – you can't fall." Peter's height gives him a little more air than the others – but the heat is oppressive and he feels claustrophobic. He senses John's body go slack, his friend's head falling against his shoulder. Around him, he hears men hyperventilating: panicking in the total blackness, struggling for breath – feeling trapped and frightened as if buried alive.

Throughout the hours they remain at anchor, the trapped men endure their individual torments: a groan, followed by the splatter and stench of diarrhoea; retching, accompanied by the acid stink of vomit – screaming, crying, praying – all in total darkness. Despite the enforced human contact, each man blindly suffers alone – frightened and miserable in his bleak isolation.

Twelve hours after leaving Bangka Island, the guards open the hold, recoiling from the rising stench. The glare blinds the men immediately under the hatch, who are dragged out by their hair. When there is room, a ladder is lowered and the men slowly emerge into the light, collapsing onto the deck.

Matt drags Peter out, returning to the ladder to search for John. Delirious with fever, John is pushed up by the men below. As his head rises into view, Matt grabs him before he can fall.

On deck, the prisoners are washed down with buckets of seawater – while the dead bodies hauled from the hold are tossed carelessly overboard. Looking around, Matt sees they are moving up the Musi river, heading towards the tall storage tanks of the oil refineries at Palembang.

Herded onto the quayside, the men are finally given buckets of peaty water to drink. Peter helps John, pouring water from his cupped hands into his friend's mouth. As if feeding hens, a guard splits a sack of rice with his bayonet, pouring the contents out among the starving prisoners.

All around, locals continue their work, loading barrels of oil onto ships – warily glancing at the dreadful condition of the prisoners. Hungry as they often are, the workers are deeply disturbed by the sight of the pale living skeletons.

Left alone on the quayside in the fading light, the prisoners try to sleep. There are no thoughts of escape any more – they have barely enough strength to stand and where would they go? Above them, Peter can see his old hospital building, lit from within. He lets his thoughts drift back in time until they settle on a memory – examining the tiger cub that John and Emily had brought to him. How the small creature had captured their hearts – except for Sister Catherina, who had been so frightened.

Instantly, his mind betrays him and he is thrust into another memory – Sister Catherina lying dead on the floor, blood soaking into her pure white robe. He pictures Sato, wondering if he is up at the hospital. Unguarded, Peter would love to go up there and try to kill him – but he is too weak, too tired even to climb the hill. Despite the aches and pains which continually plague him, Peter settles down into a deep sleep.

"Where's John?" Matt shakes Peter until he wakes. "I can't find John! He's not here!"

Peter sits up too quickly, dizziness descending like a black fog over his eyes.

"He must've gone for a pee. He can't have gone far."

"Peter, I heard a splash in the night. I was too tired to get up and see if anyone had gone in. I just fell back to sleep. For Christ's sake, Peter, he's gone!" Matt's face appears to collapse in on itself, as he imagines the worst.

Rubbing his sore eyes and getting unsteadily to his feet, Peter staggers towards the river – searching the expanse of muddy water, dreading what he may find.

"If he'd gone in, he'd be trapped in the reeds," he tries to reassure Matt. "Look, they're thick here. Maybe what you heard was something thrown off a boat, or even a night bird diving for fish?"

"So, where *is* he then?" Matt pleads. "He couldn't have tried to escape in the night – he's burning up with malaria." Desperately, Matt questions the other prisoners, but they shake their heads – no one has seen John.

The great iron wheels creak and rattle, as the train makes its way inland. Once again, they have been loaded like cattle, into the open carriages – from where they stare out at the forest and swamps, oblivious to the natural beauty of the rainforest, with its broad canopy filled with exotic birds and colourful flora. Their bodies sweat in the heat and humidity – their only relief is finding they no longer have to walk.

Matt and Peter sit together in silence, still shocked by the sudden loss of their friend. When the guards had come to move them on, they had known there was nothing they could do. The only reasonable explanation is that John had gone into the river, broken free of the reeds and floated downstream. For so long, they had watched out for one another, determined they would all stay together and survive. John's disappearance is somehow worse than finding him dead. Death at least has its own certainty, a knowledge that the suffering is over.

Chapter 27

January 1945

From the relative safety of the hospital, General Sato watches the pale dawn sky above Pladjoe: dog fights between tiny fighter planes circling high above rumbling allied bombers – releasing their deadly cargo; sowing the land with seeds of destruction.

Satisfied the allied bombers are taking heavy losses from the lethal barrage balloons, he is nonetheless unnerved by the plumes of dense black smoke rising from the damaged installation – filling the air with the acrid stink of burning oil and explosives. Despite the barrage balloons, the superior number of Japanese fighter planes and the anti-aircraft guns, the allied forces' attack is successfully destroying the refinery.

Following the American invasion of the Philippines, the bombing of Tokyo and the sinking of several ships of the Imperial Fleet, Sato comprehends that damage to the refinery risks a further serious setback – preventing the supply of aviation fuel, vital for keeping the Imperial bombers and fighters airborne.

The thunderous destruction before him stirs long-forgotten memories of the disaster that had rocked his world, changing his life forever: the Kanto earthquake that devastated Japan in 1923, when he had only just left home.

Born in the prosperous city of Yokohama, on the main island of Honshu overlooking Tokyo Bay, Sato had led a privileged childhood: the second son of a wealthy businessman. His father had made his fortune trading in silk and had taken advantage of the rapid industrial growth following the First World War, building textile factories staffed with a supply of easily-exploited Korean immigrants pouring into the city to find work.

The family thrived in the optimism of the cosmopolitan city, with its Western influences and liberal attitudes. However, Sato had been resentful of his father's obvious preference for his elder brother; the evident pride in his first-born's social ease and academic prowess. Sato's brother had been popular, clever and manipulative. He had the ability to present himself as the perfect son, a natural successor to his father's business interests – never missing any opportunity to humiliate Sato, revealing his younger brother's failings to their father by exploiting the boy's tendency to lose his temper.

Over the years, burning resentment had become a furnace of hatred, so Sato had decided to join the nationalistic Imperial Army, turning his back on the family's wealth and connections – deserting his devoted mother, whose timidity prevented her from interfering in her two sons' rivalries.

Within months, the catastrophic earthquake had struck the Kanto region of Japan: the subsequent tsunami and firestorms that raged through Yokohama devoured his entire family and destroyed his childhood home. Sato had been at the army garrison well away from the city centre. He had stared in horrified fascination at the scarlet sky and billowing black clouds of smoke – buffeted by the high winds of a typhoon, fanning the giant flames, ensuring the total destruction of the city, the only home he had ever known.

Suppressing any natural feelings of grief, Sato had devoted himself entirely to the service of his divine Emperor, supreme commander of the Imperial Army.

Having grown up mistrustful of the Koreans who worked for his father, the impressionable Sato had been prepared to believe his superiors' accusations that the immigrants would take the opportunity to rob and loot the charred remains of their masters' dwellings. Despite evidence to the contrary – the Koreans had actually helped in the distribution of aid to survivors – the young Sato took an active role in the Korean massacre which followed the earthquake. This genocide provided him with an outlet for his pent-up resentment and aggression, the physical violence leaving him calm and at peace with himself. It had always been his brother's face he imagined when killing, leaving him with an overwhelming sense of satisfaction.

Encouraged by military propaganda in the belief that the earthquake had been divine retribution against the hedonistic lifestyle of the socialist citizens of Yokohama, he had been eager to embrace the fascist views of his senior officers, adopting contempt, even hatred, for all foreign races.

Serving in the 1931 invasion of Manchuria, Sato spent the following five years fighting the anti-Japanese guerrilla armies raised by the Chinese – small local forces, familiar with the terrain, armed to harass the Japanese troops carrying out their subjugation operations.

By 1937, when Japan invaded China, Sato had become a junior officer – attached to the divisions infamous for the murder of hundreds of thousands of disarmed soldiers and helpless civilians at Nanking. Over the course of six weeks, under the influence of his brutal commanders, Sato had remorselessly butchered, raped and looted his way through the city. He considered himself an unassailable conqueror: feasting on the terror of his defeated victims, satisfying his lust as he pleased – before slitting the pale throats of the squealing young girls.

As the years passed, Sato's brutality attracted the attention of high command, so by the time he sailed with the Japanese fleet for the Dutch East Indies, he had risen to the rank of general and would be commander of the POW camps on Sumatra, once the island had been invaded and occupied.

During the voyage, Sato had been disliked intensely by the naval officers. Feeling restless, one evening he casually raped and murdered a European civilian woman, rescued from the sea in the Bangka Straits. His brutality sickened the ship's captain and crew. Sato knew there had been a collective sigh of relief when he and his cohort left the ship at Palembang: he had been amused by the captain's refusal to attend the disembarkation ceremony and gratified by the obvious fear he instilled in the crew, who had kept their eyes down, unwilling to challenge his superiority.

Refocusing on the present allied attack, Sato's fury heightens with each bomb that strikes its intended target. How dare these pale-faced devils threaten the Empire of Japan?

Despite the recent difficulties, he remains confident that the divine Emperor will prevail – certain that Japan will soon have its great victory.

Sato despises the cowardly creatures he has interned, the snivelling Europeans, who surrendered without resistance. No Japanese soldier would lie down at the feet of an enemy – it was inconceivable, dishonourable. Turning his back on the terrible scene, Sato returns to his desk to prepare his report.

Sounds of battle penetrate the delirium: the drone of aircraft engines rising to a metallic scream as they pass overhead; earth-shaking blasts of bombs striking targets; the boom, boom, boom of anti-aircraft guns; the whining engines of fighter planes circling one another – the rattle of their mounted machine guns and mid-air explosions.

The heat is intolerable – rising from deep within his fevered body. The noise of battle competes with the pounding inside his head. Gasping for breath in the high humidity, his body convulses with every painful inhalation.

Surrounding odours stimulate his nostrils: damp wood; dry fragrant grasses; the salty sweat of his own body, sour with fever. At times, he smells a cooking fire, roasting fish, boiling rice – steaming broth dribbled into his mouth, soothing his dry throat, settling his distended stomach.

Images, in vivid colours, swim before his closed eyelids: Pladjoe on fire, a burning airfield, a blood-filled hospital ward, a stifling jail, bamboo huts, boats, the burning sun, a man dropping back into the clear water – disappearing beneath the surface. He feels the cool water on his face, the refreshing fluid passing through his chapped lips, quenching the fire, making him calmer, comforted, sleepy.

As the moon rises – a white disc, glowing above the flickering red flames of Pladjoe's burning storage tanks, a truck carrying three battered airmen bumps along a muddy path. Ahead, they see lights streaming through the windows of a single-storey building – a white picket fence bringing a benign quality to what now appears to be a place of refuge, rather than retribution.

Their mission is a success, although unable to celebrate the victory with their comrades, having been shot down after releasing their deadly bombs. Picked up by enemy soldiers from the wreckage of their aircraft, the three survivors stare out from the back of the open truck, wondering at the destruction they have wrought from the sky. With the pump station destroyed, there can be no oil production for the next few weeks, even months.

For these men, the war is over. They expect to be interned for however long it takes the allies to liberate the camps. They are frightened, reports having reached them of the brutal treatment they can expect at the hands of the Japanese.

On the grass outside the front doors of the lit building, they are forced to kneel and wait. After what seems like hours, the airmen begin to fidget uncomfortably, asking for water. The guards ignore them, tension growing as the stars gradually fade, and the skies lighten in anticipation of the dawn.

A high-ranking officer finally appears through the doors – smartly turned out in full dress uniform, medals displayed across his chest. Silently, he stands before the three men, his hand resting on the scabbard hanging at his side. Looking up, the airmen see black blazing eye and thin lips curling into a sneer of contempt. With a flick of a finger, he summons one of the guards, speaking quietly in his ear. Nodding in understanding, the soldier steps forwards to speak.

"General Sato say you dishonourable men. You not fight to death but surrender. Like pigs, you squeal for mercy. General Sato say you carry shame of your people. Japanese never surrender. Japanese brave and honourable."

The three men bow their heads, having been warned about the intimidation they are likely to face if captured – the personal insults it is best to ignore. The officer speaks again with the guard.

"General Sato say he honourable man. He merciful man."

The airmen look up hopefully, all offering their thanks which the guard translates. The general nods in appreciation, then gestures for the guard to continue.

"General Sato say he give you back some honour. He allow

you to die with honour. You will die by his sword."

As if he is granting their freedom, Sato smiles benevolently, sliding the gleaming blade from its sheath.

The executions are swift and efficient – Sato allowing himself a grunt of satisfaction as he severs each head with a single stroke.

Open-mouthed expressions of shock and terror remain fixed on the three faces, whose eyes gaze up sightlessly from the severed heads, lying in the blood-stained grass beside the picket fence.

Chapter 28

April 1945

Margery and Emily agree that their plan to grow vegetables is a total failure. Despite gathering seeds from the scraps of vegetables they are given to eat, and planting them in the soil next to the wooded area, the temptation has proved too much for one or more of the prisoners – the green shoots have been plucked and eaten during the night.

"I wish I'd caught whoever pinched them this time!" An indignant Emily searches the small rows she has been tending, to see if any shoots have been left.

"Never mind, Emily. You can't really blame them – especially if it's mothers trying to supplement their children's diet with a little greenery. We could try planting the seeds in pots and hiding them near the hospital, but, as our diet is so poor now, we could never grow sufficient to distribute fairly." Margery gives a sigh of defeat. "Come on, let's see if Martha needs any help."

"Martha says Nora's bad with malaria, Margery."

"I know. It's the awful cerebral type. Poor Nora is having dreadful headaches as well as the fever."

"Is she going to die?"

Unable to reply, Margery shrugs – a lump rising in her throat as her eyes fill with tears.

"I'm so sorry, Margery. I know you've been friends for

years. I'm sure Martha and the other nurses will do everything they can. Susan's a close friend, too. She'll look after Nora."

Inside the hospital, the Australian nurses do their best for the increasing numbers of women and children falling sick due to lack of nutrition. As Emily and Margery enter, they find Susan bathing Nora with cool water, trying to reduce her soaring temperature.

"Shall I take over?" suggests Margery, noting the strain and dark circles under the exhausted nurse's eyes.

"Thanks, Margery. I'm dead on my feet. Every day we've more patients and fewer nurses. Without food or medicine, all we can do is wash them down with water. It's not enough to fight infection, especially when their bodies are so weak." Susan begins to cry silent tears of sorrow, fatigue and frustration.

"Go and lie down, Susan. Emily and I will manage, and we can ask Martha if we're unsure of anything. You look wrung out. Go and get a few hours' rest."

Martha crosses to where they stand around Nora's mat. Squatting down, she places her palm on the sick woman's brow, before looking up at Susan and shaking her head.

"The water isn't helping to get Nora's temperature down, but at least it makes her more comfortable. Susan, Margery's right. Go and get some rest before you fall down. Emily, if you want to help, then go to the well for more water. I'd rather you kept away from any infectious patients."

As Susan and Emily leave the hospital together, Martha turns to Margery.

"We're really struggling, Margery. We've lost another two patients today. One to beriberi and the other to dysentery. At this rate, the camp'll be empty in a few months. Is it worth speaking with the guards again?"

"It's always worth a try, but don't hold out much hope. I've noticed even the guards are looking thinner. There's obviously some problem getting supplies through, and we're not their priority." Margery crouches, dipping a cloth in the bowl of water and washing the perspiration from Nora's ravaged face. "Nora's not really responding. Are we losing her, Martha?"

"It's this dreadful type of malaria she's contracted. It seems to attack the strongest among us. I think she's got a bleed on her brain and is slipping into a coma. I'm so sorry, Margery. We're doing what we can, but I think you should prepare yourself."

Margery stares down at her friend. In the early days, Nora had been so full of life and optimism: helping to sort out accommodation, keeping cheerful and welcoming frightened women and children to the camp, comforting those who had lost loved ones. Margery wonders what has happened to Nora's bizarre sun hat, with its old parasol, that had made her so distinctive around the camp. Now, lying almost lifeless on her mat, skeletally thin, with wispy white hair; Margery feels a sharp sense of loss. How many more friends will she bury before this nightmare ends?

"Martha, I've spoken with the guards." Margery appears at the door to the hospital. "They say we're moving again – back to bloody Sumatra!"

Martha's mouth opens in astonishment and horror. "These women are too sick to be moved, Margery. They can't walk to the lav, let alone get to the harbour."

"I've said that, so the Japs are providing stretchers."

"And who's going to carry those, I wonder?"

"I asked that, too. I thought the older boys might manage, but the patients will be last to leave, so it'll be the nurses. I'm sorry, Martha. There's no negotiating with these devils."

"We'll just have to manage as best we can. I'm not leaving anyone behind, Margery. It just wouldn't be right."

Emily hugs Martha tightly, wishing they could all travel together. Gently, Margery pulls her away.

"Come on, Emily. We have to get going or we'll have the guards on us. Martha will catch us up as soon as she can. She'll be on the boat behind us. We're all going back to Palembang." Briefly embracing Martha, Margery takes Emily by the hand and leads her away to join the line of prisoners walking from the camp down to the harbour. Secretly, Margery is scared. Surely the patients and nurses are coming too? What if the Japs are just waiting for most of the prisoners to leave before finishing off the sick? She tries to drive these unpalatable thoughts from her mind. No, if the guards are intending to murder the sick, surely the nurses would be travelling with the others.

Stumbling along the huge jetty, hanging onto the handrail, the prisoners board the first of the boats. Fortunately for Margery and Emily, being at the back of the line means they can stay up on deck as the black stinking hold is full. Margery remembers their arrival, all those months ago. Their numbers have more than halved during their imprisonment on Bangka Island. Surely, conditions will be better back on Sumatra?

There is no conversation. The prisoners, now used to being treated as livestock, merely shuffle around, trying to find a space in which to settle for the long uncomfortable voyage. Emily stares out to sea, grateful for the cooling breeze. She wonders where the men might be – are they returning to join them or leaving them behind? Perhaps it is her imagination, but she senses she is being pulled back to Sumatra, back to Daddy, Peter and Matt.

A number of Japanese naval personnel stare in horror as the living skeletons struggle along the quayside, carrying their patients on rough stretchers. None step forwards to assist – they can only look away, unwilling to acknowledge that such human misery exists, let alone share in the responsibility.

Heads held high, the nurses stagger past, heading out along the jetty to the waiting boats.

"They can't even look at us," Martha rages to no one in particular. "It's as if we don't exist at all. Petty little men fighting their petty little wars. If I had the energy, I'd spit in their faces. They've de-humanised me. I hate the Japanese. I'd blast them off the face of the earth if I had the means."

The nurses lay the stretchers out on deck. It is an impossible choice – the merciless sun, or the black airless hold.

"Let's keep them up here and try to give them shade," Martha suggests. "I think the fresh air will be better and we can shade them with our bodies." She stalks over to the ship's rail, glaring back towards the staring men. "Yeah!" she screams. "You wouldn't want to even rape us now, would you? You're total bastards! May you all rot in hell!" Sinking to her knees, Martha gives way to despair. Never in her life has she felt so exhausted, so empty, so hopeless.

Turning around, she watches as Susan gently closes the lids over Nora's sightless eyes. As tears roll down Martha's face, Susan is roughly pushed aside by a guard – who lifts the dead woman's body, a bundle of nearly weightless bones, still warm and pliable and carelessly tosses the pitiful remains overboard.

Chapter 29

Slipping under the barbed wire fence and crawling through the dry ditch which had once been a drain, Matt moves silently away from Belalau camp, disappearing from the sight of any patrolling guards. The bright moon guides him through the trees, to the field where he has been stealing the tapioca root tubers from a local farmer's cassava crop. In his weakened condition, Matt struggles to wrench the potato-like tubers from the plant roots, leaving himself exhausted and covered in crumbling soil.

Desperation has brought Matt out foraging for food each night. Since their arrival by train from Palembang to this abandoned rubber plantation, set deep in the jungle, food supplies have been scarce, and the death toll is climbing rapidly.

Returning to the ramshackle hut, once home to plantation workers that he now shares with Peter, Matt sets to work hacking off the inedible skin with the knife Peter has kept hidden since leaving Mumtok and the hospital. Hearing footsteps, he hurriedly conceals the evidence of his night's work under his sleeping mat.

"Peter?" Matt calls uncertainly, waiting until the moving shadow resolves into a human form and Peter emerges into the moonlight. He is terribly thin and stooped from continually bending down to treat the sick men of the camp. Lines of exhaustion are etched deeply into the prematurely-aged skin around his hollowed eyes, and what little hair he has left, is now completely white.

"You've got more food!" Peter's eyes glint in the moonlight, his mouth opening in a grin, revealing several missing teeth.

"And this time," Matt's voice is firm, "you are goin' t' eat it all."

"We have to share it, Matt."

"We will, when you're strong enough. I'm sorry, mate, but you're the only doc we've got, so you're goin' t' stay alive – even if I have t' force-feed ya. I've worked out the patrol times, so I'll soon be able t' bring in more food without bein' spotted. I'll share it out, don't you worry."

Peter sinks down to his mat and begins to gnaw on the hard flesh.

"We're losing the battle, Matt."

"What d'ya mean, mate?"

"More cases of malaria and now black water fever."

"What's that?"

"A complication of malaria. A few of the men have black urine, hence the name. In their starved condition, it's usually fatal."

Matt is silent. What is there to say? He reaches out to pat Peter's shoulder before wearily climbing to his feet.

"I'll go for a wash and get water. You eat and rest, okay?"

Peter nods, continuing to chew on the root, watching Matt disappear into the darkness, wondering at the young Australian's undiminished bravery and determination. Frank, the only other man who went under the wire for food, had been caught, beaten in front of them all as an example and left to die in the sun. Peter recalls how the sobbing man had cried out for his wife, Gracie – begging her forgiveness for leaving her alone. Fortunately, he had never regained consciousness, escaping further appalling suffering.

Peter is aware of Matt's desperation to keep them both alive

– his sense of guilt at losing John by not reacting to the splash in the water during the night spent at Palembang. They rarely speak of John now – not knowing what happened had been eating away at them. How many hours had they spent going over the possibilities? Finally, they had nothing left to say, reaching a tacit agreement to drop the subject altogether.

When Matt returns from the stream which winds its way through the camp, he finds Peter asleep on the ground, the half-eaten root resting in his open palm. The doctor is utterly exhausted; taking the weight of the world on his shoulders – feeling responsible for every life lost in his personal war against infection and disease. Matt has insisted they move out to this relatively isolated hut, so Peter can have a few hours' peace each night, away from the moans and last rattling breaths of his dying patients, who haunt his turbulent dreams and every waking hour.

Matt acknowledges that his own determination to keep Peter alive is born of his fear of being abandoned. He couldn't go on without the doctor's resilience, his mental strength and support. They have already lost John, and Matt is terrified of being left alone. It is not in the physical sense – he is adept at finding food to supplement the starvation rations – it is a fear of fear itself: a terror that will paralyse his mind. An empty void, an entire universe with nothing to which he can attach his thoughts, feelings, love. Matt shudders – having allowed his mind to wander too close to the abyss into which he will fall if Peter dies.

Chapter 30

They had spent a dreadful night on board the old train at Palembang. Emily, Margery and the women and children from the first boat, had been loaded into filthy overcrowded carriages, forced to sit up throughout the night. Martha and her fellow nurses, carrying their patients from the docks, had been pushed into cattle trucks which provided barely enough room to lie the stretchers down on the stinking floor, leaving the nurses slumped against the side shutters slammed shut by the guards.

Thirsty and hungry, having received nothing after the twelve-hour voyage from Bangka Island, the prisoners had sweated, with no sanitation or sustenance, in the dark airless carriages. Unable to see the golden dawn, they had nevertheless felt the rising heat, as the merciless sun crested the horizon to begin its fiery arc across the sky.

Eventually, the guards had opened the shutters and carriage doors, handing in buckets of water and small amounts of rice. Now, the train chugs slowly westwards, past abandoned dwellings and broken-down station platforms, all of which are being inexorably reclaimed by the jungle.

As they pass to the north of the secret airfield, Emily recognises where they are and her mind fills with memories of the P2 airbase, the cave she shared with Indah, swimming together in the pool, finding and caring for Matt. There remain gaps in her memory, a swirling jumble of violence and pain she is still unable to process. Closing her eyes, Emily recalls the feel of Indah, remembering the silky fur, the deep vibration of her contented purring. Lost in her fantasy, soothed by the rocking motion of the train, Emily drifts between sleep and consciousness – jerking fully awake at the cry of a child or the screech of iron brakes as the train slows to pass through another abandoned station.

It is late afternoon when they finally stop – to the sound of hissing steam and the squeal of brakes. A rusty sign reveals their destination as Loeboek Linggau. The tiny station has no office or any other building, just an overgrown wooden platform with a rusty handrail and wooden staircase down to ground level.

As soon as the carriage doors are unlocked, the women and children pour out, stumbling on shaky legs. When the cattle truck shutters are lifted, the flies are the first occupants to leave – a buzzing black cloud rising in reaction to the sudden light, swiftly returning to feast on the flesh of the dead.

With no help from the guards, who stand and stare impassively at the appalling scene, the women and older children help the nurses carry the stretchers down the precipitous steps to the ground to what had once been a road, but is now an uneven mud track, almost lost to sight beneath ferns and grasses. At the insistence of the guards, who prod the reticent nurses with their bamboo canes, the dead are simply left where they lie and the remaining prisoners walk, or are carried, away into the jungle.

Mosquitoes are out in force by the time they arrive at the broken-down gates of Belalau, an abandoned rubber plantation. In the fading light, they finally reach a row of rundown huts and collapse onto the filthy earth floors of the damp rodent-infested dwellings – able to see the moon rise through holes in the palm roof thatch.

One of the guards leads Margery away. Emily trails behind,

unwilling to let the older woman out of her sight. He shows them a freshwater stream, a few yards from the huts, before disappearing into the night.

Within a few minutes, all the prisoners who can still walk, are either in or by the water, quenching their thirst, washing away the filth from their bodies and clothes. Haunted by images of their dead, left lying on stretchers by the station, there is little conversation. Returning to the huts, they find a sack of rice. Too exhausted to prepare the food, they chew on the grains before lying down to fall into exhausted sleep, still wearing their wet clothes.

In and out of shadows cast by a brilliant moon, the little stream meanders through the overgrown fields of what had once been a prosperous rubber plantation. Abandoned by the owners and estate workers escaping the invading Japanese, it now houses two POW camps, isolated not just from the rest of the world, but from each other. Throughout the still night, the ravaged bodies of men, women and children try to find oblivion in sleep – uncomfortable, starving, hopeless. The sick lie in rows, untreated by medicine, certain to die without dignity. Guards shift their weight from foot to foot, purposeless and hungry; wondering if supplies will be sent or if they, too, will die alongside their prisoners. From the starlit sky, an owl drops, its talons extended to grip an unwary rodent. At the sound of its triumphant screech, a solitary man looks up from where he cuts root tubers, to watch the swift ascent of the predator, carrying away its struggling prey.

PART SIX

Chapter 31

August 1945

Major Jeffrey Walker screws on the lid of his fountain pen, drops it onto the blotter and leans back in his chair, his large hands linked behind his head. His enormous frame melts in the Palembang heat and humidity, and he looks up in resignation at the slowly rotating ceiling fan, deciding it had not been worth the effort of getting the blasted thing running again. Around him remain signs of the office's previous occupant: Japanese flags, maps covered with neat little characters hanging on cracked whitewashed walls, an empty silver scabbard propped up against the far wall, blood stains on the wooden floor that refuse to be scrubbed clean.

As soon as his unit landed at Palembang airfield, he had come straight to the Japanese headquarters – to assume command and question the defeated Imperial officers. A general named Sato had been found dead on the office floor, impaled on his own sword. According to Colonel Kimuru, Sato's fellow officer in charge of the POW camps, the general had reacted with fury to Emperor Hirohito's radio broadcast announcing the unconditional surrender of the Japanese military. Through an interpreter, Kimuru described how General Sato had screamed that he would never surrender, had stormed off to his office and taken his own life, in what the Japanese believed to be the honourable manner.

In the days that followed, Kimuru had been interrogated repeatedly as he reluctantly revealed the locations of the POW camps in South Sumatra, and Walker's unit had gradually discovered the appalling conditions in which allied prisoners had been held.

Flying in from their headquarters in Ceylon, with several stops for refuelling, the allies formed part of the RAPWI, a division set up by Lord Mountbatten to aid the recovery of allied POWs interned by the Japanese. Since his arrival, Major Walker had written repeatedly, requesting urgent food and medical supplies, as well as transportation to evacuate the internees, who all needed hospital treatment. He and his men had been unprepared for the true horrors that awaited them in the camps. More than once, men had broken down in his office – unable to cope with the sick and dying skeletal remains of what had once been healthy human beings.

According to intelligence given before setting out on this rescue mission, these headquarters had been a local charity hospital, run by the Catholic church. No doctors or nursing sisters had yet been located in the camps and Walker remains convinced that Kimuru is withholding vital information. Unable to hide his rage during the colonel's questioning, Walker had sensed the Japanese officer's fear of reprisal should more camps be discovered in the same dreadful condition as those so far liberated.

Staring out of the window at the marshy grassland dropping away to the river, Walker sighs wearily. The slow progress of the rescue operation is frustrating. Supplies are taking too long to arrive, so internees are still dying from disease and starvation. Running his thick sausage-like fingers back through damp fair hair, he massages tight neck muscles to relieve the growing tension – straightening up at the unexpected knock on the door.

"Major, there's a man to see you. I think it could be important." Sergeant Roberts hovers uncertainly in the doorway. Tall and rangy, in his mid-twenties, with cropped ginger hair and a pleasant open face with large features, his anxious brown eyes look questioningly at his superior.

"It's always important," growls Walker, stretching out huge arms and rolling broad shoulders. "Okay, show him in. Bring something to drink. Water or tea. Something refreshing."

"Sir." Roberts nods deferentially, intimidated by this man-mountain. Relieved not to be bawled out by the erasable giant for the disturbance, he ushers in a stooped, fragile-looking man of indeterminate age, wearing ragged cut-down shorts, a torn shirt that hangs from his wasted body and rope sandals usually worn by the local workers. Despite the worn-out clothes, the visitor is clean-shaven with dark, silver-streaked hair. His skin is sun-browned, sallow and deeply lined and he appears exhausted, swaying on unsteady bird-like legs.

Fearing the man may collapse at any moment, the major gestures towards the chair opposite, and scrutinises the fellow lowering himself stiffly into the proffered seat.

Walker leans forward, placing his elbows on the desk, stretching his jacket sleeves tightly across his powerful upper arms. Steepling long thick fingers under his chin, the major regards the unknown man from green feline eyes beneath bushy eyebrows – too dark for his fair hair and lightly freckled face.

"What can I do for you?" His voice is deep, but the tone gentle.

His visitor looks up. From sunken sockets, his bright blue eyes are penetrating, feverish and demanding.

"My name is John Crawford, and I need your help."

For the next half an hour, Major Jeffrey Walker sits silently listening to John Crawford's life-story since becoming involved with the secret P2 airfield, at the end of 1941. John explains how he became caught up in a surprise attack on Pladjoe by Japanese paratroopers while trying to destroy the refinery's capabilities before it fell into enemy hands. How the main invasion force had landed at Palembang and he had been taken prisoner outside this very building. Describing Sato's brutality and the uneasy situation at the hospital, John's voice cracks with emotion as he speaks of his daughter, fists clenching in anger as he explains how an Australian airman had carried her for two days to seek medical help after her violent rape by Japanese soldiers. His eyes had become inscrutable as he described the appalling conditions in the Palembang prison, Matt's arrival with the dreadful news and contriving to be sent for treatment so he might see his daughter, Emily.

Graphically, John describes the shooting in the ward that caused them all to be sent to the camps – Doctor Peter, the remaining sisters, the Australian nurses with other women and children recovering from ill-treatment on Bangka Island, as well as himself and his daughter.

After a break for water, John relates the move from Palembang prison to the huts they had built in the jungle. Their joy at discovering the women's camp – where John had last seen Emily waving from the high wall. For a moment, John is silent, closing his eyes, picturing Emily up on the wall with Martha. Walker notices the slight upwards curve to John's lips before the eyes reopen and the face falls into an expression of great sorrow.

John continues, recounting the night march back to Palembang, crossing to Bangka Island, the dreadful conditions there and his vague recollection of the nightmare voyage back to

Sumatra.

"I'd recurring malaria, you see. I'd no strength left to fight it. I would've died if my old housekeeper's grandson hadn't seen me disembark and carried me off in the night to their hut. I have little or no memory of the following weeks. When I finally recovered sufficiently to wash and feed myself, Lai, my housekeeper, insisted I remain with the family until we learnt of your arrival." John pauses, fighting for breath, his distress increasingly evident. "I *have* to find my daughter and my friends. All I know is that Peter and Matt were alive when I was rescued. Lai found out they were sent west by train. While I was recovering, Lai's grandson told me he had seen the women and children loaded onto boats long after us men left for Bangka Island. He was sure they had returned during the time I lay unconscious and also disappeared west on the train. Lai heard that some of the women were nurses carrying their patients on stretchers. They were all in a bad way. Those that died were just left by the tracks."

John's voice finally fails him. His eyes fill with tears held back for too long. Now, he has made his report, and help will come. His part is done and he lets go, burying his face in his hands, releasing the flood of fear and sorrow in which he has been drowning since his recovery. Overcome with exhaustion and relief – no longer shouldering the responsibility of his knowledge alone.

For a few minutes, Walker remains still and silent, allowing John time. He cannot imagine what this man has endured. His own children are safe at home in Scotland, deep in the Highlands, hardly touched by war. Could his daughter, Emma, rosy-faced and pampered, survive in the jungle on her own? Could he bear to exist not knowing if she still lived? Unaware of the suffering

241

she has endured and may still be enduring? Walker senses the mental barriers he has carefully created to protect his mind from the true horror of what has happened here have been blasted away by John's words. Images that Jeffrey has forbidden his brain to process so he can complete his mission, now fill his head – indelible, he knows they will now haunt his dreams for the rest of his life.

Slowly, Walker rises to his feet, steps around his desk and places a gentle palm on John's trembling shoulder. Words are unnecessary – in this simple gesture, the major offers sympathy, comfort, assurance that he will move heaven and earth to find the missing internees.

"Roberts!" he booms. "Get this man some food and find him a place to rest. And then get that bastard Kimuru in here, *now*!"

Chapter 32

Captain Haku sits alone in the guardhouse, vacantly gazing into space. Small in stature, with cropped greying hair, the Japanese officer allows tears he can no longer hold back to fall freely, soaking into his dusty shirt collar.

The long-awaited truck with meagre supplies has arrived from Palembang, bringing news of the atom bombs dropped on Hiroshima and Nagasaki and the unconditional surrender broadcast by Emperor Hirohito.

In the newspapers that have finally reached Sumatra, Haku discovers photographs of the giant pillar of black smoke with its pale mushroom-shaped top, forever symbolising the destruction of his home city of Nagasaki. The written reports of the blinding white flash, the deafening blast and the thousands of broken bodies that litter the shattered streets of the city centre are brutally frank, beyond anything he could have imagined. He recoils at the photographs of burnt civilian corpses: bloated charred skin that has burst apart, peeling off to reveal raw flesh with white cooked body fat. He reads the harrowing witness accounts of survivors, searching the smoking ruins of his city for missing relatives. Haku should be there, searching for his wife and children – not stranded out here, on this derelict plantation, with insufficient supplies to feed his own men, let alone the prisoners. He is desperate to get back to Japan, to find his family. As Haku's chest tightens with the visceral agony of his enforced separation, his tears flow – an impotent outpouring of fear and despair, acknowledging the absolute impossibility of returning home.

The orders from Colonel Kimuru are to inform the prisoners the war has ended and keep them alive until relieved of his command. That he will obey is never in question, but Haku knows his superior well. Kimuru could not care less whether the POWs live or die, so such orders will have been given under duress. Kimuru must be in enemy hands.

"Peter!" Matt calls breathlessly, shaking the sleeping man's bony shoulder. Having attempted to run from the main camp to wake the doctor, he now bends over, hands on knees, gasping for breath. Peter groans. He has been working through the night, washing down fevered bodies in an attempt to extend the miserable lives of his fellow prisoners, one by one dying of black water fever.

"Wake up, Peter!" Matt's shaking becomes more insistent. "We've all been summoned to Tenko, there's gunna be an announcement."

Peter sits up, rubbing his sore eyes. Every bone in his body aches from the long hours spent in the makeshift hospital.

"Go away, Matt. They don't care if I'm there any more. They know I work nights. Come back and tell me what it's all about later. I'm too tired to move."

"No, mate. Orders are that we *all* attend today. Sorry, Peter, but you've gotta get movin'."

Still half asleep, Peter holds up a hand, allowing Matt to drag him to his feet. Swaying with fatigue and hunger, he staggers down to the stream for a quick wash. The cool water on his sweat-streaked face revives him and the two men head towards the centre of the camp, to join the other prisoners waiting for Captain

Haku's announcement.

As the Japanese guards emerge from the guardhouse, rifles in hand, Peter wonders if they have been assembled to be shot. There is so little food, with several men dying each day – perhaps it would be a kindness to end their misery?

Captain Haku steps up onto a wooden box so he can be seen clearly and looks about him, taking in the pitiful state of the human skeletons, wondering if it is even possible to keep these men alive for much longer. The disgruntled guards fidget and mutter behind him. Their behaviour is so unusual that the prisoners become agitated – casting questioning glances at one another, their shrugging shoulders lifting like jerked puppets with invisible strings.

"Gentlemen," Captain Haku begins in his carefully enunciated English, "war is over and now we are friends." He raises his hands, the benevolent benefactor conducting the anticipated celebrations, accepting their gratitude. All he receives are the silent stares of uncomprehending skulls. His words are anathema, idiotic, unbelievable. Like docile cattle, they merely gaze up at him, a bewildered congregation, until acute discomfort drives him from the makeshift podium, to stand amongst his restless men, before retreating to the guardhouse.

Peter and Matt stare at one another with complete incredulity. "Mate!" Matt's eyes are bright, hopeful. "Did I hear right? The war's over and we're still alive?" Trembling, he reaches forwards to hug Peter, who remains motionless, silent, attempting to process this incredible news.

"The war's over!" Men begin to speak the words, reinforcing the truth with their constant repetition.

Finally, Peter turns, setting off at an even pace towards the guardhouse. Confused, Matt follows, catching hold of his arm.

"What's up, Peter?"

"I have to know. I have to know if we've won or lost."

As they reach the wooden door, it opens before they can knock. Captain Haku comes out, brandishing a Japanese newspaper which he thrusts into Peter's face.

"This is what end war!" Haku points to the black and white photograph of the mushroom cloud hanging over Nagasaki.

"What is it?" asks Peter. Neither he nor Matt has ever seen anything resembling the peculiar formation of smoke or cloud, whatever the photograph represents. Haku turns the page and they are faced with more photographs: burnt corpses fill the page, lying amongst the debris of a ruined city, with ghost-like figures in torn clothing floundering in a floating sea of ash, searching for loved ones. Peter covers his eyes. The pictures are too disturbing. The broken bodies are hideous with their scorched skin, bloated and burst, oozing pale body fat.

"Atom bomb drop on my city, Nagasaki. Bomb drop on Hiroshima first. Japanese surrender. Very dishonourable for my people." Haku's eyes are haunted, despairing, defeated.

Inside the hut, Peter and Haku drop down into chairs, but Matt remains standing, looking from one to the other and becoming agitated.

"Look, I'm sorry if your family's gone but we had t' find a way t' stop you. You Japs've watched us starve and die. Your men beat us, shoot us in cold blood. You rape our women, our children. Christ almighty, your bloody soldiers raped a child in the jungle. I should've been there. I should've protected her from your bastard countrymen." Matt's voice rises to a scream. "Your general shot a nun. He shot his own interpreter. We had to stop you mad bastards, whatever the cost."

Haku stares at the ground, impassive, silent.

246

"Are we free to go?" Peter's question makes Haku look up in alarm.

"Yeah," adds Matt, more threateningly. "If we've won, then we must be in charge, right?"

Haku takes a deep breath and slowly rises to his feet. "Orders say stay here until relief come. Must come soon as not enough food. Must go to women camp to announce war over."

"Women's camp? Here?" Peter's heart begins to beat wildly, threatening to burst through his fragile ribcage. "What women's camp?"

"Other side of plantation. Two mile." Haku's tone is wary. Is it too soon to give away this information? Can he delay the inevitable uprising until he is relieved of his command by bringing the men and women together?

Emily lies on her roughly woven sleeping mat, staring up through the broken roof thatch to the threatening grey sky. In the high humidity, her long lank hair sticks uncomfortably to her damp face, tendrils clinging to her neck like clammy seaweed. Alone, she wonders how it would feel to be the sole survivor? Left alone, the last to die. The thought is so terrifying that she tries to shut out the image of complete solitude. Her limbs ache, but why move? There is no position more comfortable, she may as well remain as she is. Her head aches. She should go to the stream for water, but cannot be bothered. She is so tired all the time now, even blinking the dust from her eyes needs too much effort. At least there are no more tears. She has cried them all dry. There is no more hope. There is only one unknown – the day and time of her death. Emily's eyes close and as she drifts into sleep, she wonders if this time will be the last and she will never wake up.

Leaning back against a tree, Martha sighs heavily, subconsciously winding her fingers around the long dry grass, as if anchoring herself to the earth.

"Margery?"

"Um." Margery lies on the ground near Martha, arm shielding her eyes, chewing on a grass stalk.

"We're never getting out of here, are we?"

"It seems less likely as more time passes. There's hardly any food left. Sadly, we can't live on grass alone."

"How long've we been here now?"

"I lost count somewhere around three months. I really haven't a clue, sorry."

"We lost two more today, and Susan is really sick now." At this news, Margery abruptly sits up.

"We've got to keep Susan going. I'll go and see her. Shall I take more water?"

Martha grimaces.

"Quinine too and some nutritious food please."

Both women look up at the sound of an approaching aircraft.

"Take cover!" Martha screams. "It's dropping bombs! It's an air raid!"

"Hang on, Martha," Margery holds up an arm to stop her. "I've never seen square bombs with parachutes. Come on, let's see where they land."

Other women and children rise from their lethargy, including Emily, who crawls out of the hut on all fours to see the plane.

The parcels, with their little chutes, seem reluctant to fall, taking forever to land. As they hit the ground, the women are on them, tearing at the brown paper, exclaiming at what they find.

"It's bread! I haven't tasted bread for years!"

"Share it out! Children first!"

"Not too much everyone," Martha entreats. "Your stomachs will rebel if you eat too much after so long. Please, only small amounts."

"Martha!" Margery holds up her prize. "You asked for quinine and here it is!" Martha puts her hands to her mouth in complete astonishment and pleasure.

"Quickly, let's take it to Susan and the others. This will really help with a little food."

"So, Emily," Margery puts an arm around the teenage girl as they follow Martha, chewing on the soft white bread, "you know what this means?"

"We won't starve to death?"

"Well, yes, of course. It also means they know we're here, which means help will come."

Emily smiles wryly. "Trouble is, Margery, I'd resigned myself to dying and now I've got to rethink my whole future!"

Guards appear, staring impassively at the women and children gathered around the Red Cross parcels. They, too, are hungry but make no move to take the food. One of the few remaining nuns offers them a loaf of bread, while other prisoners stare in open-mouthed horror.

"Hey! That's for us, not the bloody Japs!" The nun turns, clasping her hands reverently.

"Mother Helena would advise us to share in our good fortune. These men are hungry."

"Now look here, Sister…"

"That's enough!" Margery intervenes. "Sister is right. There's enough to give them something. These parcels mean help is coming. Listen to Martha. If you eat too much after so long, it could make you seriously ill, even kill you."

In Kimuru's requisitioned car, John and Major Walker bump along the rutted track up to Palembang airfield.

"As I said, John, we've carried out an airdrop at Belalau and are preparing trucks to take more supplies overland. You and I will fly to Lahat, the closest airbase and take a truck from there. Please be assured, we're moving as fast as we can."

"What did Kimuru tell you?"

"I could've wrung his scrawny neck!" Walker growls. "Why he withheld the information is beyond me. He blames Sato. Said Sato had ordered Belalau forgotten, left to rot. Those were his words… after translation, of course."

"Sato," John smiles bleakly. "Still as vindictive, even from beyond the grave."

"We can fly the internees out from Lahat direct to Singapore, I've organised the aircraft in principle, but we won't know the numbers until we've been to the camps. From what we've found already, conditions in the camps are so appalling that every survivor needs hospital treatment, so there's little point in bringing them back to Palembang first."

"I have to admit, major, I'm half hopeful, half terrified. I'm pinning all my hopes on Emily being at the women's camp, but they've been there for five months without supplies, if Kimuru is telling the truth. We can't be sure there're any survivors. Thanks for letting me tag along, I know it's not procedure but I simply couldn't wait any longer. Will I be able to go to Singapore too?"

"If we find your daughter, I promise you'll accompany her to Singapore. I'm a father, too. Wild horses wouldn't keep me from boarding that plane if it were my Emma."

"She'll be fifteen now…" John falls silent. He cannot imagine his child almost a woman. Blocking the possibility of her not being at Belalau from his mind, he tries to imagine how she will look – even more like her mother, he suspects. He considers how she had been before the war: her constant chattering, her vivacity and confidence. How confident she had been with the cub – how she had come to love Indah. It is hard to reconcile the tiny stumbling cub with Matt's description of a ferocious tiger ripping out the throats of Emily's attackers. How will she be coping with her trauma? Hopefully, Martha has been with her. He hadn't known the Australian nurse well, but Peter spoke so highly of her and he trusts his friend's judgement, despite the obvious bias due to their mutual attraction. How will he find Peter and Matt? They must be at Belalau; it fits with the information he gleaned from Lai. Suddenly, John feels a rush of adrenaline flood his body – his whole future depends on what he finds at Belalau prison camp. The thought is overwhelming. They could all be dead – maybe all he will find are earthen graves marked with small wooden crosses.

Chapter 33

Martha and Emily kneel by Susan in the small hut chosen to be the hospital because the roof is still intact.

"Will the quinine make her better?" Emily gently washes Susan's face with water she has collected from the stream.

"Hope so, Em. Keep going with the cool water, that really helps too. I've softened some bread with water and she's taken a bit. I daren't give her too much though."

"How does the quinine work, Martha?"

"It kills the parasite that causes malaria."

"How are we doing?" The women look up to see Margery stride into the hospital – the food plus the hope they will be rescued have restored some of her old confidence. "The guards tell me Captain Haku is on his way with some sort of announcement. They couldn't, or wouldn't, say what the news is, but they don't look happy about it."

"We've hidden the medical supplies in case they try to take them from us." Martha gets to her feet, stretching out her aching back. "It must be something to do with the food parcels – I can't believe our manna from heaven was dropped by the Japs."

"Can you do without Emily so she can hear the great announcement? We'll come straight over here to let you know what's going on."

Martha nods, before kneeling next to Susan, continuing to keep her temperature down with the cool water. The younger nurse is restless and still delirious, muttering and crying out between bouts of unconsciousness. Like Margery, Martha feels more positive since the airdrop – the food and medicine will save lives. For the first time since arriving at Belalau, there is hope.

As she works, it occurs to Martha that she had given up, accepting they would all die here. For months, she has been living a nightmare existence, administering the most basic and inadequate care to the dying. In the heat and humidity, trying to cope with the febrile temperatures of the sick, she has pictured hell reaching up with giant fiery fingers, dragging them inexorably into its burning depths. Only Mother Helena had passed away peacefully, her face serene as her soul slipped away. The others, Nora, Grace, so many others, had fought against death: faces contorted in agony, bodies burning with fever in the grip of hell's flaming fingers.

Unexpectedly overcome with a wave of fear and nausea, leaving her floundering in a world with sharpened clarity – a world that is intolerable – Martha hunches over, burying her face in her hands, helpless to prevent her carefully constructed dam – filled with despair, grief and terror – from collapsing around her. The torrent of horror being released smashes through every barrier, waves cascade over disintegrating defences, roiling and writhing, until she is drowning under the sheer weight of her misery.

Margery and Emily watch the convoy of trucks trundle up the dirt road leading into their camp. They recognise the short slight figure of Captain Haku clumsily levering himself out from the passenger seat of the front vehicle.

"He looks terrible, Margery" Emily whispers as Haku – eyes bloodshot, face pale and gaunt – stumbles forwards to address the surviving women and children. Expecting only Japanese guards in escort, they do not at first notice the tentative ragged figures emerging from the rear trucks. All eyes are on Haku, who holds up his arms for silence.

"War is over. Now we are your friends." His voice is clear, but without inflection and it takes a few moments for the meaning of his words to penetrate the prisoners' desensitised minds.

As they stand motionless, stunned silent statues, it is the children who first notice the male prisoners approaching. They tug at their silent staring mothers, pointing towards the trucks disgorging their pitiful cargo. The women look from Haku to the human skeletons, then back to Haku, as if waiting for further explanation, unable to trust their eyes. But Haku's head has fallen to his chest, having withdrawn into his own personal misery. All Haku sees are the black and white images of burnt bodies lying in a storm of ash.

The male prisoners approach the unbelieving women. Hesitant, as if one false move could shatter this fragile scene. Emily's eyes search, flitting from one emaciated figure to another, seeking familiar faces in these brittle cadaverous men.

Matt and Peter climb down from their truck, watching the women and children's reaction to Haku's words – shock, disbelief, confusion. They search the haggard faces for Martha, Emily and Mother Helena. They view a child's drawing: a tableau of stick women and children, dressed in rags, faces taut, large hollowed eyes bewildered and fearful.

A father seeks a young wife and small boy. His wife searches for her youthful handsome husband. Shocked by one another's appearance, the family reunites. Man and wife aged and careworn, their sturdy boy a starved youth – his child's eyes no longer bright and innocent, but dark and knowing, expressing knowledge of the countless horrors he has witnessed. The three cling together, desperate to form a ring of security: a fragile whole, created from the jagged pieces of their broken lives.

Emily recognises Matt's white-blond hair. Hesitantly, she walks towards him, stopping when she realises the tall skeletal man beside him with wispy white hair and sunken eyes is Doctor Peter. Her hand covers her mouth, trying to block the cry of anguish rising from her chest as she takes in the appalling appearance of the two men. No longer a child, they do not recognise her until Margery steps forwards to place a hand on Emily's trembling shoulder.

"Emily! Are you all right?"

"Where's Daddy?" She stares at the men, her huge brown eyes pleading, switching from Matt to Peter and back, trying to read their expressions. "Where is he?"

"We became separated, Emily. We don't know where he is. I'm sorry. We tried to stay together..." Matt's voice falters.

"No!" she screams. "No! He must be here! Daddy! *Daddy*!"

Emily runs towards the empty trucks, calling for her father. Her cries mingle with the wails of every grieving prisoner. The men make to follow, but Margery shakes her head.

"I'll go. Is he dead?"

Matt shrugs, raising his hands in a gesture of helplessness.

"We really don't know but he was real sick."

Peter steps forward, gripping Margery's arm as she tries to follow Emily.

"Martha?" His deep voice cracks with emotion, his eyes full of desperate hope. Margery glares down at his hand and he immediately withdraws it. Peter drops his eyes as they meet her withering look, but then she softens, pitying him and points to the hospital hut.

"She's in there – caring for the sick."

Standing in the open doorway, Peter gazes impassively at the atrocious condition of the sick women, lying on inadequate palm mats on the dirt floor of the miserable hut. It is a scene so familiar to him, there is no sense of shock. A woman, emaciated and pale, sits on the ground between the mats staring vacantly into space. Her despairing green eyes sparkle with tears in the half light of the shabby interior – a vivid contrast to her sallow skin and hollow cheeks, lined with exhaustion and privation. Unable to speak, he shuffles forward, the noise attracting her attention, bringing her back to herself. The mournful green eyes lock with his, and time stands still while they assess one another.

"Could you use some help?" Peter steps carefully around the prone patients, offering her his hand.

"Yes, please." Martha clasps his proffered hand, allowing him to pull her to her feet.

Gently, with his free hand, he pushes a loose strand of her lank hair behind her ear. The gesture brings a tentative smile to her ravaged face. Encouraged, he steps forwards, letting go of her hand and wrapping his arms around her trembling shoulders, pulling her into his bony embrace. Instantly, she stiffens, pulling away. Peter refuses to relinquish his hold and gradually, her instinctive fear subsides and she relaxes against him, her arms moving cautiously around his waist.

"Have you come to rescue us?"

"Unfortunately not. It seems we've been neighbours for quite a while. Haku only told us about your camp this morning when he announced the end of the war."

"It's over?"

"It's over. The allies dropped two atom bombs on the Jap mainland and they surrendered. Haku only found out this morning when supplies came in from Palembang with newspapers."

"What's an atom bomb?"

"Whatever it is, the results are apocalyptic. Haku showed me the photos. The ruined streets are filled with burnt bodies. Christ, Martha, it was a terrible thing to do to civilian people but it's probably saved our lives."

"Is Emily's father with you? Is he all right?" At Peter's lack of response, Martha steps back and looks up into his tear-filled eyes. "Oh no! What's happened to him?"

"We stayed together for years but John had bouts of malaria and when we got back to Palembang from Mumtok Jail…"

"Peter! Not there! No! Not Mumtok Jail! I was terrified we were going there when we were taken over to Bangka Island. In the end, it was not so bad at our camp. Well, not so bad compared to this place."

"Yes, I remembered what you'd told me and the jail was every bit as dreadful as you'd described. When we were there, the Japs had opened up a walkway through to a hospital. Still concrete slabs for beds, but less crowded. It was run by monks who'd tried to get out of Singapore. They did what they could, but with no medicines and barely any food, most there died. John survived though, but he was feverish when we sailed back to Palembang about six months ago. We were left on the quayside for the night. When we woke in the morning, he'd disappeared. Matt thinks he heard a splash in the night. We can only assume John went into the water."

"Oh, poor Emily. She'll be devastated."

"She is. There's a stern-looking woman looking after her. She told me where to find you."

"That'll be Margery. She's our sort of leader and Emily's

always by her side. They've become close. Margery never married and has no children. They seem to have adopted one another."

"Right then." Peter rubs his hands together, a habit he has acquired to increase his poor circulation. "Tell me what I can do to help."

Emily sits by the empty trucks, huddled into Margery's embrace. Around the camp, the men, women and children, experience heightened emotions – a maelstrom of relief and anguish. Those reunited hold fast to one another, others offer comfort to the grieving, or sit alone, lost in a private hell of disappointment and despair. None has much to say. To speak of the last four years is to burden one another with more guilt, more horror. Empathy binds them all, a wall of steel, a solidarity, a means of survival. Haku and his men retreat, driving away in convoy – defeated, returning to the guardhouse at the men's camp to await their fate.

Chapter 34

Ears popping as the plane begins its final descent, securely strapped into his seat for landing, John gazes through the window of the Douglas Dakota transport plane, to where the lush lowland rainforest spreads out to the distant horizon. He feels the vibration of the undercarriage being lowered, watches the wing tips almost clip the tree-tops of the impenetrable canopy and winces at the bone-shaking thud of touchdown, gripping his seat as the plane bounces and skids along the unkempt runway into Lahat.

Unclipping their seatbelts, he and Major Walker clamber out, emerging into a brilliant sunset, to be met by Roberts' ginger hair flashing like a welcoming beacon against the spectacular pink and orange sky.

"Is everything ready?" Walker's booming voice disturbs the exquisite peace replacing the constant drone of engines and rattling fuselage that had assaulted John's ears throughout the flight, ending with the shrieking protest of engines thrown into reverse, finally bringing the plane to a shuddering halt.

"Sir." Roberts salutes, standing stiffly to attention. "We've carried out an airdrop and have a convoy leaving for Belalau at first light, carrying more food and medical supplies. Another is on its way overland from Palembang. Turns out the Japs have been hoarding Red Cross parcels for years. Most are still usable so we're reasonably well provisioned."

"Good work, Roberts. John and I will join the convoy. Have

you found us a billet for tonight?"

"Sir. If you'd both like to follow me." Roberts leads his commanding officer and John to a wooden structure, originally used for the storage of supplies intended for the local rubber plantations. "It's very basic, but seems weatherproof, so we've made this our base."

John clenches his fists, digging fingernails painfully into palms, frustrated by yet another delay. Of course he knows the dangers of driving through the jungle at night, but is he mad enough to steal a truck and head out right now? Clamping down on his rising desperation, John tries to be calm, breathe deeply and wait patiently for the morning. The same haunting questions spin around inside his head. Is Emily at Belalau? Is she still alive? What will he do if she is not there? If she is dead? Tormented, he stumbles restlessly around the dark airfield, reliving memories, fantasising emotional reunions, fearing earthen graves with little wooden crosses. Every nerve and fibre of his body is on alert, straining for release, desperate to be on his way to Belalau.

Major Walker stands alone: hidden by long shadows cast by the moon rising above the forest canopy, smoking a cigarette, watching the tormented man tramp around muttering to himself, wound up like a tightly coiled spring. Apart from the airdrop – returning pilots have confirmed signs of life – the allies have had no contact with Belalau, so Walker has no idea what to expect upon their arrival tomorrow. Bringing John may have been a huge error of judgement. Unless they find his daughter alive, the man could become unmanageable, too distressed to listen to reason and to follow orders. Walker does not believe John is a danger to anyone, other than to himself, but Walker is taking a risk by allowing the man to accompany the convoy. Still, the decision has been made and, without John's input, they may never have known about the Belalau camps.

Crushing the discarded cigarette beneath his boot, Walker clears his throat, alerting John to his presence.

"Come inside, John. Roberts has found us a bottle of brandy. You can't make the sun rise any faster. You're exhausted man, still not recovered from the malaria. Come and get your head down for a few hours. The brandy will help you relax. We'll need you rested for the drive. From what you've told me, you've far more knowledge of this jungle than any of my men."

"I just want to get there, to know if Emily is alive? I can't stand the waiting. It's driving me mad!" John runs his hands through his greying hair, clenching fistfuls and tugging, using the pain to ground himself. "It's almost worse now we're so close."

"You definitely need that drink." Walker puts a comforting hand on John's shoulder, guiding him to the wooden hut, where the convoy personnel lie on wooden pallets, sweating in the sultry heat, waiting for the dawn.

Exhausted by the food in their stomachs, and the strain of the day's visceral emotion, the prisoners sleep restlessly around the dying embers of cooking fires. Some huddle together, frightened to wake and find it has all been a dream. Others sleep alone, away from the reunited families, hiding their grief away from confused children – so recently reunited with complete strangers they are told to call Daddy.

An owl glides through rising air currents far above, circling, hunting for the small rodents feasting on fallen crumbs around the silent humans.

Matt sits, cooling his feet in the stream, dispirited and alone now Peter has found Martha. For years, he has imagined finding Emily – dreamed of taking her hand, allowing her soul, so carefully cradled within his heart since he carried her to safety, to find its way back to her, reigniting her spirit, witnessing her eyes regain their sparkle. Instead, he has failed her, failed to keep her father safe, failed to bring him back to her. Since John's disappearance, Matt has existed to keep his promise, to look after Emily. He has prepared his explanation, imagined it would be within his embrace that she grieved. But he had made a complete mess of it, not even recognising her. In Matt's imagination, Emily had remained a child. To be confronted by a young woman, grown up despite the privations she had suffered, was such a shock that he had floundered, forgetting his carefully prepared explanation.

Now, he experiences a sense of rejection, jealous that Emily has turned to the unknown Margery for comfort. His acute loneliness has driven him from the camp, needing to be away from Emily, away from Peter and Martha. Feeling abandoned and overwrought, Matt ties the palm leaf coverings around his damp feet, rises stiffly, and sets off to follow the stream the few miles back to the old hut he had shared with Peter. His tears act like cataracts, flaring in the moonlight, blurring his vision, causing him to trip and stumble over every rock and bush he encounters, adding to his sense of injustice, increasing his bitterness towards his ungrateful friends. In this unendurable misery, he throws back his head and howls – hating the world, determined to die alone, to make those he loves feel guilt for abandoning him, to escape his own guilt at failing Emily and John.

Beside Margery, Emily wakes to the sound of unbearable pain, the mournful cry reaching her through the forest, carrying across the loose-linked foliage of the jungle. Perhaps it is the lost soul of her father, or Indah, roaming the dark forest, unable to find peace. She senses its pull, being drawn to the tormented spirit, as if it calls to her alone, crying for the protection of her living warmth, seeking her heart as its final resting place. She listens, but it does not come again and all too soon, in her exhaustion, she falls back to sleep within Margery's enfolding embrace.

Chapter 35

Seated around a small cooking fire, Martha, Margery, Emily and others barely look up as they hear the rumble of trucks approaching the camp. Assuming it is the returning Japanese guards, they continue their conversations.

"I haven't seen Matt since last night," Margery replies to Martha's enquiry.

"Peter's really worried. He's been looking since first light but there's absolutely no sign of him anywhere." Martha frowns in concern, turning to watch clouds of dust rising around the approaching convoy.

"Those aren't Japs!" Emily shouts, rising to her feet, screwing up her eyes to get a better look.

"I think, ladies, we are finally being rescued." Margery gets stiffly to her feet, brushing dust from her hands, before hugging Emily in delight.

As the sound of engines fades, the prisoners all stand, staring in fascination at the well-fed European men stepping out to greet them.

Advancing towards the emaciated prisoners, whose eyes appear huge and accusing in their skull-like heads, Major Walker subconsciously removes his cap in deference to these people who have suffered so dreadfully at the hands of the Japanese. His eyes fill with tears at the piteous sight before him – silent bundles of bones in rags. Slowly blinking eyes and small muscle twitches are the only discernible movement in this tableau of human suffering.

"My name is Jeffrey Walker, Major Jeffrey Walker, and I'm so sorry it's taken so long to find you." Walker's voice cracks, he cannot continue.

"We're very glad to see you, Major. I'm Margery and, on behalf of us all, I welcome you to our camp." The bony woman steps forwards, holding out her hand, its fragile tapered fingers firmly gripping his massive paw-like hand. Behind the major, she watches as a much thinner man in civilian clothes steps out from the lead truck, scanning the faces of the prisoners.

"Daddy!" Emily streaks past Margery and the Major, hurling herself into the waiting arms of her father.

"Hello, you." John clings to his daughter in sheer relief. "I've missed you, darling."

Peter wanders down by the stream, guilt-ridden for leaving Matt, especially after Emily's hysterical outburst. How could he have been so selfish, forgetting Matt in his relief at finding Martha alive? It had been hours, working alongside Martha in the hospital, before he had come back to where he had left Matt earlier. Most of the camp had been asleep, Emily curled up against the older woman Martha had explained was Margery. Matt, always cheerful, hid his own emotions, supporting Peter through the last few months by bringing extra food and making sure Peter rested. But Peter had known Matt was afraid to be left alone. After losing John, he had stuck close to Peter, literally keeping him alive. Now, in Peter's selfish joy, he had abandoned his friend in his hour of need.

"Daddy!" Peter's head jerks up at the sound of Emily's cry. He has also assumed the approaching trucks are the returning Japanese guards. Now, he tries to run, his uncooperative legs giving him a shambling gait. Is it John? Can it really be John back from the dead? Is Matt with him?

"So, let me get this straight." Peter sits close beside Martha, having listened to John's tale. "Lai's grandson – the one I patched up all those years ago – rescues you in a boat from the harbour and hides you in their family home, where Lai nurses you back to reasonable health?"

"In a nutshell." John grins at his friend from where he sits, wrapped in Emily's possessive arms.

"And then John comes to you." Margery nods towards Major Walker, also seated on the ground with the group, who inclines his head.

"Yes," he agrees. "Thanks to John's story, we *persuaded* Kimuru to reveal your whereabouts."

"And now you've found me," John looks questioningly at Peter, "you've managed to lose Matt?"

Peter's head drops into his hands, Martha rubbing his back, trying to comfort him.

"I was so intent on finding Martha, then helping her, I completely forgot about him. I'll never forgive myself if anything's happened to him, John. He's kept me going since we came here."

"If Matt felt so alone that he went away, where would he go?" Margery looks from one to the other, hoping for suggestions.

"I heard something in the night," admits Emily. "It came from over there." She points towards where the stream disappears into the thicker forest. "I thought it was Daddy's lost soul, or Indah's. It seemed to call to me. I tried to listen for it again but I was so tired, I fell asleep and have only just remembered. Could it have been Matt?"

"What's out there though?" the Major looks questioningly at Emily, finding her words a little disturbing.

"Wait!" Peter claps his hands together. "If Matt followed the stream, it would bring him back to the old hut we shared outside the men's camp. Quick! Major, may we take one of your trucks?"

John enters the broken-down hut Peter and Matt have been using since they arrived at Belalau. On the drive over, Peter had described how Matt had slipped out at night to gather extra food for the camp, risking execution if caught. Now, John studies the sleeping man: white-blond hair with tufts of unshaven beard frame the emaciated nut-brown face, sallow and haggard, ragged shallow breathing the only sign of life.

Dropping to his knees beside Matt, John gently strokes the sleeping man's arm, not wishing to startle him. Matt's eyelids flicker and he lets out a moan of pain and desolation.

"Well, that's not a very friendly greeting, I must say!"

Matt's eyes spring open, trying to focus. "John?" The whisper is barely audible, hesitant, questioning. "Am I dead, too?"

"Not dead, you bloody idler!" John watches Matt's mouth slowly turn up at the corners, smile lines crinkling around his sunken eyes.

"You found Emily yet?"

"Yes. She heard you last night. That's how Peter guessed where you'd be. She's waiting for you, Matt."

EPILOGUE

South Africa 1948

Margery stands, one hand on her hip and the other shading her eyes, on top of Table Mountain overlooking Table Bay and Robben Island. The day is clear and the panoramic views are magnificent. She had considered hiking up the mountain but decided to risk the precarious-looking cable car. Now, with her feet back on solid ground, she feels a wonderful sense of freedom and achievement.

Breathing in deeply, enjoying the fresh breeze on her face, Margery decides she must now consider her future. At the end of her odyssey, the meandering travels across East Asia to India, the voyage to Durban – accompanying immigrant Indian workers destined for the sugar cane fields of Natal – she has made her way down the East Coast of South Africa, clambering out among the rocks at Cape Point to watch the Indian and Atlantic oceans collide, before heading up the west coast to Cape Town and the longed-for Table Mountain.

She recalls the camp at Belalau, where she thought they would all die, and where she had last felt close to Emily. It had been Matt, who, having been found at the men's camp, had walked silently up to Emily and taken her hand. Margery could never have explained what had happened between them: a brightness had entered the girl's eyes. She seemed to have more energy, more spirit – as if the contact had brought the girl back to a life of colour, after the grey years in the prison camps. Margery admits to herself she had been jealous, the secure bond that had held she and Emily together had quickly dissolved, leaving Margery purposeless and lonely. She had not been jealous of John – he was Emily's father. It had been Matt she had resented, held responsible for the girl's loss of interest in her.

At the hospital in Singapore, they had not seen much of one another. Recovery had been slow. Margery had found it difficult to gain weight. Her appetite could not be persuaded to grow. With her height and bony frame, she considers herself rather like a stork, striding around on long stick legs.

She pictures Martha, who had good reason to recover. She had fallen in love with Peter and intended to return to Melbourne with him. For Peter, there was nothing left for him in Europe and he was looking forward to starting a new life in Australia.

John, Matt and Emily, had become an inseparable trio. John would never fully recover, and Matt had become his strength, growing closer to Emily with every day that passed. Only Susan had spent time with Margery. She had given her account of the massacre on the beach on Bangka Island to Major Walker. Having unburdened herself to the authorities, she felt she could now return home.

After the months of rehabilitation, they had all decided to go to Australia, except for Margery.

"I want to travel," she had told them. "To see more of the world before I get too old and senile."

"Will you go to Table Mountain?" Emily had asked. "I remember you telling Martha and me that's where you'd like to visit. To be as free as a bird."

"I hope so, Emily. It's where I'm aiming for."

"Then will you join us in Aus, Margery?" Martha's

invitation had touched her deeply.

"Yes, Margery. You must come when you've travelled enough." Emily's eyes had been gratifyingly pleading.

"Oh, you don't want an old bird like me hanging around. I should go back to England."

"Do you have family there?" John had asked.

She had shaken her head.

"Not any more. My parents are both dead and my brother was killed at the start of the war. That's why I left Europe."

"Please come to Australia, Margery. We're going to Matt's farm in Canberra," Emily had explained. "*Please* say you'll come."

So here she stands, trying to decide. She may still have a few years of teaching music left in her and could probably get work in either country. The royal family had not long visited South Africa, also coming to Table Mountain, and that made her nostalgic for the old country. Then again, she would know no one. No one who could empathise with the suffering she had endured during the war. At least in Australia, she had friends, comrades even.

A child, chasing a butterfly, stops beside her, looking up with interest at the tall, thin, statuesque woman staring fixedly out to sea.

"What do you think, young man?" Margery asks, as if they are mid-conversation. "England or Australia?"

He stares, mouth open, uncomprehending. Then he holds up a finger, breaking into a wide smile. "Oh! You mean the cricket!" The boy's Afrikaans accent is strong. "Well, Don Bradman's Australia beat England four-nil in the Ashes!"

"Right. Thank you. Australia it is!"

Author's note

Although this book is a work of fiction, and all the characters are imaginary, the story broadly follows the events surrounding the Japanese invasion of southern Sumatra during the Second World War. Pladjoe refinery, the Charitas hospital and the P1 and P2 airbases all existed, with P2 remaining hidden during the allied defence. There were camps at Palembang, Bangka Island and Belalau Plantation. Lord Mountbatten's RAPWI Division based at Ceylon was set up to rescue the POWs, and Belalau camp was one of the last to be liberated. However, my account of the rescue mission and liberation is fictional.

In locating an area where wild Sumatran tigers still existed in the 1940s, I became aware of Palembang, its oil refineries, and its strategic importance to the Japanese military as a source of oil. Further reading brought in the evacuation of Singapore and the tragic encounter with the Japanese Fleet in the Bangka Straits.

The personal accounts of the POWs I have read are very disturbing, but their bravery, strength of will and determination to survive is inspirational. Through my imaginary characters, I have attempted to portray some of the atrocities carried out against the civilian POWs through fictional settings.